The Me List

Julee Balko

Black Rose Writing | Texas

First printing

ISBN: 978-1-68513-361-0
Library of Congress Control Number: 2023943074
PUBLISHED BY BLACK ROSE WRITING
www.blackrosewriting.com

Printed in the United States of America
Suggested Retail Price (SRP) $20.95

The Me List is printed in Minion Pro

*As a planet-friendly publisher, Black Rose Writing does its best to eliminate unnecessary waste to reduce paper usage and energy costs, while never compromising the reading experience. As a result, the final word count vs. page count may not meet common expectations.

PRAISE FOR *THE ME LIST*

"You know those books you can't put down? Where you find yourself cheering for the characters, dreading the pain you know is coming, laughing as if you're among friends and crying for the sake of love? *The Me List* is THAT kind of book–a marvelously poignant, relatable, unforgettable read!"

–Kathryn Inman, author of *Counting Spoons*

"Balko's writing is pure magic and has the potential to change the world! She shows us what's possible when two very different people are able to move past their assumptions of one another and truly accept each other as they are, mistakes and all. It's a must-read for today's divided world."

–J.D. Greyson, founder of *Move Me Poetry*

"This is the kind of story women search for. A story of unusual friendship, surprising support, and lasting knowledge."

–Bambi Sommers, author of the romantic suspense series, *Hart Investigations*

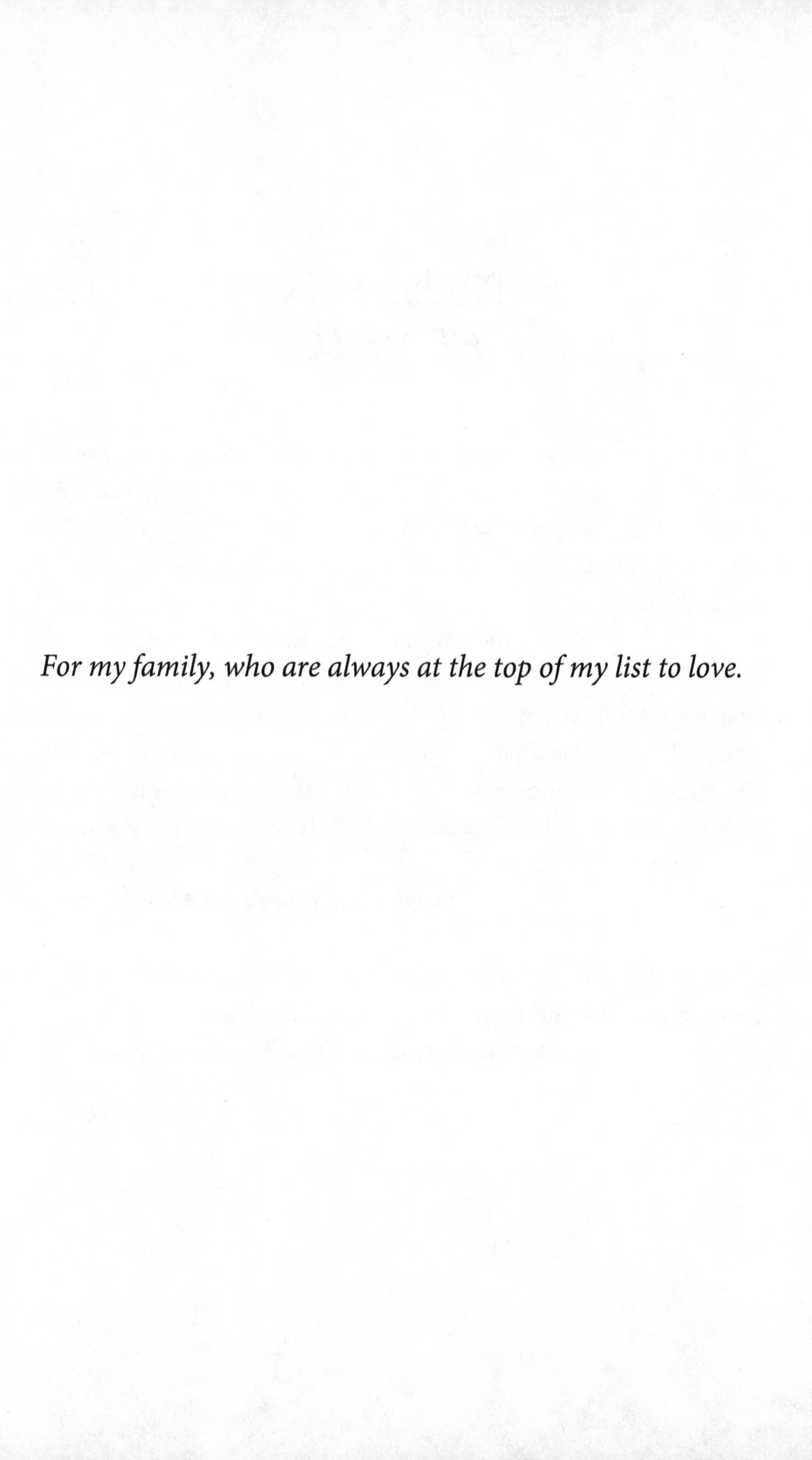

For my family, who are always at the top of my list to love.

The Me List

CHAPTER 1
SALAD

Olivia's life felt like hard piled on hard. And then some piles of laundry. And a sink full of last night's dishes. And not nearly enough wine.

She rifled through the clearance underwear at Target and knew her marriage was in trouble. Who had she become? She didn't even think about sexy lingerie. She nabbed a nude-colored pair for two dollars and threw them into her cart. Could anything scream boring more loudly than nude underwear that was on sale?

She tossed a bag of coffee on top of the underwear to hide her dismal life. What else did she need to pick up today? Not that underpriced panties were technically on her list. She scanned her phone: bread, milk, cereal, those granola bars that Sammy liked. The usual. Oh, and wine. Olivia definitely needed more wine. Especially after that frustrating call with her mother earlier today.

Olivia pushed the cart through the aisle, distracted by her issues with her mother, and hit the corner of the end-cap display, knocking a few Tupperware containers off the pile. Rolling her eyes, she picked them up, and they fell again. Olivia scrunched her nose with hate at the little plastic bowls nestled into themselves with their right-sized lids and thought, *how do they magically get these to stay?* She balanced the last bowl on the corner and walked away. About two aisles down, she heard them drop to the ground again. She quickly took a left and the Tupperware problem was out of her sight.

Olivia glanced at her watch and saw she still had two more hours until Samantha finished school. If she walked around Target long enough, could this count as exercise? She had told herself she was going to go to the gym every day this week. Yet here it was, Wednesday, and the closest she had gotten to the gym was a Target run, without any actual running.

Olivia heard Patricia's voice before she saw her. It oozed authority and money and polished hair. She slowed her cart, hoping to avoid her, but wouldn't you know it, Patricia turned right into her aisle.

"Hello there." Patricia held the phone away from her face, put her hand over the receiver, and whispered, "It's a client." Olivia gave a wave like she was still a dork in eighth grade. It was like even her hand couldn't be cool.

Patricia walked right over and picked up the fancy cleaner. You know, the kind that costs a lot, has a hip-looking label on it, and is only made from essential oils and freshly squeezed hibiscus flowers or something. Olivia judged her while secretly thinking she should buy the same one.

Patricia hung up the phone and said, "Ugh, it's been a day."

Olivia nodded her head in agreement, even though her day had technically only been stressing about her mother, ignoring the dishes, avoiding exercise, and then coming here.

"Work's been so busy, I didn't even eat lunch. Have you tried that little salad place next door?"

"Oh, no. Sprouts? It looks good, but I haven't."

"Perfect. We should go."

"Yeah." Olivia only said that to be nice. It's the kind of answer you give when you assume you will never go to the fancy salad shop with your fancier-than-you neighbor. If Olivia wanted to eat salad, which she didn't, she would eat it at home and then do the respectable thing—eat brownies two minutes later while hiding in her closet so her kid didn't see.

"Let's go grab some now," Patricia said. There was no uptick in her voice as if it was a question. It was a statement, a sentence with a period and no wiggle room.

And Olivia's lips betrayed her by saying, "Oh," which sounded enough like "okay," before she could stop them. Technically, she had two hours to spare. But eating salad was not her idea of a good time, and eating salad with perfect Patricia was pretty close to Olivia's idea of torture. And yet here she was, pushing her cart behind Patricia. Behind her! Not even in front of her. Pushing it behind her like an odd duckling following a swan. Olivia wished Patricia would stop short so she could accidentally clip her ankle. But there was no breaking Patricia's speed. It was like the sea of Target shoppers could feel the powerful energy of Patricia, and they parted ways to let her through. Olivia's heart rate was pumping just to keep up. Seriously? When Olivia shopped, it was usually sluggish old ladies at every pass. How did this woman clear the aisles of humans with just her presence?

Olivia's armpits felt sweaty. *Damn stupid natural deodorant,* she thought, and she saw a little sweat appear on her gray shirt. *Pit stains and pea shoots, I'm a regular class act,* she thought as she joined Patricia in line.

"Hello, Sandra." Patricia greeted the Target employee by her actual freaking name. Who does that? Not Olivia. Olivia was a quick upward glance and get through the transaction as quickly as possible with as little discussion as necessary kind of shopper.

"Find everything you need?" the Target employee, apparently named Sandra, asked.

“Oh yes. Everything was quite in order,” Patricia said, and flashed a smile.

Meanwhile, Olivia tried to think of how she could get out of the salad fest. Vomit? Could she spontaneously vomit? A call from school? No, her phone wouldn’t ring. An email from school about Samantha? What if Patricia asked to see it? She was nosy like that. And before she could think of an excuse, Sandra, the quickest scanner she had ever met, was already scanning her things, until beep.

Dammit, the clearance nudes.

Beep. “Um, miss, these aren’t scanning. Where’d you get them?”

Patricia peered through her glasses at Olivia and seemed annoyed at the inefficiency of the underwear purchase.

“They were on sale. In the clearance bin.” Olivia straightened her posture and tried to say it with poise and grace. Nothing to be ashamed of. So she liked boring underwear at a good price.

Sandra held the tag on the underwear and typed in the number. Beep.

“Hmm, not working.”

She tried the number again. *Think of something to say, brain.* Olivia wished her mind could make small talk so the underwear silence would be broken.

“Let me call my manager.” Sandra picked up the phone and said, “Bob, I need your help with a clearance garment.”

“That won’t be necessary. I don’t need them. Really. It’s okay.”

“Are you sure?” Clearly, Sandra thought the nudes were worth the effort.

“Yes. My friend and I are about to get lunch.” Hold up. Did Olivia just call Patricia her friend? Out loud. Could this day get any worse? Now she was going to have to go eat cold greens. There better be cheese options. Creamy dressing.

She grabbed her bag, and all Patricia said was, "All set? Great." And out the door they went, Patricia wearing a black tailored dress with appropriate heels and Olivia in a grey shirt and yoga pants that had never seen the light of an actual yoga studio.

No surprise, Patricia walked right up to the counter and ordered her salad while Olivia fumbled with the menu and searched for something that sounded good. Tex-Mex turkey, no thank you. Loaded kale. Absolutely not. Caesar, nope, that's the nude-underwear salad of conformity. Olivia scanned the menu, looking for just the right blend of healthy and not. Finally, she decided just to make her own.

"Hi, can I do a build-your-own salad?"

"Yeah. What greens?" The young man did a Vanna White hand motion to the various salad combinations.

"Whatever is the most normal and has no kale." Olivia was not in the mood to play salad games.

"Okay, our combination sounds like the right choice for you." His perky mood only made Olivia hate everything about her salad situation even more.

"You get four toppings of your choice."

Nothing about this is my choice, thought Olivia.

"Um, tomatoes, chickpeas, cucumbers, and cheese. Lots of cheese."

"We've got goat, blue, parmesan, cheddar, and mozzarella. Oh, and feta."

"Goat. Load it on there."

"I can give you a double amount for an extra charge, ma'am."

"Yes. Thanks." Olivia hated being called ma'am. It made her feel like she was seventy and should have a knitting ball and an old orange cat. She started to walk away when the perky salad man shouted with a little too much enthusiasm and urgency, "Your dressing, ma'am. Which dressing?"

"Oh, I don't know." Olivia scanned the 42 choices and thought, *why does salad have to be so difficult?* She saw her choice and said, "Green goddess," nodding her head as if the salad dressing described herself. She peered over the crowd to see where Patricia was sitting. Patricia was on her phone again looking important, but she smiled and gave a big wave.

"That'll be $12.99."

"What? For a salad?" Olivia gawked. The woman at the check-out, who looked about the same age as her, did not look amused.

"Well, you did get the extra cheese."

Olivia handed over her debit card, feeling slightly cheese-shamed, and hoped this was going to be the best salad of her normally non-salad life.

"Would you like bread?"

"Yes, please."

"I put an extra slice in there for you," the woman said. Olivia smiled and said, "Thanks," although she was pretty sure the lady figured a cheese loader was also a carb loader. Olivia sat down next to Patricia, who had gotten the chicken Caesar salad (who's a boring nude-underwear salad lover now?) and went straight for the goat cheese.

"Is it good?" Patricia asked as Olivia had salad hanging from her mouth. She mustered an "uh-huh" while her shoulders slunk down in defeat. Could she feel more like a grazing cow? She watched Patricia stab her salad with the right amount of bite and effort. The woman even ate salad with powerful elegance.

"I've actually been meaning to run into you," Patricia said after patting her lips with a napkin.

"Oh?" Olivia replied, not sure what Patricia and she had in common besides these overpriced greens today.

"Your daughter started school, yes?"

"Yes. She's in kindergarten this year. It's quite a change. But she's doing great."

"Wonderful. And you?"

"Me?" Olivia suddenly felt very shy. "What about me?"

"I just remember when my Christopher started school, I got a little lost the first few months. That's when I pursued getting my real estate license. And now look." Patricia said it as if her monumental success was all around her, which it sort of was. It was in her fine haircut. The way her brown, shiny hair lined up perfectly on her shoulders. Her nice clothes. The way she carried herself.

Olivia felt compelled to defend her lack of a job. "Well, you know Steve travels a lot for work. It makes sense right now for me to be home to help Sammy get through the next few months."

"Oh, yes. Yes." Patricia's eagerness to agree did nothing to convince Olivia that she did, in fact, agree with her.

"It's just...if you had time." Patricia paused, and Olivia knew she was pausing to make her inquire what she was going to say next. Oh, how she hated this type of verbal warfare. It was why she avoided Patricia in the first place. That and the fact that she was always dressed to go out, while Olivia was dressed most definitely to stay in. Olivia looked her straight in the eyes. She would give her direct contact, but she was not going to give her any words. She was a strong woman, too.

Finally, Patricia gave in and said, "It's just, I lost my assistant and I thought maybe you had a few hours here or there to help. Weren't you a..."

"Project manager," Olivia filled in her sentence. Damn it, she fell into her word trap.

"Yes, yes. I remember thinking it was something to do with organizational skills," Patricia said in a way that wasn't supposed to sound demeaning but made Olivia's entire career, which was quite successful, suddenly feel basic, like she arranged stationery for a living.

"You could do it from home. You have a computer, right?" Patricia asked. And again, Olivia felt like this woman was killing her with each condescending question. Why on earth would she ever say yes?

"I'll think about it."

"Wonderful. You won't regret it!" Just like that, Patricia took Olivia's "I'll think about it" and turned it into a commitment.

"Well, listen, I have to run to an appointment, but I'll stop by tomorrow with the details and we can talk further. I bet I can convince you that it'll be great with a capital G." With that, Patricia picked up her fancy salad, put it into her fancy black bag, and left.

Olivia started picking the goat cheese out of her salad and wondered what on earth had just happened? And what the hell could she eat for dessert? She stopped at a drive-through Starbucks on the way home. Hey, she deserved it after that salad lunch.

As she drove, she pushed Patricia out of her mind, and thoughts about another challenging woman pushed in—her mother. Olivia was stressed about her last conversation with her mother and how desperate she sounded for money. How was she going to tell Steve she had caved and sent her mom cash from their savings again? Or worse, that she had used the account they set up specifically for their future vacation? When was the last time they had gone on a vacation? Before Samantha was born. And with every withdrawal she sent her mother, she knew the chances of a vacation got further away. She wanted to believe her mom would pay her back. She wanted to believe a lot about her mother and none of those things ever came true. This would be the last time she gave her money, Olivia promised herself.

With Starbucks in one hand, Olivia loaded way too many Target bags onto her other arm in her driveway. She balanced about ten bags on one wrist, cutting off her circulation and leaving the drink hand to shut the heavy trunk of her SUV. As she closed it, she saw a man sitting on Patricia's porch. He wasn't sitting as much as slumping against the wall. He wore a hat that covered his face. As Olivia shimmied forward to get a better look, she felt one of her bags break.

Please be the coffee beans and graham crackers, she thought, even though she knew from the noise it was neither. She looked down and saw three broken jars of tomato sauce and a stream of red tomato blood oozing down her driveway. *Is it Monday?* Olivia wondered, because everything certainly made this feel like a crappy Monday.

Olivia brought the bags inside and tried to assess the man next door at Patricia's place as she walked back to her tomato crime scene. She delicately picked up the shards of glass and got her hose to clean up the sauce. The man still hadn't moved. Was he dead? Should she call 911? She gave him a friendly wave as she sprayed her tomato sauce, but he did not wave back.

But then again, she wouldn't have waved at herself either, because now she had a big river of red flowing down her driveway, like something out of a horror film. Just then, Patricia pulled up and got out of her car with her phone attached to her ear. She looked over at the bloody mess with raised eyebrows and disgust. Olivia shouted, "I didn't kill anyone!" Part joke, part just her mouth working faster than her brain, making her seem as awkward as possible. Patricia lifted her chin ever so slightly to indicate she had heard Olivia.

And then Patricia looked toward her house and saw her houseguest, who was now lying down, and rushed forward to talk to him. Olivia thought about asking if she needed help, but she was too embarrassed by her sauce explosion, and besides, it seemed like Patricia was talking comfortably and the man was moving into her house.

Olivia finished cleaning up the bloody stream of sauce and walked into her home. She had been spending a lot of time here by herself since Samantha started school. It was a bit lonely. Even yesterday, when she went to a coffee shop to read a book, she could feel herself trying to blend into the background of the café. Not wanting to stand out in the crowd. Not sure who she was anymore out in the real world when she wasn't being Samantha's mom. Instead of reading, Olivia watched all the people at the shop and wondered what their lives were like. She stared at two women who were clearly friends and thought longingly about how most of her friends had gone back to work. And now here she was in her kitchen, contemplating working for the uptight lady next door. Was she that lonely? But she could use the money. She could put back what she had lent her mother. Maybe she wouldn't even have to tell Steve?

Olivia took out a pen and piece of lined white paper and did the only thing she knew would help her. She wrote pros on one side and cons on the other side of the paper.

Pro: I've been bored. Con: Neighbor is bitchy. Pro: Need money. Con: Conversations with neighbor always leave me feeling stupid. Pro: It's a job. Con: Patricia's hair always looks good.

Olivia stared at the list and added a few more. Con: Already feeling insecure because of Patricia's perfectness. See hair comment. Pro: Job given to me with no effort and might be a way to warm up to going back to work without missing Sammy. Con: Job is with Patricia.

Olivia looked at the list and crumpled it up in frustration. She decided to learn more about the job. If it worked with Sammy's schedule, she would consider it. But she wasn't going to do her hair for the conversation with Patricia. After all, she had standards, too. They were just low, easy, and required minimal effort.

Just then, Olivia heard a commotion coming from outside. It sounded like shouting. As she pulled back her living room curtain ever so slightly, she could see a police car in front of Patricia's house. The man, the same man who had been looking quite tired, was now looking quite animated. Olivia couldn't make out what they were saying. She pressed her ear to the window, but it was still too muffled. Olivia looked out the window again and watched as Patricia touched the man's arm. He elbowed her away.

"Fuck you," he shouted.

Yes, Olivia definitely heard those words. Patricia's smile didn't change. It was cemented on her face, as if the sureness of her smile could transform the situation from being an embarrassing fiasco with cops to an upscale wine tasting. The police officer grabbed the man and, in the scuffle, the man's hat fell off. That's when Olivia realized it wasn't just a man. It was a young man. And it was Patricia's son. Olivia watched Patricia's son get in the cop's car, and she swore Patricia was looking right at her through the tiny crack in the curtain.

Olivia jumped back and waited a few minutes. Her mind was aflutter with so many questions. Why would Patricia have her own son arrested? Why didn't she invite him in? Maybe Patricia wasn't so perfect after all? Then Olivia peeked again without moving the curtain so it was just a little line of sun, but she could see that Patricia was gone.

CHAPTER 2
JOB WITH A CAPITAL J

Samantha had just boarded the school bus when Olivia heard a knock on the door. Samantha's cereal bowl was still on the table, as were a few scattered Cheerios and milk spills. Olivia's hair was unwashed and she was wearing her slippers. She opened the door expecting to see an overzealous Amazon delivery driver, not Patricia.

Patricia was ready for the morning, her chocolate brown hair smooth and shimmering in the sun. Gray slacks. A black leather bag with her computer. A charming maroon button-down sweater. Gold bangles on her wrist that lightly chimed as she held up two Starbucks lattes.

"Hello there. I hope this isn't too early to talk. I picked these up on the way home from the gym." She had been to the gym. Already. This woman was ridiculous.

"Come on in. I was still getting my morning going after getting Samantha on the school bus." Olivia smiled—or at least tried to smile—but her lips weren't ready to spread cheer just yet.

"Oh yes, I remember those days." Patricia came right in and paid no attention to the fact that Olivia was not dressed nor ready for a morning visitor. She sat right down on a kitchen chair, took out her computer, and then carefully put her arm down on the table, avoiding the milk splatters.

"Kids are messy. Sorry, let me wipe down the table. I would have cleaned up, had I known we were meeting up this early."

Olivia grabbed a towel and sprayed down the table as Patricia leaned back and enjoyed her sips of coffee. Did Olivia think about spraying Patricia with the cleaner and messing up her perfectly ironed outfit? Of course she did. Did she do it? Unfortunately, she did not. Instead, Olivia sat down with her not-shiny messy brown-haired bun and insecurity and took a sip of the latte.

"So…?"

She wondered if Patricia was going to mention her son. Olivia didn't dare bring it up.

"I'm here because of what we discussed yesterday."

"Oh." Damn, no son gossip. But Olivia took a gulp of latte and responded with, "Yes."

"I hope you are considering it. Do you have experience with Excel and programs like that?"

"Yes." Boy, Patricia went straight to the nitty-gritty. No pleasantries. She went from lattes straight to what she needed.

Patricia glanced around the kitchen as if she was evaluating it to sell. "Did you put in this light?" Patricia stared at the light fixture above them—a mixture of wooden farmhouse and simple modern features.

"Yep. Steve put it in," Olivia answered, not sure if her taste in light fixtures was good or gaudy in Patricia's eyes.

"You painted in here too, yes?" Patricia glanced around the room.

"Yes, I like calming colors," Olivia answered, feeling like her kitchen and her design skills were on a job interview.

Patricia looked back down at her computer and changed the conversation back to work. "You could work around your daughter's schedule. There are no specific work hours. Although there might be a time or two in a pinch when I might need your help after school. But we'll keep those to a minimum." Patricia winked at Olivia.

Olivia felt like she was at a used car lot and Patricia was giving her the hard sell on a car she didn't even know she wanted.

"I can send you the paperwork later today and they'll have you in the system by tomorrow, so you can start tracking your time. We can pay you hourly. I'll have HR send you all the details—what we pay, if you are eligible for benefits, which I don't think you will be if you want to keep your hours low. But we can make anything work."

Patricia put her hand out and before Olivia had even showered, she now was shaking Patricia's hand in some weird business act that had closed the job deal, even though Olivia had never uttered the word yes. And now the momentum that was Patricia had Olivia looking at her computer like she was a marionette who had lost the ability to control her own body.

Patricia showed her property listings and yammered on about vendors, painters, stagers, and lockboxes. Olivia wanted to stop her and crack her business veneer. She wanted to say, "Let's talk about the cops." Not because she cared about Patricia's life, but because she was curious about its imperfect splotches. And this was the first one Olivia had ever seen. She had walked past Patricia's perfectly planted petunias. Her seasonal wreaths. It was all so damn pretty. But yesterday did not have a bow. Yesterday had cops.

Just as she was about to ask, Patricia said, "That's probably enough for one morning. Here's a little homework." Again, Patricia gave her the used-car salesperson wink and handed Olivia a few listings to look over to get used to the various categories.

"This will be great with a capital G," Patricia gushed.

Olivia smiled and thought, *this might suck with a capital S.*

Olivia walked Patricia out and closed the door. And it hit her. She now had a job. Is this what happens when you eat a healthy salad?

Olivia started going through the list of things Patricia had left. Olivia looked at all the properties that would need a For Sale sign when an address caught her eye. 406 Willow Street? That was her street. That was next door. That was Patricia's house! She's putting her house on the market? Olivia quickly went onto Zillow to see what she could learn. The price they were asking was reasonable. A good profit from what they bought it for fifteen years ago, but not overly greedy considering they just put on that new screened-in porch Olivia had ogled every day while she sweated in the mosquito heat with Sammy.

But why was she selling? Did it have to do with her son? Why hadn't Patricia mentioned it? And Olivia so wanted to go to the open house and spy on everything in Patricia's house. Olivia had watched when they redid the floors. She could see from the sidewalk as they laid the beautiful, wide, rich maple planks. Nothing like Olivia's scratched, skinny wood floors which had faded to a strange orangey-yellow. Olivia had noticed when Patricia had someone paint a chandelier just the right color and put it on the front porch to dry. Every Friday, when Olivia took the trash out, she could see Patricia's chandelier shining elegantly through the window. And every two weeks, Olivia watched from her slightly brown lawn as Patricia's lawn crew came to keep Patricia's perfectly green lawn perfectly green. Olivia had never seen Patricia's husband, Paul, mow, or trim, or rake leaves. To be honest, she hadn't seen much of Paul lately, or his cool, always-clean Audi.

Olivia got so caught up in her homework that day, mainly looking at everyone's pictures of their houses for sale, she lost track of the time. She heard the brakes of the bus and ran to the front door, opening it just in time to wave to Samantha as she got off the bus. Her bookbag was about the same size as her body. Her little legs came running straight towards Olivia.

"Mommmmmmyyyyy," she squealed as she flung her arms around Olivia's waist.

"How was your day, sweetie?"

"Good."

"Oh good. Guess what?"

"What?"

"Mommy got a job."

"Yay, Mommy. Can I have a snack?" That was the end of the job discussion and the day moved on to playing outside, skinned knees, dirty fingernails, and some goldfish cracker eating.

That night, when Olivia's husband, Steve, came home late, Olivia had already tucked Sammy in for the night and sat with a glass of wine in her hand.

"Hi, sweetie." Steve kissed her forehead. "Tough day?" He raised his eyebrows at the wine.

"Actually, no. Good day." Olivia smiled. Steve walked over to the kitchen counter, poured himself a glass of red, and sat down next to her.

"Tell me. Sammy cuteness?"

"No. I mean, yes, she's always cute. But good because of me. I got a job today."

"A what?"

"A job. Patricia from next door hired me to be her assistant."

"The Patricia you called the spawn of the devil once?" Steve took a big gulp of wine.

"I didn't call her the spawn of the devil."

"Oh yes, you did. She was wearing that pink tracksuit, and you said the only person who would wear a pink tracksuit must be the spawn of the devil. I remember because I laughed my ass off. And then every day that week, every time we passed one of her realtor signs with her face on it, you'd wave and say, just in case the devil is watching."

"Okay, yes. Well, I stand by that. A pink tracksuit is utterly ridiculous and possibly a sign of a hellish demon. However, for now, I've chosen to forget about the pink and take advantage of this situation. We could use the money." Olivia thought about telling Steve at that moment about her mother and the money she'd lent her, even though she knew it would lead to a fight about how her mother always took advantage of her. And where they both knew the money really went. She was just about to when Steve said, "Yes, we can. It's great you've found something productive to do."

As Steve stood up to get Olivia a little more wine, she ruminated on the word productive. That sounded shitty. Was taking care of Sammy not productive? They had agreed she would take time off from her career to stay home. Olivia took another sip of wine. She decided to keep her money-lending secret to herself for now. Instead, she said, "How was your day? Good dinner meeting? Was that French place good?"

"Is it French? I don't think it was French?"

"I don't know. It had bistro in its name, so I made it French."

Sometimes a conversation with her husband was difficult. Especially lately; it seemed like Steve worked more and more while Olivia was stuck doing more and more of the grunt work. Why did her life feel like all work? She had chosen to stay home. But now every time Olivia had to clean the bathroom, wipe up spilled milk, or pick up everyone's socks, shoes, you name it—well, it made her hate Steve just a little.

"It was good. I had steak. I was going to bring you dessert, but the client didn't order any and I didn't want to make him wait."

"That's okay. Thanks for thinking of me. I'm trying to eat healthier anyway," Olivia said, thinking about yesterday and her cheese salad. Not about the entire package of chocolate chip mini muffins she'd eaten today.

"Look at you, making healthy changes." Steve held up his wineglass to her.

Olivia took a sip of hers, clinked his glass, and said, "Well, not too healthy. Although wine is technically a grape."

"Just don't start wearing pink," Steve said and made a grossed-out face.

"No chance of that, buddy." Olivia settled into her chair and felt a sense of something wash over her. A little bit of excitement. A little bit of dread. And a whole lot of warmth from the wine.

CHAPTER 3
MUD

Olivia took the job. Every day she woke to an email from Patricia with a list of to-dos—pick up lightbulbs from Home Depot, order flowers for an open house, and schedule the painters. Every day Olivia accomplished them and felt good about her work. She had forgotten that feeling. That little inner clap you give yourself when you know you're kicking ass.

For some reason, it was important to show Patricia that she could do this. Maybe it was because Olivia thought of every job done well as a little shiv into Patricia's side. Or maybe it was because Olivia had been ready to transition. She had focused so much on making sure Samantha was ready for kindergarten that she had never thought about herself. Now, thanks to a few hours every day of real estate logistics, Olivia realized she was ready.

Sometimes Patricia would run over and give her signature knock. One time hard, four times faster with a little rhythmic flair. Was there nothing Patricia didn't add a little pizzazz to? Patricia would hand Olivia brochures for recent houses on the market, or some handwritten notes highlighted in pink for Olivia to update. Patricia was an interesting blend of old-school—write it out on paper—and new-school—she could design a brochure in a pinch. But most of all, Patricia was uptight. Shoulders back as far as they could go, spine straight, voice taut, she'd give Olivia passive-aggressive compliments. "You're getting better at these promotional updates. Just remember, periods at the end of everything. We're always looking to make a statement with a capital S."

Inside, Olivia would vomit a little. Outside, she'd look Patricia in the eye and say, "Periods. Got it." Patricia had quickly become Olivia's white whale. If she could overcome her and capture her approval, Olivia knew she could take on anything. And maybe a job at an actual company could be her next endeavor.

Olivia would finish tasks early with a sinister delight, just to show Patricia she was efficient. Then she would ask for extra work, to show Patricia she had underestimated her.

When Patricia was unhappy, her knock sounded different. There was no melody. Four quick knocks hard and fast would make Olivia's heart race. What had she done wrong?

"You put the wrong address on this just-sold postcard. Here, I marked it up. Details, Olivia. A great realtor is all in the D-E-T-A-I-L-S." She smiled and tapped her foot slightly on the pavement outside Olivia's front door. These little conversations happened with Olivia inside and Patricia outside. As if the threshold of Olivia's door was just too far for Patricia to step over.

Olivia was sure it took Patricia longer to mark up the document with a pink highlighter and pen than it would to just open the document and make the change herself. But she would never say that out loud. Olivia suspected Patricia was lonely and enjoyed the jaunt over to her house. Because a simple email would have done the trick. Was pretty Patricia a princess stuck in her castle?

That night, after Samantha went to bed, Olivia pulled out a spreadsheet.

"Look at you. Patricia working you to the bone?" Steve asked as he put an arm around her.

“Nah, I just lied and said I got this spreadsheet done when I didn’t.” Olivia stuck her tongue to the side as she concentrated on the updates. The rows and rows of numbers made her eyes water.

“And why are we lying to our boss already?” Steve smiled to show he was more teasing than serious. But Olivia was in no mood. She raked her fingers through her hair and pulled at the ends. She’d also promised Patricia she’d work on the flyer for the open house, too.

“Because fuck Patricia and her perfectness. I can be perfect and efficient, too.”

“Even though it’s a lie.” Steve laughed.

Olivia swatted him hard with her hand without taking her eyes off the spreadsheet.

“Ow. That hurt.” Steve rubbed his stomach. “Does Patricia know you pack a punch? ’Cause she should watch out.”

“Funny. Now let me finish this.”

“I thought we were going to watch the next episode of that show we liked? Can you work and watch too?” Steve grabbed the remote and gave her sad eyes as he said, “Please.”

“You just want to watch the gratuitous sex scenes.” Olivia rolled her eyes and put her face closer to her computer to concentrate.

“There’s a plot too, you know. In fact, there are some very nice plots.”

“You are disgusting. Why did I marry you?” Olivia teased, but she wanted to finish her work without the TV in the background showing her women with body parts that had never had a baby or a cookie.

“Because I’m disgusting and I love you?” Steve hugged her again.

“Okay, we can watch TV while I work. Just let me get this done.” She looked up. “And make us popcorn.”

“Telling me what to do. You have been hanging out with Patricia.”

Olivia shot Steve a look that said “enough.” He walked over to the microwave and tossed in a bag of popcorn.

Two more rows to go and she’d be done with her updates. Olivia knew it was silly that she wanted Patricia to think she was capable of more than she actually was. But somehow, this made Olivia feel more energized. Could spite be her motivation?

It was with this newfound empowerment that Olivia opened her email and read Patricia's message about a staff meeting at her house the next day. Olivia was Patricia's only staff. But the smell of popcorn had put Olivia in a good mood, so she didn't bother to take offense at how absurd and overly official the email sounded. Instead, she forged ahead with her work and gave Steve one more whack on the belly for good measure.

Next up, the open house flyers. She looked at the file Patricia had given her to replicate. Olivia could see there was room for improvement. She would show Patricia she was capable of more than copying and pasting. After all the Instagram posts Olivia had made over the years, she knew a thing or two about design aesthetics. Yeah, those posts were of Sammy or crafts. Even so, she was about to get Pinterest-pretty on Patricia's ass. By the time the not-very-plot-driven show was ending, Olivia was still changing colors and fonts on her flyer. None of it looked right, and it was all harder than she had thought it would be.

"Ready for bed?" Steve peeked over at her screen.

Olivia put her hand up to cover up her work. "I'm still working. You go to bed. I'll come up when I'm done."

"Okay, but don't work too hard. You don't want to like overload yourself and then suddenly Sammy hasn't eaten in days and you don't remember who we are."

"Seriously?" Olivia looked at Steve. He rumpled her hair with his hands to lighten her mood.

"You know what I mean." He bent down and went to kiss her lips. "I was trying to be nice."

She moved her head, so he kissed the top of her scalp instead. "Then be nice. And let me get this done."

The next morning, Olivia decided to do her hair and wear a light blue button-down shirt with black slacks and black flats. Like she used to wear for work. The flats were scuffed, but they still fit. The slacks were more than a little tight. She tried to inhale as deeply as she could, but the button just wouldn't close. She heard the doorbell and sucked in her stomach so much it hurt and jammed the button in. Take that Patricia. And take that Steve. She grabbed the flyer off the printer to show Patricia and ran down the stairs.

Olivia felt her stomach bulge push against the top like a cupcake expanding on the top of a baking pan. As she rushed down the stairs to get the door, her button popped off. Olivia looked down. Her shirt was long. The zipper was still up on the pants. You'd have to look closely to notice the top of her pants poking the shirt. And if the meeting went well, Patricia shouldn't be staring at her crotch.

Patricia looked her up and down and said, "Change of plans. Our meeting is happening in the car. I need you to come with me today. We are going to meet with a photographer who is taking some pictures of one of our high-end properties. I want to introduce you because you'll be booking her for future projects. Poppy is going to meet us there, too. She's our designer who stages the homes. Everything should be in order, but you just never know."

Olivia thought about running upstairs and changing pants, but Patricia was already walking towards her car. Tight unbuttoned pants for the win.

As Olivia sat down in Patricia's spotless car, Patricia asked, "What's that in your hand?"

"Oh, it's the flyer I worked on for you." Olivia could feel her face get splotchy and red. Why did her skin have to betray her like this? She needed a confident complexion. "I stayed up late finishing it." Could she sound more like a twelve-year-old trying to impress a teacher?

Patricia took one glance at it and put it down by Olivia's feet. "That won't do."

Patricia then went on about the details of the house they were driving to, like the flyer discussion had never happened. She talked about all the parts of the house the homeowners had painted, cleaned, and improved to get it on the market and fetch a full price.

"You sound like you know this house well," Olivia said as she looked down to see how noticeably her pants were pushing up at her shirt. She looked over at Patricia's pants, which were a nice wool blend. Expensive. Probably the type that needed to be dry-cleaned.

Olivia stopped herself for a second. Was she staring at Patricia's crotch? She quickly looked down at her own shoes and the flyer on the ground next to them. "Can I ask why the flyer won't do?"

"You really want to know?" Patricia kept her eyes on the road.

"Yes, I'd appreciate the feedback."

"Your fonts are too big. The colors a bit, I don't know? Garish. And that box around the outside of the flyer is thicker than my aunt's thighs. And she's a very large woman. Beautiful. But build like a redwood tree." Patricia paused as she looked at the road sign.

Olivia thought Patricia was done. But the feedback kept coming. "This flyer isn't for a garage sale. These are expensive houses. Everything needs to represent elegance with a capital E. Down to the font choice. What is that, Courier? No one likes a serif font." Patricia turned the steering wheel and smiled. "And here we are."

Her mouth moved from disparaging remarks to pleasantries so quickly that Olivia could find no response and just sat there quietly. The flyer feedback churned in her stomach.

She felt the bump of the driveway as Patricia's car pulled up to a gorgeous blue house. Round manicured bushes and a row of yellow and purple flowers lined the front. A happy and inviting red custom door with a beautiful wreath accented it. Money sure did make it easy to sell houses. "I do know this couple. They were friends with my husband."

Olivia chewed on that statement for a second. Friends with her husband, not her. And past tense? Were they no longer friends?

"No one's here yet. Let's do a quick walk around the property to make sure everything is in order. A picture can sell a house but we need it to be perfect with a capital P." Patricia walked up to the front door as Olivia watched, feeling like the awkward friend who shouldn't be at the party. Actually, she felt like the enemy who wanted to ruin the party.

Patricia adjusted the wreath as if only she could see the angle it needed to be at to reach perfection. She took a step back and stared at the wreath and adjusted it another inch to the right.

"Selling houses is all about the details, Olivia. Like I told you with the flyer, D-E-T-A-I-L-S matter," Patricia said with a teacher tone that made Olivia's insides curl with annoyance. Olivia was about to open her mouth and mention the one detail Patricia didn't see—that she was dangerously close to the edge of the concrete—but instead she let Patricia fall back and get her gloriously fancy navy pumps muddy.

"Details, got it." Olivia tried not to smile.

Patricia gave Olivia a look that said she did not appreciate the mud on her shoe or Olivia's smirk.

"The ground is still wet from all that rain. Be careful, Olivia." Patricia walked forward with her head high as she kicked the mud off her shoe. "I want to go around back. I gave the homeowners a few tasks for the backyard, and I hope they did them. Because their deck was in terrible shape the last time I saw it."

Olivia couldn't imagine how a house this pretty had a deck that wasn't in tip-top shape. She walked along the side yard and her foot caught a root. She tripped and her knee went down into the grass hard. Patricia laughed. "Karma, my dear. Karma. Good thing we don't need to be in the photos today."

Olivia straightened up and felt her zipper give way a bit. She tried to dust off her muddy knee while also adjusting her zipper. Mud and mooning Patricia might be a little too much karma.

"Why do I deserve karma?" Olivia shot Patricia a look.

"Don't think I didn't notice your little smirk back there when my shoe got dirty."

Olivia rolled her eyes.

"Like that. I see you rolling your eyes at me. When all I do is try to help you, Olivia. If it wasn't for me, you'd still be stuck inside your home, staring out the front window." Patricia took a big step forward and this time her leg slid out. The grass wasn't just wet; the side yard had entirely turned to mud.

Olivia held her laugh in as her brain realized Patricia had seen her stare out her window. She wanted to push her into the mud and run away from her snobbery and the job. Instead, Olivia held out her hand and tried to sound magnanimous.

"Need a hand?"

"Yes." Patricia put her hand out and grabbed Olivia's so hard she slid a little too.

"Jesus, Patricia, I wasn't ready." Olivia's shoes got completely covered in mud.

"Your shoes will recover. Mine, however, won't."

"You know what?" Olivia let go of Patricia's hand. She was tired of the invisible crown of superiority Patricia wore. "Great, you've got nice shoes. My shoes are fine. I used to have a job, then I stayed home and took care of my daughter. And now I'm supposed to be helping you. But honestly, Patricia, you make it so hard."

Patricia got herself up and said, "I just meant my shoes are suede. I hadn't sprayed them yet with a waterproof protector. I should have gone home and changed when the photographer called and said he could squeeze this house shot in. Your shoes look like they are made of a washable material."

"Oh."

Just then, they heard a high-pitched, "Helllooooooo."

Patricia yelled out, "Stay there, Poppy. We are coming. Don't brave the side yard." She walked over to Poppy and introduced Olivia as she explained away the mud.

"Don't worry, we will both be taking our shoes off for the inside photos." She winked at Poppy and Olivia. And with that, the day moved forward as only Patricia's will could force it to.

It was a quiet drive home, with Patricia occasionally mentioning something for Olivia to add to her list. They got out of the car, and each walked to their own home wearing mud and embarrassment. Both took their shoes off as soon as they got inside. Both took their shoes to the sink and scrubbed away the mud to try to salvage them. Both finished their muddy chore, washed their hands, and then sat on their thrones, which were nothing but the couches in their living rooms. And both thought about the other with a little bit of annoyance and a lot of judgment.

CHAPTER 4
SIGN

The next morning, Olivia woke up early so she could work on the flyer again with Patricia's original design and font choices. She squinted at the fonts with hatred. Was it too early to hate fonts? She quickly showered before she got Sammy off to school. She blow-dried her long brown hair and put on jeans with a sweater.

"You look nice," Steve noticed. "Hot date?"

"You wish. No, just a staff meeting." Olivia smiled and sat up confidently. Calling it a staff meeting did sound better than a coffee meeting at the neighbor's house. Maybe Patricia was on to something.

"Well, have a great day. And hey, I know I was teasing you the other night. But I am proud of you."

Olivia and Steve walked out of the house together and exchanged vanilla suburban kisses on the cheeks. Their love life was all vanilla lately. No swirl. No chocolate chip. Just plain been married for a few years and would rather get in bed with a book than with each other.

As Steve got into his car, Olivia walked over to Patricia's house. She noticed the For Sale sign in the yard. There was no running away from this conversation now. Olivia was so curious about what Patricia was going to say. Her mind wondered if this was why they were meeting. And then, more importantly, Olivia wondered if Patricia had stopped at Starbucks after the gym? Olivia could go for a fancy coffee drink right now. She knocked on the door and waited. Nothing. Olivia rang the doorbell and stood awkwardly, wondering if a knock and a doorbell ring seemed rude or too eager. A few minutes passed. Should she knock again? Ring? Olivia got out her phone and checked the email. It said to meet at 7:45 for a staff meeting. It was now 7:53. Olivia knocked again, this time with a little more force. A knock seemed less intense than a doorbell. She looked around and waved at someone she did not know who was walking a dog. Why did she feel so uncomfortable? She was supposed to be here. Patricia had invited her. She had a flyer she designed for Patricia in her hand.

Olivia devised a plan in her mind. "Okay, I will ring one more time and if she doesn't come, I will walk home and send her an email." She pressed the doorbell. This time, she heard feet. Fast feet.

Patricia opened the door. She was not showered. Her hair was back in what Olivia guessed was a slept-in ponytail. She was not dressed. Patricia's hands clung to her gray plush bathrobe and her pajamas, silk cream with delicate roses, stuck out from the bottom of her robe. She wore matching cream slippers and a look of absolute mortification.

"I'm so sorry," Patricia said. "Come in, come in. Coffee is on. This morning just…"

And when Olivia looked at her boss, because that's how she thought of her now, not her uptight neighbor who she sometimes hated, but her boss, she realized Patricia's eyes were red, as if she had been crying. Olivia gazed down at the very clean wood floor. Was it sparkling at her? She passed the sensible vase filled with fresh flowers on the probably handmade hutch. She walked down the hallway, painted that perfect slate blue color that's soothing but smart. She made her way to the kitchen, where on the table sat four bamboo placemats accented by a grey tablecloth with a print that had various types of flying birds in a darker grey. Olivia knew a designer must have picked out the tablecloth, because no ordinary person could know how to make birds look this chic.

"So, I'm sure you saw the sign." Patricia gestured to the front of the house with a flourish of her hand.

"Yes," Olivia said quietly. Where were Olivia's words? Where were Patricia's words? The yes sat there between them on the table, but no other words followed from either of them. Patricia waited for Olivia to ask why. Olivia waited for Patricia to tell her why the house was for sale.

Finally, as if Patricia was blowing up a balloon and she was right at the end where she could not muster any more breath, Patricia squeezed out the words, "I'm divorcing Paul. We are selling the house." And then exhaled all the air out of her body.

"I'm so sorry," Olivia said. She thought about patting Patricia's hand, but Patricia's eyes somehow communicated, "Do not touch my skin." Instead, she said, "I redid the flyer" and placed it on the table. She expected Patricia to say something. But they both sat there quietly staring down at the paper until finally, Patricia broke the silence with, "He cheated on me."

Patricia's words were hard and cold. "I came back early from a real estate conference because I had just lost my assistant and I was upset."

Olivia nodded and figured someone like Patricia, who likes order with a capital O, might be ruffled by changes like losing your assistant.

Patricia lowered her voice and said, "She died. Breast cancer. She was only 34."

Olivia felt awful for not realizing that loss meant real loss, like dying. And she felt a wave of sympathy for Patricia.

"Oh Patricia, that's awful. I'm so sorry."

And this time Olivia's hand did not waver. She put it right on Patricia's hand. And Patricia did not move her hand for a good ten seconds. She looked down at Olivia's hand like it was a fly she'd like to swat.

Then she moved it away and said, "Yes. It was terrible. We had just done this walk for cancer the month before. I bought the entire real estate office pink tracksuits, and Peggy was so touched. Who would have guessed that one month later she'd be gone?"

Olivia felt like a total jerk. She had judged that pink tracksuit down to its pink core. And here Patricia was doing a cancer walk. Olivia frowned as she thought, *well, who is the spawn of Satan now?* Olivia briefly got lost in her self-pity of hate until she realized Patricia was still talking. Had she uncorked Patricia's inner verbal dam?

"And then I come home and he's having breakfast with the new salesperson, Cynthia. He wasn't even supposed to be in town. He was supposed to be away on a business trip."

Olivia started to say, "Breakfast doesn't have to mean…" but Patricia cut her off. "She was naked. Like full-on naked, sitting on my chair. I had to scrub it afterward. Who sits on a chair and eats naked? It's disgusting. She's disgusting. He's disgusting. And so now you know why the house is on the market." She said the last bit like it was a wrap-up and she was moving on to whatever was next. Patricia got up and grabbed her computer like she was officially ready to talk business.

"So, forgive my robe and my unprofessionalism this morning, but I just got caught off guard when I saw the sign this morning. I knew it was going up. But to see…" Patricia got quiet and steadied herself. "Well, anyway, enough about me. Let's get to what I need from you. The flyer looks fine. So that's done."

Olivia got out her pad of paper and pen and made a list of all the things Patricia needed to have done that day. Listings, emails, a few follow-ups with inspectors. The list felt longer than Olivia had expected. And even though she was smiling like the perfect assistant, internally she was stressing about how she was going to get it all done, clean the house, and still take Sammy to the park like she promised. When Patricia finished, Olivia stood up and said, "You know, Patricia, if you ever need anything, not real estate related, I'm here for you."

Patricia looked up at Olivia with uncertain eyes, and then her phone rang. "Got to take this. Thank you with a capital T," she said and gave her a dismissive smile, turning her body toward her computer. Olivia took that as her sign to leave and made her way out of the house. She shut the door quietly behind her, using both hands to close it gently, as if that was somehow treating Patricia gently, too.

Olivia went home and thought about what Patricia had said. It made her sad and stressed, so she began straightening up before digging into work. But she wasn't in the mood to truly clean, so she broke out her little hand vacuum and cleaned up a few crumbs here and there. Before she knew it, Olivia was bent over, cleaning her entire rug with her hand vacuum, which she knew was stupid. She owned a real vacuum, but she was too tired to go upstairs to get it, and somehow, she felt better doing it this way. She vacuumed the ground hard, as if her husband had just been there naked with a girl. And she realized she was mad for Patricia. Mad at men. Definitely mad at cleaning and the endless dirt that women had to deal with in their lives. She also wondered if all this cleaning counted as exercise. She tightened her stomach muscles as she bent over with her little hand vacuum and then let them go. That was enough of all that. Time to get to Patricia's list.

CHAPTER 5
LOTUS

Over the next few weeks, Patricia and Olivia talked about many things. Open house schedules. Mortgage rates. That odd collection of creepy dolls that fell out of the closet at a house showing, killing the buyer's interest. The one thing they didn't talk about again was Patricia's For Sale sign. Patricia hadn't mentioned if the house had seen a flurry of interest. Olivia certainly wasn't going to bring it up. But she was starting to feel like she was an essential part of Patricia's team so, as her employee, didn't she have a right to know what was going to happen to her job if Patricia moved?

Olivia wanted to broach the subject because paying back her vacation savings was weighing heavily on her mind. Especially since the last three calls to her mother went straight to voicemail. Although she had received a text from her mother last night: *Been busy, talk soon!*

She was at Patricia's for a morning meeting to talk about the next steps for a property when Patricia wrapped up with, "Okay, any other questions?" It was like a welcome mat for Olivia. Well, it was like a very uptight and please-don't-step-on-me kind of welcome mat that didn't even say welcome but had a decorative bouquet on it that you should never put your dirty feet on.

"Yes." Olivia's voice was small. Dammit, where was her womanpower now? Instead, her voice sounded itty-bitty and nervous.

"I'm sorry, yes what?" Patricia asked, since she had already moved on to the next task and assumed Olivia would just make her way out.

"Yes, I have a question."

Patricia stopped ruffling her papers for a second and said, "Go on."

"What's next for you? I mean, for me? When you sell the house? We haven't talked about that."

"Oh," was all Patricia said. And then sat there quietly for a while, nodding her head slightly to show she was thinking about her answer.

"It's funny you should ask that. Because I saw this today." Patricia handed over a property listing of a little bungalow with a thatched roof. Olivia scanned the listing. Just north of Placencia. Private beach. Near a charming local village in Belize.

"Sounds beautiful. Who is this for?"

"Me. It's been the top thing on my Me List that I've been too scared to do."

"Me List?" Olivia was confused.

"Oh, everyone has a list. Things you want to accomplish. Things you push yourself to do." She pointed to the property listing. "I traveled here and always wanted to retire in one of these adorable cottages. Of course, I thought I'd have Paul with me. But maybe that's the point of all this. To do it for me. I don't know, maybe it's crazy."

"It looks amazing." Olivia stared at the picture and thought about how beautiful it would be to just walk out to the beach each morning. Enjoy coffee on the sand. Catch fish for dinner. Although Patricia was not a catch-for-dinner type of woman. She was a pay-a-local to catch fresh ocean fish for dinner and do all the nasty deboning and stuff.

"What else is on your list?" Olivia's curiosity overcame her. She hoped Patricia was in a sharing mood.

"Honestly, every year on January first, I write myself a list of ten things I want to do in the New Year. This year, I accomplished all but the house and…" Patricia got quiet.

After a long pause, she added, "It's not something I want to admit." Patricia's tone wasn't haughty or mad. Patricia's voice sounded vulnerable. Could this force of a woman be letting some of her walls down?

Olivia waited.

"I told you about Peggy. The woman who worked for me, who had…"

"Breast cancer." Olivia finished the words for her, so Patricia didn't have to bear the weight of them.

"Yes. Well, she was distraught when she lost her hair. And she was so beautiful, honestly, even without hair. I thought, wouldn't it be a sign of support if I shaved my hair too? But as a realtor, I'm too concerned about how I look. Okay, as a woman, I'm too concerned with how I look. So, I put it on my list. But everything happened so quickly and, well, you know how this story ends."

Something in the room shifted, and Olivia suddenly knew what she had to do.

"Come with me." Olivia grabbed Patricia's hand. She didn't wait for an answer. She took her by the hand with such force that Patricia, though surprised by this new authority, got up.

"We're going to my house. I know exactly what to do." And believe it or not, Patricia followed. Without words. She followed Olivia down the steps, across the grass, and into Olivia's home.

"Don't mind the toys," Olivia said as she kicked a bunch of stuffed animals to the side. She brought Patricia to her round white kitchen table, which had no tablecloth but a few remnants of red permanent marker thanks to a craft by Sammy gone wrong. "Sit here. I'll be right back." Patricia sat on a green chair with a pillow tied to the back that had seen many days of cereal spills and pasta meals.

Olivia ran upstairs to her bathroom and grabbed Steve's clippers.

"You are not shaving my hair," Patricia said at once when she saw the clippers dangling out of Olivia's hands.

"Just wait. I want to show you." Olivia lifted her ponytail to reveal that underneath, where it met the neckline, the hair was shaved into the shape of a small lotus blossom. "It's my secret symbol of strength. Lotus flowers can bloom even in muddy waters," Olivia said quietly, suddenly aware she was revealing something personal, too. "I do it when I need to remind myself..."

Olivia couldn't quite find the words to explain why or when she started doing it. Honestly, the first time she did it, it looked like an angry frog. The hair would grow back and then she'd look in the mirror and attempt again. A little secret warrior patch all for herself. And she didn't want to tell Patricia she'd been so stressed recently by balancing her job and family life that she needed the lotus. Because on more than one occasion, she had thought about quitting. Until she remembered she still hadn't told Steve about the money she gave her mom. And that her mom had been avoiding her calls ever since.

"I could do it under your hair. No one would see it. But you would know. And it would be a way to honor your friend."

Patricia was quiet. And suddenly Olivia noticed the dishes on the counter, the shoes by the door, and wondered what the hell she was thinking, bringing this pristine woman into her cluttered house and thinking she'd let her touch her hair. Her face blushed. She began to back away when Patricia said, "Do it."

"Really?" Olivia's energy went from deflated to a giddy schoolgirl in two seconds flat. "I promise, I'll make it look great. I won't mess up." Olivia said it to herself, as much as to Patricia.

"Here, hold your hair up with your hands." Patricia pulled her hair forward. Damn, it was silky. What on earth did Patricia condition it with?

"Are you ready?" Olivia asked. Her finger slid the power switch on and the vibrating blades of the razor hummed.

"Ready as I'll ever be." Patricia stared straight ahead, too afraid to move, and held onto her hair as tightly as possible—as if her hands were a seatbelt that would get her safely to the other side of this adventure.

Olivia concentrated hard and quietly narrated to Patricia everything she was doing. "First, I'm just going to shave a little patch.

Now, I'm going to take the blade off so I can etch the first flower petal. It won't hurt. One done. Now the next petal. It's looking great."

And before Patricia could argue or question how on earth she had let the day change so dramatically, Olivia was finished.

"Come into the bathroom and look," Olivia said, suddenly praying that Sammy had flushed the toilet before leaving for school that morning.

Patricia angled herself so she could see her hair. Olivia glanced down and was happy to see no floaters in the toilet. Patricia put her hands to the back of her head and touched it where her hair used to be. She followed the lines of the little lotus flower and said only one word to Olivia: "Thanks."

The two women had walked into the bathroom one way. But they walked out of the bathroom differently. It was too early to use the F-word. They weren't quite friends. But they were no longer boss and assistant. They were in a middle ground, yet to be defined.

As Olivia walked Patricia to the door, Patricia said, "Olivia, I have an assignment for you for tomorrow."

"Oh, let me grab my pen."

"No need. It's simple. Bring your Me List tomorrow to our meeting." And with that, Patricia closed the door and walked home.

CHAPTER 6
THE ME LIST

That night, Olivia tucked Samantha into bed, snuggling next to her and slowly running her fingers through Sammy's thin, long brown hair in the way that made her relax.

"Sammy," she said. "Can I ask you a question?"

"You just did," Sammy said and smiled proudly to herself.

"You little stinker. That's my line. I say that to you."

"Yep."

"Is there anything you wish you could do? Like if you had a list of fun stuff you wanted to do this year, what would you put on it?"

Sammy scrunched up her nose, her sign of deep thinking, and said, "You know what I've always wanted to try?"

"What?" Olivia sat up a little, excited to hear what Sammy would confess.

"Bowling."

"Bowling?"

"Yeah; we've only gone that once. And there's that cool place that also has the games."

"We can definitely do more bowling. Anything else? Think more adventurous than bowling."

"Hmmmm. Well, I know one. But you'd never do it."

"Why?"

"You're scared of heights."

"Oh. What is it?"

"That zipline place. Zoe went, and she said it was amaaaaaazing."

"Saturday."

"What?"

"We're going this Saturday. Deal?"

"Are you serious? You'll go?"

"Yep. I'm putting it on my list. You and I are going. Daddy too. It's about time I stopped running from fun stuff like that. What's a little fear of heights, right?"

"Oh Mommy, I'm so excited. I'm so excited." Sammy hugged Olivia tightly.

"Now less excitement and more sleep, okay?"

"I'll go right to sleep." Sammy pulled up her covers and squealed with delight.

"Love you," Olivia said as she turned off the light.

Olivia crossed the hallway to their bedroom, where Steve was reading on their bed.

"How'd bedtime with Sammy go?" Steve asked.

"Good. She was sweet." Olivia grabbed a notebook off her nightstand and wrote the numbers one through ten on it. She wrote Zipline in the number one space.

"Steve, you know that zipline place?"

"The one outside of town with the crazy ropes?"

"Yeah. Sammy really wants to go. We don't have plans Saturday, right?"

"Nope. I can take her."

"Yeah, I want to go too."

"Sure, sounds great. I can go up there with her. My guess is at her age she'll need a parent."

"No. I want to do it too."

Steve put down his book and looked at his wife. He moved his dirty-blond hair out of his eyes, a habit he had but didn't know he had. His hazel eyes were wide and bright. "It's up high, you know."

"Yes, I understand what zipline and rope course means. I want to do it." Olivia looked at him with her "I'm serious" eyes.

"You remember the old church steeple, right?"

"Yes. But that was years ago. And I want to do it. I can do it."

This time, she sounded very sure. Yes, she'd had a panic attack in an old church steeple that time when she looked down from the bell tower and realized how high up she was. And yes, she'd cried with every step they took, her back pressed against the wall, eyes closed as Steve led her down the stairs one at a time. And yes, she could still hear the old lady chuckling at her as she connected with solid ground. She'd sat down, kissed her hand, and touched the ground because she was so thankful. Still, zipline was going on the list. She was going to face her fear of heights, for herself and for Sammy.

Olivia thought about asking Steve about her list, but something inside said to her, "No. This list is mine." And besides, after he'd joked about the zipline place, she didn't want his input. This was important to her.

"I'm going downstairs for a bit. You coming down or reading up here?" Olivia asked.

"Let me finish this chapter; then I'll come hang."

"Read for as long as you like." Olivia kissed him on the forehead because that was the answer she wanted. She wanted to be alone with her list.

Nine spots left. Nine ways she could improve her life, take a chance, or just do something for herself. Olivia shuffled uncomfortably on the tan couch. She propped a yellow pillow behind her back and looked down at herself. Not in a judgy, self-hate kind of way. More in a loving, what-do-you-need kind of way. And it was with her body and heart in mind that she knew what to write for number two. She had never done it, but she had the pants. Number two: Yoga.

Number three called to Olivia from deep within her heart. Something she used to do all the time but hadn't done in years. But as she wrote the word—Sing—it felt foolish. Do adults still sing? She wasn't a church choir kind of girl. But who was she to judge herself? Singing brought her happiness, and this was her list. She'd figure out the how later.

Number four would not go over well with her husband. But there was something she had wanted since she'd been a little girl. She could still see its little scruffy fur and big, round eyes. She could still hear the "no" her mother had said, and she could still feel the "no" too. Her whole life, she had always wanted a dog. But her mom was allergic. And so was Steve. She didn't think to ask during the dating period about allergies. But would that have stopped her from falling in love? She thought of the dog she met at the rescue fair when she was little. She thought of her husband's eyes. Surely, she could have both sets of eyes in her life. There were so many new breeds that were hypoallergenic. With confidence, she wrote down number four: Rescue Dog.

How else could she make this a great year? Who did she want to be? There was a simple one she could put down. Everyone likes to have one easy thing to cross off their list, right? Danielle from down the street had been bugging her for a while to join the neighborhood book club. The thought of hanging out with Danielle and Suzanne, who always had beautiful hair and Starbucks, made her want to hurl. But books were good. More adult contact was good. Even if it meant she had to blow-dry her hair. And there would be wine to drown out Suzanne. She needed more books in her life. Plus, it would be good for Samantha to see her reading. Olivia used to read books all the time, but now, besides a parenting book here and there, she couldn't remember the last book she read. Olivia wrote Book Club next to the number five. She was halfway there and feeling excited. Looking at the list made her smile. She wanted all these things in her next year.

The simplicity of books felt good. Olivia tried to think of another simple pleasure. She smiled to herself. Coffee. She loved a good cappuccino or latte. But they were expensive, and she always felt guilty indulging. Could she learn to make one at home? Buy a milk frother or a decent coffee machine? Maybe she could ask Steve to get her one for her birthday? Being her own barista could be pretty cool. She wrote Make My Own Coffee Drinks next to six.

Four more to go. The last two were easy. Olivia decided this one should be hard. What would be a hard thing that would improve her life? There was one looming impossible thing in her life. Could she do this? Did she actually want to tackle this? Would it make her life better? Yes. Did she think about it every day and stress about it? Definitely. But the thought of actually mending this relationship seemed larger than the ocean. Olivia didn't even know how big the ocean was, but that's how big the rift was between her and her mother. And that rift had become even wider after she lent her mom the money. For Sammy's sake, she had to give it one last try. Olivia wrote Mom next to the number seven.

Three more spots. Three more things that would be just for herself. She hadn't thought this much about herself in a long time. Maybe that was the point? Damn, that Patricia was smart. This Me List was a good idea.

"Whatcha' working on?" Steve asked.

"You scared me. I didn't even hear you." Olivia folded her list in half as a feeling of slight embarrassment washed over her.

"Is that something for Patricia?" Steve asked. He sat next to her and brought her legs over his lap, rubbing her feet a little. The act of sweetness made Olivia feel a little more like sharing.

"Sort of. It's something she wanted me to do. But it's actually for me. It's a list."

Steve rubbed her feet and said nothing, so Olivia continued, "It's like a list of stuff to improve my life."

"Am I on it?" Steve gave her his cheesiest smile.

"It's not like that. It's not a people list. Although I guess my mom is on it."

"Your mom! Is it a things-that-drive-me-crazy and treat-me-like-crap list?" Steve was always quick with sarcasm. His jokes had made

Olivia fall in love with him. He brought happiness and laughter to her life when she felt low. But now his jokes stung more than they should. A byproduct of marriage. The slow disintegration of once-loved habits.

"Ha. Funny. No, it's things I want to do or work on, or basically anything I want to be a better me. Is there anything you'd want me to put on it?"

"Sex 365 days a year."

"You. Are. Killing. Me. I'm being serious here."

"So am I. It would be awesome."

"How about date nights? We could try to get a babysitter once a month to go out."

"Works for me. It would be great to have some non-Sammy time together."

"Agreed. And who knows, if you're lucky…"

Steve smiled. God, men are so easy. Steve's list probably would be sex listed one through ten. When was the last time they had sex? Olivia couldn't remember. Instead, she wrote Date Nights next to number eight.

"I've got two more."

"Can I see the list? What else is on there?" Steve peeked over Olivia's shoulders.

"I don't know." Olivia felt like she was a child again, being asked to share an intimate poem with a class.

"You don't trust me," Steve said, pouting.

"I trust you to make a joke. And I'm taking this seriously."

"This list?"

Olivia sighed. "Yes, this list." This list was turning out to be like the thirty other little things in her day that Steve didn't take seriously. Like her new job. But she didn't know how to talk to him without it all sounding trite, so instead, she tilted her list towards him.

"I think you meant to write hot dog on number four."

"I knew you'd hate four. But we'll figure it out. I get lonely at home and I've always wanted a dog. And it'd be great for Sammy. And lots of breeds have less dander."

"Okay. Okay. I get it. But is 'I want my husband with red eyes and a constantly drippy nose' on that list?"

Olivia frowned. She knew Steve wouldn't understand her list. She wanted a dog. There were options. And she realized at that moment she was taking the list very much to heart. That each one of those words or phrases next to a number represented something she truly wanted. She moved her legs off Steve.

"Hey, I have a good one for you. If you want. It's your list, so you don't need to do it. But it's sort of one that includes our whole family."

"What?" Olivia said it with just a hint of "I'll cut you if you say something stupid" in her tone.

"Well, we've been saving for years to take that vacation. I think it's time we make it happen."

Olivia's stomach dropped. She should tell him now about the money. But he'd already made the comment about her mom. On one hand, every day she waited to tell him, it got harder. On the other hand, she was still hoping her mom was going to pay her back like she promised. But she knew from her mom ignoring her calls that she wasn't going to get the money back anytime soon. Olivia would have to keep working and figure out another way.

"Yes!" Olivia forced a smile as she wrote Vacation next to number nine. That left just one spot left. Lucky number ten.

Steve seemed to sense he should leave before he pissed her off again. He kissed Olivia on the head and said, "I'm heading upstairs to finish that book. You've got this. That last one is all you. As long as it's not a cat." He smiled warmly at her to show that he loved her. Olivia knew he secretly hoped she'd write another three-letter word that wasn't cat but started with S, ended with X, and would make him purr.

One more spot. Olivia looked around her room. She certainly could put Get More Organized on her list, but that did not thrill her. What would make her feel better? Become more self-confident? And then, when she thought of it, she let out a little giggle. I mean, it would make Steve happier, too. But there's no way she could let Patricia see the words. The yoga was going to make her fitter. And hopefully, the dog would make her walk more. So how could she write the last few words that would show she'd change? Number ten waited for the right words. "It's my list," Olivia said to herself and wrote the words Fancier Undergarments as confidently as she could.

Ten things, all for her. It was done. And somehow, seeing the words made her excited about what the year held. She was a little nervous to show it to Patricia tomorrow. All she knew about Patricia's list was that it involved big plans, like buying a home in Belize and supporting a dying friend. Those were huge. But Olivia stuffed those feelings of insecurity down. This was her list, to be as big or as small as she wanted. And tomorrow she'd share it with Patricia.

CHAPTER 7
YOGA

Olivia felt a little nervous that morning. She wasn't the most open person, and this list made her vulnerable. Being vulnerable was one thing, but being vulnerable in front of perfect Patricia was another. She steeled herself and knocked on the door.

Patricia opened it with a phone to her ear and gestured for her to come in.

"The Bakers' house just got an offer," she whispered to Olivia along with a thumbs-up, which seemed not quite like something Patricia would do. Somehow, it seemed a thumbs-up gesture would be beneath someone with so much polish and dry-cleaned clothes. And before Olivia could stop herself, she gave a thumbs-up back. Great, now they were like middle-school boys who just scored a basket.

Patricia hung up the phone and smiled at Olivia. "Big commission on that house. I can't believe we got full price." And she went right into the details of what had to happen next. Scheduling an inspection. Radon testing. Lead paint testing because of its age. Olivia took copious notes. At the end of their meeting, Patricia gave her a little speech.

"Great. Thanks again for all this help. I know we've had a few bumps. But overall, I think it's gone well." She paused, but only briefly. "Actually, there is something I want to ask you."

Olivia was ready. She knew her list was folded in half and in the back of her notebook.

"Next Thursday evening, what are you up to?" Patricia asked.

"Oh, um. Let me check my..." Olivia pulled out her phone and clicked on Thursday, even though she knew Sammy had nothing that night and neither did she. "It's open. What do you need?"

"You. The real estate firm is holding an appetizers and drinks event down at the Bard Hotel. I was hoping you'd join me in toasting to a challenging but successful few weeks." Patricia smiled and added, "Free drinks."

"Um. Yes. Let me double-check with Steve. But I think that should work. Anything else?" Olivia felt a bit disappointed. She didn't want to show her the list if she didn't ask. She felt as if she had done her homework and then her teacher had forgotten to collect it.

"Yes. Did you do it?" Patricia gave her a warm smile. Not her usual terse, slightly bitchy, "I'm better than you" smile. It was a big welcome mat sort of smile.

"Yes."

"You don't have to share it if you don't want to. I mean, it's for you. But I'd love to see it. Maybe there are some I can help you with?"

Olivia touched the list gently and knew she was about to be judged. But she wanted to show Patricia because that would make it real and she needed to be accountable. Otherwise, it'd be just another thing she'd started without following through on. Like that blender she bought. She'd made one kale smoothie that tasted like crap and never used it again. No. This was not going to end up like kale. Olivia handed the list to Patricia and immediately started babbling to make up for how uncomfortable she felt.

"I tried to pick big and small things. Things just for me. A few that might involve Sammy or Steve."

"It's great. What are you doing tomorrow morning at eight-thirty?"

"Uh. Probably something for you."

"Well. Meet me here. We can go to hatha yoga at nine."

"What?"

"Number two on your list. I love the class and the instructor is fabulous."

"You should know I've never done yoga. I don't even own a mat."

"I have an extra."

"Great. I mean thanks. Number two. Here we go. Number one is happening this weekend."

"You're on your way, aren't you!" Patricia beamed. Clearly, self-empowerment was her thing.

"Thanks for the suggestion. I think this is going to be good for me."

"I'm so glad. And don't forget to let me know about Thursday evening."

"Will do." Olivia left Patricia's house with an odd feeling. She wasn't leaving her boss's house. She wasn't leaving her neighbor's house. She felt like she was leaving her sort of friend's house. Could it be? Could Patricia go from being the spawn of Satan to a friend who was helping Olivia find herself again? Life was weird.

Olivia went home and typed hatha yoga into her computer. Okay, to be honest, she entered "Is hatha yoga hard?" into her computer. The answer made her feel better. Hatha yoga was great for beginners. It focused on static poses. She clicked on a video clip. This girl was fit. Pretty. Really pretty. Not that it mattered. Strengthening, stretching, relaxing—this didn't sound so bad. But the lady talked slowly. Was she too impatient for yoga? Olivia skipped ahead in the video. Child's pose. She could handle that. How long can one pose last? She would try to have a better attitude at the actual class tomorrow. New Olivia was going to slow down and breathe and be one with the moment or something like that. Maybe she should wear one of those lavender oils her friend gave her tomorrow. It might help. It definitely couldn't hurt.

At 8:29 the next morning, Olivia was wearing black yoga pants that had never done yoga, a grey T-shirt, and the only sports bra she owned. She'd barely knocked on Patricia's door before it opened. Patricia stood in front of her, looking fit and ready. One purple mat and one pink mat were tucked under each arm. She wore burgundy yoga pants and a matching burgundy and grey tank top. Her hair was in a bun. If there was a poster for calm and kick-ass yoga, Patricia would be on it. Olivia would be a small, badly cut-out picture on the bottom of a sad-ass flyer someone had made on their home computer of moms who needed to try yoga.

"You ready? I'll drive." Patricia's words were more of a statement than a question.

"Yep. Ready as I'll ever be. First yoga class coming up."

"I do think you'll like it. I leave feeling stronger and ready to start my day. I go three times a week ever since...Paul and naked bitch."

Olivia laughed. She couldn't help it. She had never heard Patricia sound anything but polite.

"I'm sorry. I shouldn't have said that. But my therapist said I shouldn't hold in my feelings and, well...you're a safe space." Patricia looked at Olivia with a softness in her eyes, like she wanted to make sure it truly was safe.

"Of course. You can say anything you want. I think that's a fair deal. You're helping me on my yoga journey. I can help you express yourself. That's one area I'm pretty good at. I mean, I'd have loads of words for bare butt."

Patricia laughed. "Bare butt. That's going to make me laugh every time I think of it."

"My job here is done." Olivia grinned and noticed how different she felt around Patricia. The air seemed less tense. Their yoga pants were both going to yoga together. This was surely a moment.

The yoga studio was decorated in pale wood tones and tasteful greenery in big white vases that sat on the floor. The smell of cedarwood hung in the air. Delightful music played. In about twelve seconds flat, Olivia had sized up the other women. A few were thin, athletic, and ballerina beautiful. Three were blond and chatty; not her type. Two were older and refined like Patricia. She got a few bashful smiles thrown her way, since she was new.

Olivia was thankful that Patricia put her mat down on the floor and with Olivia's next to it. It made her feel like she belonged. There was one woman who put her mat in front of her. "Hi, I'm Chrissy. Just had a baby three months ago and trying to get back to whatever it was I was before." Olivia liked her immediately.

"This is my first class," Olivia admitted.

"Well, don't watch me. I never know what I'm doing, but I figure it can't hurt."

Chrissy settled onto her mat and started stretching, so Olivia sat on her mat and started stretching too. Her toes had gotten farther away from her. Couldn't she reach them before? Just then, a beautiful red-haired and sun-kissed woman walked in, her whole body moving with relaxation and ease.

"Instructor," Patricia whispered, as if it were a naughty secret.

And because Olivia was feeling a tad out of her element, she gave her the thumbs-up sign. A sign that solidified that she was, in fact, a total lame-o. Her thumb stood there, pointing up for longer than it should. Why couldn't she put her huge thumb down?

"Yes? Do you have a question?" the instructor asked. Olivia realized she was looking at her. Damn thumb. She shoved her hand under her leg.

"Nope. I'm good." Olivia could feel her face blush. Stupid cheeks, always giving her away.

"You're new?" the instructor inquired.

The warmth of the lights felt hot. What was this, a yoga interrogation? Okay, it was only two questions. But still. It was more attention than Olivia wanted in a class where she knew nothing.

"Yep. New. Starting today." And because Olivia's mouth wouldn't stop her, she then said, "Right-o," which were words she never had uttered before.

The instructor smiled and said, "Well, my name is Sequoya. If you have any questions, feel free to ask as we go along." Olivia nodded and kept her mouth shut—mainly because she worried what words might come out next.

Olivia breathed deeply as Sequoya led them through some stretching. And while all the women around her appeared to be enjoying inner peace, Olivia's brain was going something like this: *You wanted to do this, Olivia. Take advantage. And breathe. Did I pack Sammy's snack? I should check on that listing Patricia told me about to see if there was an offer. I wonder if that lady in front of me had a boy or a girl. I bet it was a boy. I could go for some cheese. It's too early for cheese. The French eat cheese anytime, don't they? I would love to take Sammy to Paris. Remember when I went with Steve? That was before kids. Well, kid. We sat around and ate and drank. It. Was. Heaven.*

"And now let's stretch the other side." Sequoya's long arms gracefully reached to the tip of her pointed toes.

Olivia switched sides and watched Patricia, who looked intently focused, like this was a test she was going to ace. *Maybe I need more focus,* Olivia wondered. *I wonder if Patricia's brain is quiet. She looks quiet. Be quiet, brain. We are focusing on inner peace here. Cheesy piece of pizza. Damn stomach. Pipe down. Next time I will eat a bigger breakfast.*

"Let's move our bodies to a nice, relaxed downward dog. Feel the stretch through your hands. Let go of anything bothering you through the palms of your hands." Sequoya's voice was soft but firm.

Olivia's shoulders were hurting. *Downward dog should be my friend. I like dogs.* She closed her eyes so she could concentrate and release all the stress through the floor. She was starting to relax. *Steve better let me get a dog,* she thought, tensing up. *No, no, no, mind, relax,* she scolded herself and breathed deeply again, trying to quiet her brain.

"Now rotate and put one arm up to the sky like this. Reaching, with palm up."

Olivia turned and reached and felt her leg shaking. She wasn't embarrassed. She needed this. Her body needed to get stronger. At least shaking meant she was trying. Suddenly, she felt proud of herself. She was trying something new. And it could lead to healthier roads ahead. Yes, she could do this. But she was hoping Sequoya would move to the other side before her leg and arm gave out.

Forty-five minutes later, with more sweat than Olivia's body had seen since she had Sammy, the class was over. Olivia could not even reach for her cell phone without her arms feeling like little T-Rex arms.

But she felt good. Bad good. The kind of good when you know if you just kept doing it, it would eventually lead to good.

"Thanks, Patricia, that was great."

"Oh, I'm so glad you liked it. Now let's get home and start our day!" Patricia's arms did not look like they were anchors of pain and sorrow like Olivia's.

"Sounds good." And on the way back, Patricia turned into work Patricia and discussed all the things she needed from Olivia that day. Olivia was relieved none of them involved using any muscle besides her brain.

CHAPTER 8
WINE

Thursday came and Steve made it home from work just in time so Olivia could go out. He sat on the bed with Sammy and watched Olivia blow-dry her hair and get dressed.

"You look pretty, Mamma," Sammy said as she twirled her hair through her little fingers.

Olivia had texted Patricia about the dress code and decided on a simple black dress. It was the dress she wore to weddings or funerals. It was that black dress. Not too short, not too sexy, but black. The only actual black dress she owned, and it would do just fine for drinks and networking. Her stomach rumbled a little. Why was she feeling so nervous? This wasn't a date. This was a work opportunity. But it had been a while since she had been around other adults in a non-kid setting. Sure, she had gone to the occasional work party with Steve, but that was different. For one, she didn't talk much. And she mainly hung around the sidelines, waiting for the whole thing to be over.

For some reason, Olivia wanted to do better for Patricia. In some weird way, she wanted Patricia to be proud of her. As Olivia applied her lipstick, she peered into her own eyes in the mirror and accepted that she looked pretty. And that it was okay she was looking for validation from Patricia. Deep down, she knew her mother had been hard on her most of her life and it didn't take a therapist to understand that Patricia triggered her insecurity.

"I'm ready. What do you think, guys?" Olivia twirled around in a little circle and smiled bashfully.

"You look great," Steve said. Sammy gave two thumbs up.

"Now, Sammy, I want you to be good for Daddy. Go to bed when he tells you, okay?"

"I'll be good, Mamma."

Sammy jumped off the bed and gave Olivia a big hug, rubbing her nose and lips all over the middle of her black dress, which meant it now had a faint smear of Sammy's snot. Olivia gave her a hug and a kiss on the forehead and went back into the bathroom and took a towel to the snot stain. Now she had a wet spot in the middle of her dress. The doorbell rang. Patricia was right on time.

"Can you go tell her I'll be down in one sec?" Olivia gave Steve her 'please, I beg you' eyes.

"Will do. Let's go, Sammy."

Olivia took her blow dryer and aimed it at the wet oval around her navel. Snot drying before a night out was a clear sign she was a parent. When it looked dry enough, Olivia gave herself one last look in the mirror, checked her nose for anything gross, checked her teeth for cleanliness, raised her armpits to make sure her deodorant hadn't left any marks, and decided she was good to go. She walked down the stairs as if she was heading off to prom and Patricia was her date waiting with a corsage. Okay, no corsage was in her hands. She texted someone on her phone as she hugged a smart-looking black clutch under her arm.

"Ready for a night out?" Patricia smiled—a little curtly like a boss, a little warmly like a friend. She stood in two-inch heels and a black lace dress that looked sophisticated and expensive. Olivia was sure that Patricia probably owned at least five black dresses. She probably never had to worry about relatives looking back at wedding photos and noticing the same dress year after year after year.

"Ready," Olivia said more confidently than she felt, which she gave away by glancing down nervously to see if her wet spot had dried. She smoothed out her dress one last time.

"I won't bring her home too late," Patricia said to Steve, patting him lightly on the shoulder as if familiarity existed between them.

On the way to the restaurant, Patricia gave Olivia the run-down of who all would be there.

"John. He runs finance. Good person to know, especially when you need to pull a few strings." Patricia winked at her. With every person they discussed, Olivia felt more honored that Patricia was treating her like an active part of her team. She really did want her there, not just as a plus one.

"Ugh, there's Kelly. She's got short blond hair. Don't even talk to her. If you open your mouth, she won't stop talking for days. Avoid her like the plague."

Olivia laughed. "Good to know."

They pulled up to the restaurant and approached the valet. As they walked through the doors, Patricia stopped for a second and said quietly, "Thanks for coming with me. It's my first one of these without...without Paul."

Olivia instantly grabbed her hand and said, "Of course."

The restaurant was big and modern, filled with dark woods, candles, and accents of moody artistic paintings. To the right was the bar, featuring a big sign with scriptwriting that read, "Welcome Smith & Holden Realtors."

Olivia had the sudden worry that maybe Patricia would see people she knew and leave her on her own. But instead, Patricia said, "Oh there's Bob. I'd like him to meet you," and grabbed her hand, pulling her along to make the introduction. And that's how it went from person to person. Olivia was never pushed to the side. Patricia made sure to introduce Olivia in every conversation. Olivia remembered to order white wine, so she didn't have to worry about her teeth staining red if she drank too much. The conversation and wine flowed easily. Maybe too easily. Olivia's heels were hurting. She sat down at a high-top table as Patricia talked to one of the other "high performing" realtors.

"Do you mind if we keep being boring and talk numbers?" Patricia asked Olivia politely.

"Of course. Just giving my feet a rest." Olivia adjusted herself into the chair and suddenly felt the exhaustion of having to be so "on" with people. Not in a bad way, but in a way she hadn't pushed herself to do in a while. And that's when she felt the table jiggle a little and found herself staring at a short-haired girl who had plunked herself into the chair across from her.

"You don't mind, do you? My feet are freaking killing me. Every time I wear heels, I say I'm never going to do it again. They're evil. Probably designed by men." Kelly dropped one black shoe at a time below her seat and said, "Yes. Much better."

Olivia giggled. A bit from the wine and a bit from what Patricia had told her earlier about this woman.

"I'm Kelly." Her handshake was firm and quick. "I'm drinking mojitos. You want one?" She beckoned a server over. "Two mojitos please." When the server left, she winked and said, "Don't worry, I'll drink yours if you don't want it. You're Patricia's new conquest. I've heard all about you." Kelly smiled but Olivia wasn't sure if this was a good 'I've heard about you,' or a bad 'I've heard terrible things about you.'

"You know, Patricia is always one of the leading realtors," Kelly said. "She doesn't need a hotshot helper to make her ego even bigger."

This sounded positive, but the conversation was happening so quickly that Olivia couldn't tell if hotshot was good. One thing she did realize was she hadn't even told Kelly her name yet. She had yet to even speak a word. Olivia started to say her name when Kelly talked over her.

"I've asked for an assistant. For three years. Can you imagine? Three years asking for something so you can do your job better. But do I have one?" Finally, Kelly was quiet. She raised her eyebrows to show this was when Olivia should speak. To finish Kelly's thought.

"No," Olivia said.

"That's right. No. No, I don't. I have me. Me. Me. And, me."

Just then, Olivia heard the welcome sound of a familiar voice. "Oh, there you are, Olivia. We must be going. Your husband said ten o'clock." Patricia looked down at her watch, which was more like a gold bracelet with a teeny tiny watch face.

"Oh, yes. Thank you." Olivia jumped off her chair and said, "Bye. Nice to meet you."

Kelly waved just as the server set down two drinks. Olivia looked back one more time to see Kelly take both drinks and cheers herself with one glass in each hand.

"Let's escape to the bathroom and we can talk about the plan." Patricia laughed as they walked across the restaurant.

"Thanks for rescuing me." Olivia hiccupped.

"Yes. She is something, that Kelly, isn't she?"

"Yes. I thought you were exaggerating, but..." hiccup, "you were not."

The two women looked in the mirror at the same time. Patricia was slightly taller than Olivia and her hair fell perfectly into a nicely edged long bob. She was probably about twenty years older than Olivia, although she never felt comfortable asking.

"I have an idea. Do you have another hour in you?" Patricia asked. Truthfully, staying here for another hour did not sound fun. All Olivia wanted was to be in her pajamas in her bed.

As if reading Olivia's mind, Patricia added, "We won't be staying here. We have one more stop on the way home. Because of your list."

Olivia looked up, interested. "Which one?"

Patricia laughed and said, "Oh, I'm not going to tell you. Let's just go. And it'll be a surprise so you can't back out."

Olivia stared out of Patricia's car into the night. It seemed so much later than it was. There were so many other cars out and about. *I guess the world doesn't go to sleep when I do,* Olivia thought. Parenting was just so tiring. The night was something she had let go of. A time she could do without.

They pulled up to a small red building. It was unassuming and old. The building looked well-loved, with a worn sign and barely-there shrubbery. It did not look like a place Patricia would touch, let alone go into.

"We're here." Patricia's voice was practically singing with excitement.

"Is this a tattoo parlor?" Olivia was sure she had not put a tattoo on her list.

"No. Follow me. You'll see soon enough."

As they walked into the bar, the bartender looked up at them. The bar was small and square and also painted red. That's when Olivia noticed to the right of the bar was a stage with pretty white lights hung all around it. And someone was on that stage singing.

Patricia leaned over and whispered, "It's a karaoke bar." And the smile that spread on her face was the biggest one Olivia had seen yet.

"Oh, my goodness." Olivia was feeling buzzed, but not sure she was drunk enough to sing in front of Patricia. But as she looked at Patricia's face, which looked so hopeful and excited, she thought at least they could sit and watch others sing.

Next up was a man wearing a blue dress and a curly wig. When he grabbed the microphone and sang the words to a country song, Olivia was in awe. That he was so comfortable with who he was. That he sang so beautifully, full of heart. Watching him made her wish she was as brave. She opened the book in front of her with all the different songs and looked for a few of her favorites. Maybe Beyoncé? But Patricia didn't seem like a Beyoncé girl. Adele? That might be too much. Her stomach flipped and her anxiety reminded her that she hadn't sung in years.

"Let's do it together. It'll be fun." Patricia pulled the book over from Olivia and started paging through it.

"I don't know. I think tonight we should just watch."

"Come on. Live a little," Patricia teased. "It's called a Me List, not a sit back and watch list."

"I know. It's just I haven't drunk this much in quite a while and..." Before Olivia could finish her sentence, Patricia wrote something on a piece of paper and brought it up to the lady running the karaoke machine.

"Oh no." Olivia hiccupped. Her stomach was really on fire now at the prospect of singing in front of everyone. Why did she put that on her list? Because she thought maybe she'd get voice lessons or sing more in the shower, not on a stage with Patricia. Her Me List was suddenly feeling like Patricia's controlling list. "You're not even going to tell me?"

"Nope. Not until we're up there. But it's a song everyone likes." Patricia smiled. "Until then, one more drink so I don't back out?"

Back out? I might black out. Olivia looked down at her feet, which felt numb, and wondered how her legs were going to get her to the stage. Patricia placed two shots in front of them.

"Liquid courage. Let's do this." In less than a second, Patricia downed her tequila shot and bit into her lime.

Olivia heard the karaoke lady say, "Next up are Patricia and Olivia with Love Shack." Olivia picked up her shot glass and dumped it down her throat before she had time to second-guess herself.

The stage was about six by six feet. To call it a stage was generous. It was more like a small platform, but that didn't matter. The lights. The microphone. It all made Olivia nervous. She looked at Patricia and tried to smile. But even her lips were too drunk to move. She heard the background music start to play. It took a second before she realized what song it was, and then she went to open her mouth, but nothing came out.

Patricia sang into the microphone and waved her hands to encourage Olivia. Olivia shakily held onto the microphone, with a barely audible voice. She heard a few "woos" of encouragement. Patricia's voice was decent. She sang without embarrassment. Olivia heard the word "love" and tried to join in but this time when she opened her mouth, she felt like something was going to come out. And out. And out. And all over the stage.

The music kept going. Olivia covered her mouth and ran off the stage, knocking over a chair and a beer on her way out. She wanted to yell sorry, but she just needed to get outside and feel the cold air. And to never see Patricia or a stage or whatever that last shot was ever again.

Olivia sat down on the curb and put her head in her hands. She should text her husband to come pick her up, but it hurt to move. She doubted Patricia was going to let her in her car after she almost ralphed on her shoes. And then suddenly those same black shoes were right next to her.

"Olivia, are you all right? I thought you went to the bathroom, and I was worried when you weren't there. I gave the waitress a tip and grabbed your purse."

Olivia nodded her head without looking up. She didn't want to see whatever look was on Patricia's face. Disgust? Judgment? Disappointment?

"Paul always told me my singing was pretty bad. Didn't know it could make someone almost sick, though."

Olivia heard an odd, high-pitched squeak. She finally lifted her head and realized Patricia was laughing.

"Oh dear, I think we should call an Uber. I don't think I should drive either. I'll go get a bag from the back of my car just in case I try to sing again and it makes you ill." Patricia laughed again.

And then perfectly polished Patricia sat on the curb next to Olivia. Olivia wondered if Patricia's bottom had ever been so close to dirt. Or karaoke? The cold air felt good on Olivia's face. She turned around and noticed the big bushes in front of the bar—just in case she got sick.

Patricia looked at her phone and said, "The Uber will be here in five minutes. Do you need water or anything? How are you feeling?"

"Better. I think my nausea has passed. I don't usually drink this much because of…" But Olivia let the next words disappear without saying them.

"Is it odd to say this night has been fun? Despite it all. I haven't been out much since…" Patricia's voice got quieter as she said, "Paul. And I haven't drunk anything since…"

Olivia waited for her to finish her sentence. She could tell Patricia was holding in a secret just like she was. A sad one. Patricia looked out into the night and the two sat quietly with the moon above until Olivia tried to lighten the mood.

"It has certainly been an interesting night," Olivia said. "Guess I should have put 'Almost puke at a karaoke bar' on my list instead of 'singing.'" She wanted to laugh, but she didn't want to jostle her stomach any more than she had to.

"I think I'll let you cross singing off your list another time, and maybe without me." Patricia let out a little laugh. It was high and squeaky, but Olivia didn't mind.

They rode in silence in the Uber on the way home. Their silences came together in the darkness of the car and hung together almost like a hug.

CHAPTER 9
ROPE

On Saturday, Olivia pretended she wasn't nervous. Samantha was so excited about the family's big ropes course and zipline adventure that she chatted all the way there. She kept saying to Olivia, "Are you excited, Mom? Are you nervous? If you are nervous, I can help you."

Steve would look over and pat Olivia's leg and smile. Olivia looked straight ahead, trying to quiet her racing heart.

"I'll be just fine Sammy. It's mind over matter, right?" What Olivia didn't say is that the previous night her mind had blessed her with three different nightmares where she fell to her death. They pulled up to the ropes course where a sign with two big trees held up a rickety bridge that spelled welcome, but it did not seem very welcoming to Olivia.

"Mind over matter," Olivia repeated to herself.

They parked and walked to the office where they met Todd, a twenty-something outdoorsy-looking dude who Olivia did not feel was adequate for saving her when all went south. He said "all right" with way too much enthusiasm and way too often in the conversation. Todd informed them they first needed to watch a safety video. Olivia breathed in and out and tried to find comfort in the word "safety" but felt uneasy about the word "harness." It didn't look like much. Just a few tan straps and three black buckles. *The wire that connects the harness to the safety line should be thicker.* The video gave a run-through of the course's two ziplines. One at the beginning and one at the end. Twenty-five obstacles in between. *Twenty-seven scary-ass things to get through,* thought Olivia. Twenty-seven was a big number. But it could be worse. The video daringly showed aerial bridges, nets, planks, and all the adventurous things they'd be doing. Samantha's face beamed with enthusiasm. Olivia's face was somewhere between white, worried, and I'm about to have diarrhea.

"Are you ready, Mom? Are you ready?!" Samantha pulled Olivia's hand.

"Yep. Let me just go to the bathroom first." Olivia smiled.

"You all right?" Steve asked.

"Yep. You guys get fitted in your harnesses. I'll be right back."

Olivia went straight to the bathroom and to the sink. She splashed cold water on her face. She stared at herself in the mirror and tried to give herself a you-can-do-it look. She had already failed karaoke. She didn't want to fail this. Not in front of her daughter.

Olivia tried to calm her breathing and summon her courage. She walked back out and got fitted into her harness. After Todd tightened her straps, she pulled them even tighter. The harnessed family took the stairs to the top of the zipline that would take them to the course. So. Many. Stairs. At every stair platform, Samantha would check in and say, "You okay, Mom?" And Olivia would nod her head, too out of breath to speak. Olivia did not look down. But seeing the tops of the trees did not make her feel any better.

"Who wants to go first?" asked Todd.

Steve looked at Olivia. "Do you want to go first?"

"Are you crazy?" Olivia's voice was screechy and totally uncool.

"You go first. Then Sammy, so you're there on the other side to help her. I'll go last," Olivia said as she pulled on her harness one last time to make sure it was tight.

"If you change your mind, it's okay." Steve squeezed her shoulder.

"I'm fine. Stop fussing over me. You're making it worse." Olivia shot Steve a mean look. His worrying was annoying her and making her feel worried, which didn't help.

"She won't change her mind, will you, Mommy?" Could her daughter's face look any sweeter? Damn that sweet face. Olivia couldn't bail now. Not when Sammy believed in her.

"I'll be fine. I'll watch you guys and be brave." Olivia's voice only shook a little.

Steve hooked his carabiner onto the wire. Smiled at Olivia and Samantha, and before Olivia even heard Todd say, "Ready," Steve was flying down the line screaming, "Wooooooo." Olivia turned her head away, too scared to look.

"He made it Mom! Look! Dad looks happy."

In the distance, they could hear Steve yell, "That was amazing!"

"Yay! I'm next." Samantha walked right up and Todd helped her get situated. "Do you want a push, or can you do it yourself?" Todd asked.

"Mmmm. I can do it," Samantha answered. "Don't worry, Mom, you'll do great. I'll cheer you on."

Olivia was trying to hold it together, but tears started streaming. "I love you, baby. Be…"

But she'd barely gotten out the word "careful" and Sammy was on her way down the line. Not screaming but looking pleased as punch. And then it hit Olivia. She was next. She was next! She was about to leave the safety of the platform and dangle her legs way above the ground on a stupid wire and tiny zipline. Why oh why did she ever put this on her list? Why didn't she put something much, much closer to the ground?

"Ma'am, you ready?" Olivia heard Todd's voice, but she wasn't quite ready to answer. Her entire body was shaking.

"I'm afraid of heights," Olivia whispered.

Todd laughed. "Well, today's the day you learn heights are awesome. Just take a deep breath. And imagine you're close to the ground. Just enjoy the ride, you know. It's no problem; a lot of people get a little nervous."

But Olivia wasn't a little nervous. She was heart-racing, bones-shaking, and might have just peed a little in her pants nervous.

She stared ahead and could see Sammy's little body jumping up and down excitedly on the platform.

"Fucking list. Fucking Patricia," Olivia murmured.

"What did you say?" Todd asked.

"Nothing. Just give me a minute." Olivia tried to take a deep breath. She reminded herself that people did this all day long. She was paying to do this. It was just a swing. She just had to sit. And not think that she was super high up in the air.

"Why don't we get you strapped up and we can do this on a count of ten. We can take it real slow." Todd was suddenly Olivia's favorite person in the world.

"Slow. Slow sounds good." Olivia could hardly get her carabiners onto the wire because her hand was shaking so hard. She tested her harness safety straps one last time. She pulled them so tight she could barely breathe. Was it possible to have a panic attack on a zipline?

Todd's walkie-talkie beeped. "Everything all right there? What's taking so long?" Olivia could hear the voice of another worker.

She heard Todd say quietly, "Yep. Just afraid of heights over here. But we're working on it." He turned back to Olivia. "Your family is ready for you. Are you ready?"

Olivia nodded her head. And before she knew it, Todd had pushed her. She was ziplining.

"What happened to ten?" she screamed.

She looked back and Todd was smiling and waving. *I knew I shouldn't have trusted him.* She put her head as high up as she could and did not look down. It took her a minute to realize the sound she was hearing was her own screaming. "Oh my God. Oh my God. I haaaatte this so much."

And then there they were, Sammy and Steve laughing, crying, and holding their arms out, ready to hug her. Olivia felt her feet on the solid platform as tears streamed down her face. She hugged her family hard.

"You did it, Mom." Sammy hugged her hard.

"I can't believe you did it." Steve hugged her, too.

Olivia sobbed. Snot dripped down her face and she felt a moment of relief until she heard Samantha say, "Mom, wait until you see what's next!"

"Oh God. Can't we just stay here for a while longer?"

"Don't worry, honey, we'll take things slowly."

The worker added, "Yes, you can take the obstacle course at your own pace and then there will be another worker at the end when you are ready to take the final zipline. That one is even more awesome."

Olivia thought about how much she hated the word awesome. She looked down at her knees because they were shaking so hard, they were hitting each other. Then she glanced forward and saw the itty-bitty wooden pieces that made up the bridge that took her to the next platform.

"I'll go first!" screamed Sammy.

"Go for it," encouraged Olivia, while secretly thinking, *anything that buys me time to not do it sounds amazing.*

Sammy took one wobbly step at a time while holding on to the rope that kept her upright. Olivia didn't know if it was more stressful to watch or not watch her daughter. Either way, she wished Sammy would slow down so she wouldn't have to go. But sure enough, Sammy made her way to the next platform and screamed, "Who's next?"

Steve hugged Olivia and said, "You are doing amazing. Why don't you go next so you have support on both sides?"

"Or do you mean so I have to not chicken out?"

"That too. But look how far you've come. You can do this. Just look ahead to Sammy."

Olivia put one shaky foot out and said, "I hate you. I love you. But I hate you right now."

"Hate me all you want. Just keep going forward."

Olivia looked down at the small step that was practically floating in the air. *Who makes this stuff?* she wondered. *Carpenters? Engineers? Psychotic people looking to kill other people by having them plummet to their death?*

She clutched her rope and as she stepped onto the itty-bitty wooden step. It pushed forward and she fell. Quicker than a second, she was dangling like a wet noodle. It was her absolute worst fear. But her harness kept her tight until she shakily got her foothold back.

Olivia heard a quiet, "You okay?" from behind her. She calmed herself and steadied her body on the step. Her hands were so tight around the rope, they hurt. Her heart was beating too fast to say, "Yes." Instead, she took one more step forward. Each time wobblier than a baby donkey. Each time righting herself until she felt calm. If Sammy did the path in four minutes, it took Olivia twenty. Twenty agonizing one-tiny-wooden-platform-at-a-time steps. This was no bridge. It was steps to hell and back. Olivia finally got both feet on the last platform and sat down. Sammy gave her a big hug. And in what seemed like no time, she felt Steve's arms around her too. She looked up at her family and smiled. "How many more obstacles to go?" she asked sheepishly.

Steve leaned down and whispered to Olivia, "By the way, totally scary as shit when you fell. I can't believe you fell and kept going. You are a badass."

Olivia smiled up at him and he put his hands down to lift her body to a standing position. She breathed deeply and looked on to what was next. A big net. She had done one of these when she was younger at an amusement park. She didn't love nets. But at least she could do it on all fours. And at least she couldn't fall through the net.

"I'll go first," Steve offered. And ran across the net, falling and getting back up as the net jostled under his weight.

"Me next?" Samantha questioned.

"Sure honey. You go." Olivia smiled reassuringly.

Samantha took the nets by going on her hands and knees. "Hey, nice form there, Sammy. Nothing wrong with that," Olivia cheered and knew she would tackle the nets the same way. It took Samantha a little while until she made it across. She shouted some pearls of wisdom.

"Hey, Mom, it's super creepy to stare down. Maybe close your eyes or something."

Olivia gave a thumbs-up but really wanted to give the middle finger to the nets and take an elevator down to a bar where she could put her feet up with a glass of wine. She started going across. Her daughter was right. Staring down sucked.

"Trying something else," Olivia shouted, more to herself than to her family. She twisted over and sat on her butt. Then she scooched backward like a crab. Not looking down was better. Every obstacle brought Olivia closer to one thing—the ground. And the ground meant she could scratch this off her list and probably never, ever do it again for the rest of her life.

By the time Olivia couldn't take any more daring heights, they were at the last zipline. The zipline that would take her down to the blessed grass. This time, Olivia volunteered to go first. She closed her eyes, told the guy to push her, and rode down in total silence. She gripped the rope so tightly her hands were sweating.

The grass and ground under her feet felt so wonderful. She turned around and cheered for Samantha. She cheered for her husband. But mainly she cheered inside for herself. She had done it. It had been awful. Scary. Terrifying. And she would never ever have to do it again.

Samantha gave her an enormous hug and said, "Mom. You did it! You know what we should do next? That skydiving place."

Olivia smiled and said, "I might let your dad take you to that one."

CHAPTER 10
FUR

The next week of Olivia's life was business as usual—which meant scrambling to get Samantha up and ready for school, listening to the occasional whining that she didn't cut her sandwich right, working with Patricia to tackle whatever she needed, feeling guilty about not doing much exercise, and drinking way too much coffee. And when Steve gave her the compliment of how "amazing she was doing at balancing it all," the last thing she was going to admit was that she was barely balancing her coffee cup.

It was during one of Olivia's latte runs to the cute little coffee shop down the street that she noticed a flyer from a local pet rescue. In big bold print were the words "Foster homes needed." Dogs of all sorts and colors were pictured under the words. A brown and white fluff ball. A black lab with white paws. A spotted terrier that looked barky. And then the saddest looking one with little brown ears, a curly mop of hair, and mournful eyes. His name was Marven. He reminded Olivia of the Shih Tzu that used to live next to her when she was a little girl. Those sweet eyes were what made her jot down the email address. Maybe fostering a dog was a way to get a dog in her life, get her walking, and get her husband on board, too. Plus, life was already a messy disaster. What was one more thing to add to her unbalanced life, especially when it was so cute and furry?

Olivia got home and right to work. That is, got right to writing the rescue an email:

Hi,

I saw your poster at the Woods Coffee Shop. I'm interested in fostering a dog. I work from home and have a fenced-in yard and I love dogs. I do have one daughter who respects animals and can help to socialize the dog with kids. I was especially drawn to the little brown dog on your poster named Marven, though I'm happy to foster whatever loving dog needs a home. Please let me know what the next steps are.

Thank you,

Olivia

Olivia read over the email; she sounded eager yet sincere. Yep, it worked. She included her cell phone number in case they wanted to call, pressed send, and carried on with the rest of her day. It wasn't until dinnertime, when she was chit-chatting with Steve and cleaning up dishes, that she got the call.

"Hello?" Olivia did not recognize the number.

"Hi. This is Jen from Last Chance Rescue. We got your email about Marven."

Steve gave Olivia the "who is it?" look. Olivia just smiled and put her finger up, implying she needed a minute, as she walked to the other room to have the conversation without him hearing. Somehow between peas and pass the whatever, Olivia hadn't mentioned the foster dog poster at dinner. It hadn't even been a thing yet. It was a wish. A silly email. And, well, now it was a hushed phone call. It was real.

"Hi! Yes. I'm so glad you called."

"Marven is a special case. I'm happy to tell you about him. And then I can ask you a few questions. And we can decide if you want to take the next step. Of course, there'd be a home visit, references, and all that. But I'll get to that."

Olivia glanced around her home. A home visit! Was her house dog-friendly? Would she pass muster as a foster mom? Before she had a chance to doubt herself and her animal abilities, Jen continued.

"Marven came into our program about two weeks ago. He's a very sad case of neglect. He's a Shih Tzu. We think he's about nine years old. When we found him, his eyes were so matted over, we don't think he'd been able to see for some time. We got him groomed and cleaned up. But his eyes still needed care, so he needed to see an eye specialist. And he needs daily eye drops. And there's a good chance he still might need surgery or he could lose his eyes. He's a sweet little guy. Very social, even though he's been through so much."

Olivia thought about his soulful eyes that he could lose just because someone didn't take care of him. And she knew this was the dog for her.

"I want to help Marven. Tell me what I need to do."

"Oh, that's wonderful. I'm going to email you an application. I'll need two personal references and the name of a vet if you have one. Once I get that, I can bring Marven to your home, and we can see if it's the right space for him. You'd foster him until we can get him adopted. But we need to find out if he needs eye surgery first before we can get him adopted, so my guess is we're looking at a two-month fostering need, possibly longer. We take care of the vet bills, food, and, well, you take care of Marven."

"Two months. Got it. No problem. I work from home, so it'll be great for me too. Oh, my goodness, I'm so excited. We're going to give Marven the best home ever."

"Do you have any questions? I'm sending the application right now to get the ball rolling."

"I'm sure I'll have lots of questions. But for now, no; I'm just excited to help."

"All right. Great, Olivia. I'll be in touch soon."

"Bye." Olivia hung up the phone and felt nervous and thrilled at the same time. She walked back into the kitchen. It was more of a sashay. She needed to pull out all her wifely swagger to win Steve over.

"Who was that?" Steve raised his eyebrows in suspicion.

"Oh, just something I wanted to talk to you about anyway." Just then, Samantha walked in with her Lego set. "Mom, will you help me build this part?"

"In a sec, hon, I was about to share some exciting news with Dad and well, you can hear it too. We have an opportunity..."

"Oh no." Steve hid his face in his hands.

"Wait. What? Why are you hiding?"

"Every time you tell me we have an opportunity, it's bad news. Did you buy a couch?"

"What? No. Why? A couch?"

"I don't know. I could just tell it was something big. Probably something expensive that you've done."

"Hey, that's not fair. I don't buy expensive things without you."

"Uh, Mom." Samantha motioned out to her swing set, which Olivia had bought without talking to Steve until it showed up in super heavy boxes. It had taken Steve about three weekends to put it together.

"She loves that play set."

"I do." Samantha dumped the box of Legos on the table and began sorting.

"This won't cost you anything. That's part of it. We don't have to pay for anything. We just need to..." Olivia paused and suddenly felt nervous. He wouldn't say no, would he?

"What do we need to do?" Steve looked at her, more confused than anything.

"Let Marven live with us."

"I'm getting a brother?" Samantha flung a Lego accidentally across the room.

"What?" Steve looked scared. A little like he had to poop or vomit. But definitely scared.

"We are not getting a brother." Olivia looked at Samantha. Then she turned and looked at Steve to reassure him. "It's not a human. Marven is a dog."

"Noooooooooo." Steve was pacing. "We talked about this. Allergies." He pointed to his nose.

"Marven is hypoallergenic. And he's almost blind, and he needs us. And it'd only be a few months."

"A few months!" Steve wrung his hands. "Why would you mention this in front of her?"

"Yay. We're getting a dog. Can I see a picture?" Samantha sidled next to Olivia and looked at her phone.

"Um, I'm not sure if I have one. Let me see if he's on their site."

"Olivia." Steve had the tone of an intense father who wanted desperately to stop his kid from making the next move.

"Oh, he's here. Look." Olivia held up the sad pictures of Marven before and after he got his hair cut.

"Aw, Dad, look how sad he was." Samantha's frown and eyes showed the confusion inside her heart after looking at an animal that was so abused.

"He looks like a big sausage," Steve said while already scratching his arms at the thought of Marven's fur.

"And we can help him?" Samantha asked.

"Yes. If your dad's on board, too. We can."

Steve sat down, shaking his head back and forth in defeat.

"And how do we help him?" Steve's voice sounded doubtful, but it wasn't a no.

"He stays with us. We take him for walks, love him, show him he can trust humans. The lady said he's social and happy." Olivia gave Steve her best 'I really want to do this oh please' eyes. Samantha's whole body was bursting with electric glee.

Steve said, "How long, again?"

"Only two months."

"Two months with a chubby sausage dog." Steve pondered the words. But to Olivia, the words sounded like an agreement. She began hugging him and bouncing up and down, which made Samantha get up and hug them both, also bouncing up and down.

"You won't regret this."

"I'm already regretting this. I'll buy allergy medicine in the morning and call my doctor."

"It'll be good. For Sammy. For me." Olivia clung to his shoulder, squeezing it.

"For Marven!" Samantha added. *Nice touch, kid,* thought Olivia.

Steve didn't smile. He merely said, "I'm going to go cut the grass." Olivia knew Steve wasn't happy. But her happiness had been on the back burner for so long, she didn't feel guilty choosing her own happiness this time. She always chose Samantha and Steve before herself. Whatever happened to prioritizing the woman in the mirror? Besides, she was going to make a needy dog happy, too.

And that is how, two days later, Jen came to be sitting in her living room with Marven and his wagging tail.

Olivia felt like she was in an interview. Except she wasn't sure whether she had to impress the human or the dog.

"And how would you train Marven if he started showing bad habits?"

"Only positive training, of course. I mean, we all respond to the power of cheese, right?" Olivia laughed. But neither Jen nor Marven looked amused. Olivia had expected Marven to just love her, so she was a little sad that he hadn't left Jen's side.

"I'm just going to grab some water. Do you need anything?" Olivia asked as she stood up. Marven's ears went down at Olivia's standing posture.

"I'm good. Thanks. I brought my water bottle," said Jen.

"Think Marven wants a drink?" Olivia smiled at Marven, still trying to show him she was the nice one he should love.

"Sure, let's try. It might warm him up," Jen said.

Darn, she noticed he's not into me, thought Olivia as she went into the kitchen. She filled her glass with water and had an idea. She opened the fridge and took a tiny piece of turkey from the deli bag and hid it in her hand. *A tiny piece won't hurt his belly too much.*

Olivia put the water bowl on the floor and sat next to it, hoping Marven would come. She put her hand on the ground, the one with the turkey, close to him. His little nose vibrated as he sniffed. Slowly, he made his way to her, and she opened her hand just a little so he could sneak a bite. Olivia gently patted his back, being careful not to raise her hand too high above his eyes or ears in case that made him nervous.

"That's a great way to pet him. Marven's sight still isn't great because his eyes had such a severe infection from his matted hair and being left in such dirty conditions."

Olivia looked at the fluffy pup and couldn't believe he had ever not been cute. But she had seen the pictures. It was hard to think about everything the little guy had been through.

Marven took a few licks of water and then wiggled his little body onto Olivia's lap. She kept gently petting him, while inside her heart was bursting.

"Should we take Marven to your backyard so I can see what kind of fence you have? We don't need to worry about little guys jumping over the fence, but you'd be surprised what a small dog like him can squeeze through to get out. Remember, he's been through a lot, so sometimes rescue dogs have pretty strong flight instincts and try to run away. I would always make sure you're out with him in the yard so he doesn't get in any trouble." Marven gave a yip as if he agreed he just might cause some trouble.

"Sure, let's go out. Come on, Marven," Olivia called and put on his little leash. Marven's little tail flicked back and forth like a quick windshield wiper.

"He's doing great with you." Jen smiled.

They made their way out back, and as Jen looked around, Marven rolled in the green grass, more excited about showing his tummy than peeing. Olivia bent down and stroked his warm pink belly.

"Your fence looks good to me. I wasn't sure about behind those flowerpots, but I didn't want to move them. You should check to make sure there isn't any room for him to get out. But overall, I'm feeling good. How are you feeling?"

Olivia smiled up at her, not wanting to take her hand away from Marven's belly. "I think he's going to do great."

"I'm so glad. Let's go in and I'll walk you through how to do his eye drops and we can talk about when his next vet appointment is. I have food in the car to give you, too."

After about thirty more minutes of talking through eye drops, food, and exercise, Jen was on her way and Olivia and Marven were home alone together. At first, the dog just wanted to stay next to her. Olivia got a little red fire hydrant dog toy, but Marven just looked at it like she was nuts.

"Did you not have toys, Marven?" Olivia was on all fours talking to the dog in the same way she would have talked to her daughter.

Olivia got a ball and rolled it across the floor. Marven watched the ball roll. Olivia got her computer and sat next to Marven on the floor. Marven closed his eyes and fell asleep. Olivia stopped every so often and looked at the little mess of hair next to her, breathing with his eyes squeezed tight, and a small smile would creep across her face. She loved her new co-worker.

To surprise Samantha, Olivia decided that she and Marven would greet her at the bus. She put Marven's leash on him so they could walk around a little beforehand. He was not a very fast walker. He seemed to stop at every blade of grass or bush. Olivia was not going to get much exercise if this was how Marven walked. She heard the squeal of the bus brakes and began heading toward the stop, but Marven pulled the leash hard in the opposite direction. He was not a fan of old bus brakes. He peeked through Olivia's legs, watching tentatively as Samantha ran up to them.

"Is it him?" Samantha instinctively lowered herself to the ground. "Don't be afraid. I won't hurt you. We'll be best friends."

Marven ran to Samantha but returned quickly to hide behind Olivia's legs.

"This is Sammy, Marven. Don't worry, she's kind."

Olivia bent down and gave Marven a little pat. She handed Samantha a treat and whispered, "Give it to him." Sammy slowly opened her hand. Marven's nose sniffed the air, and he slowly walked forward and ate the treat. Sammy gently petted him behind his ears. He didn't run away or shrink from her hand.

Sammy whispered, "Look, Mom, he's letting me pet him." Olivia smiled. "Can I walk him home?"

"Yep, take the leash. Let's take it slowly, okay?"

Sammy held the leash and Marven made his way to the grass, sniffing the road and walking leisurely toward their home.

As Sammy took the stuff out of her bookbag, Marven was quite interested. She took out her lunch box and Marven sniffed it. Then he took two steps back and barked at it.

"It's a lunch box, Marven. Want to see?" Sammy opened it up and found a few leftover pretzel sticks. "Want to sniff these?" Marven slowly crept up to them and licked one. Sammy giggled. Marven wagged his tail.

By the time Steve got home from work, Marven, Sammy, and Olivia were a tight little unit. Olivia was reading a book to Sammy on the couch, and Marven was sitting on her lap. When Marven heard the door, he was ready to protect and fight for his loved ones. He jumped off the couch, yipping like mad, with a little growl in between barks.

Olivia and Sammy quickly followed to see Steve up against the door looking very, very scared, and tall. And Marven looking very, very tiny, but menacing.

"Marven, that's just Steve. Calm down, boy."

But Marven would not calm down. He grabbed Steve's shoe.

"Marven, no." Olivia shouted as Steve shook his shoe off the dog and said, "This is the dog we have to live with? He's a mean little sausage."

"Stop calling him sausage; he's not that chubby. His name is Marven, and he just got scared." Olivia tried to calm Marven's barking. "Sammy, quick, go get a piece of turkey from the fridge." Samantha ran and brought back the whole bag. "Here, take a piece and give it to him."

"He'll bite my hand off." Steve looked scared.

"Marven wouldn't hurt anyone." Sammy bent down and stroked the dog.

"Marven bit my shoe." Steve looked down at the dog, cursing under his breath. "I told you I didn't want a dog."

"You scared him. He didn't mean it, did you, boy?" Marven cocked his head to the side and gave Sammy a lick.

"Why don't you try to give him the turkey now that he's settled?" Olivia encouraged Steve by shoving a big chunk of turkey into his hand.

"Here, evil little sausage." Steve hovered the turkey over Marven's nose. Marven sniffed it and then finally decided turkey was more important than intruders and gobbled it up.

"Marven, Steve. Steve, Marven." Olivia smiled. Sammy smiled. Steve did not smile. He took a tiny, tentative step forward. Marven, though, was more than happy to play with Sammy, deciding not to care about Steve or his feet.

After dinner, the family played in the yard. Steve picked up a ball. Olivia said, "Don't bother, he doesn't know what to do with it."

But Steve threw it anyway, and when it bounced, Marven ran to it.

"It's a boy thing," Steve teased.

Olivia gave Steve a dirty look, annoyed that he didn't listen to her. And annoyed that Marven proved her wrong. But she was glad that maybe the dog and Steve could bond after the rough start.

The next day, Patricia wanted to have a quick meeting about the Heller house. It was an expensive home, and the family was high maintenance. They were driving Patricia mad with their questions.

Before going over, Olivia called. She didn't email or text. They were now people who called each other. An unspoken, casual level of friendship.

"Would you mind if I brought my foster dog to your house with me? It's only his second day here and I'm not sure what he'd do at home."

"Sure. No problem. Does he drink coffee?"

"Funny. No, just water. I'll be over in five."

Olivia got Marven ready in his collar, looked at him, and said, "All right, you're coming with me to Patricia's and you need to be good. Because then you can come with me more often. Patricia seems scary, but she's not." Marven tilted his little head to one side as if he were listening, then did a little tip-tap happy-dance with his feet when he realized Olivia was putting on his leash.

Olivia gave Patricia's beautiful wooden door three light knocks and then pushed it open. "Come on, Marven, let's go." Marven followed Olivia's footsteps slowly into the new space. He stopped and sniffed the wall and carpet, taking in the unfamiliar smells.

Olivia could hear Patricia's voice. "Paul, I don't care what you do. Just sign the papers." Patricia put her phone down and took two deep breaths.

Marven barked.

Patricia exhaled and looked over. Marven ran right up and jumped up on her.

"Oh, my goodness. I'm so sorry. He's never done that before."

"It's okay," Patricia said as she petted Marven's head. "Anyone that wants to give me love today is welcome."

"Bad call?" Olivia shifted her feet and looked down. "I couldn't help but hear you were talking to Paul."

"Ah, is that still his name? I have so many names I call him in my head." Patricia looked at Marven and said in a sweet, sing-song voice, "What if we call him shithead, or cheater, or trying to nickel and dime his way through this divorce?" Marven's body wiggled with happiness, only hearing the uptick in her voice and not the gravity of her words.

"You are cute, aren't you? Next time I'll get a dog instead of a husband." Patricia gave Marven one little pat and then lifted his little body and put him on the floor.

Then she got down to business. "I'm hoping I can give you a few more hours if you're willing to take these digital videos off my hands. Have you ever made a video like this?" Patricia turned on her computer and showed Olivia the slow panning of a house and all the rooms inside. "It's basically just putting a bunch of clips together."

"Ha, yeah, I make videos all the time to send to my mother."

"Oh?" Patricia's voice was raised in a question, not because of Olivia's ability, but because she had never once said those words yet in all their talks. The word "mother" was not a word that fell easily from Olivia's lips, because Olivia's mother was not an easy woman. But Olivia wanted her mother to have some relationship with her daughter, so short video clips of Sammy being adorable seemed to be the safest way for Olivia to say, "See, don't you want to be a grandmother?"

Her mother had been avoiding her ever since Olivia had lent her money so she wouldn't lose her apartment. She hoped her mother had spent it on rent and not on alcohol. Because the actual truth was that month after month, her mother chose a wine bottle over Sammy. And not just one wine bottle; many wine bottles. And not just alcohol, but often pills too, if she could score them.

Yes, Olivia's mother had not quite been a mother most of her life. When she was younger, Olivia didn't know words like bipolar, depression, or addict. Her mom had glasses of wine with dinner. But once her parents divorced, the wine glasses moved to lunchtime, and sometimes before. Sometimes her mom had gone days before wondering if Olivia had washed her hair. Other times, she'd wake Olivia up at midnight with ice cream sundaes. But Olivia wasn't ready to talk to Patricia about this; not yet. Just like Patricia wasn't ready to tell Olivia what had really happened on that phone call, or what had happened weeks ago with her son. Some things open you up too much for judgment; when you're used to being shut tight like a clam or oyster, it feels safer to stay closed than to reveal your emotional frailty. Trust is a pearl that you'll never believe another human can keep safe. It's like showing someone what your real house looks like on a typical Saturday, not the house you clean up for someone to see. The mess of our lives is only for a chosen few.

Patricia showed Olivia some places on social where they showcased the videos of the houses—fully aware that between them was an invisible fortress of personal walls that kept both women sitting uncomfortably straight until Patricia said, "Do you smell something?"

Olivia popped up, her eyes searching quickly for Marven. "Oh shit. Literally. Oh, Patricia, I'm so sorry. This beautiful rug." Olivia went to the kitchen to get paper towels. "Tell me what to clean it with."

Her hands shook as she looked for some way to rectify Marven's stinky mistake.

"Bad Marven," Olivia said firmly. Marven gave her the saddest ears-down look.

Patricia casually walked over and grabbed a cleaner from under the sink. "Here, spray it with this. And don't worry, Paul wants the fucking rugs. He said he bought them. And he fucked her on it. Don't worry about cleaning it that well." Patricia smiled.

"What an asshole. I'm so sorry you're dealing with this." Olivia's eyes met Patricia's briefly.

"It's all right. We should have divorced years ago. But we were comfortable. Comfortable is not happy though. That's when my list started. I thought if I could have a list of stuff that would make me happy on the outside, I'd be happy inside. But I guess happiness isn't something you can check off on a list." Patricia paused and looked ahead quietly.

Olivia wasn't sure what else she should say. So, she said, "I'm going to take Marven out now, so he doesn't have any more accidents. Is there anything else you need besides the videos?"

"No. That will be a huge help." As Olivia grabbed Marven's leash, Patricia said, "Olivia?"

Olivia turned. "This is working out quite nicely, don't you think?" Patricia added.

"Yes. It is." Three words Olivia never thought she'd say. Olivia hooked Marven's leash and smiled.

CHAPTER 11
BOOKS

Walks with Marven broke up Olivia's day. One day, she was feeling proud of herself for her increased walking when she spotted Danielle from down the street.

"Shit," Olivia said under her breath. She tried to turn around and walk back, but Marven was having none of that. He planted all four feet into the ground and pulled his neck in the other direction. Why was he being so difficult? Normally, he'd walk wherever Olivia went.

"Olivia!"

Olivia could hear Danielle's high-pitched voice. She turned and looked over her shoulder and gave a polite wave. "Hello, there." Olivia looked down at Marven, pleading with her eyes for him to budge. Instead, he wagged his tail and kept pulling towards Danielle.

"I'm so glad I ran into you," Danielle said, as she waved at the dog like he was a small child. "Hello, there puppy. You're new, aren't you?" She took one step backward, keeping her long-flowing dress away from his paws.

"Yes, he's our new foster dog," Olivia said as she pulled his leash a little. "And he has very specific ideas on where he wants to walk today."

"Oh, foster dog. I could never do that. I would just keep all of them." Danielle chuckled, even though she had no pets in her home and barely liked it when her two daughters brought in even an ounce of mud on their feet.

"Mmmhmm," was all that Olivia could muster, mainly because she knew what Danielle was going to bring up next and that her answer would be no.

"Have you read the book club book this week? It's tonight at eight, remember? That gives us time to get the kids to bed and well, I'll need to clean my mess of a house."

Olivia knew Danielle only said this so she would say, "Your house is always clean." Ugh. Olivia hated that she had said those words. She also hated Danielle, which is why this whole book club thing was a bad, bad idea. But Olivia had put it on her list. And she had told Danielle that she would join. The only thing she hadn't done was read the damn book. Okay, she hadn't even purchased the book. How long could the book be?

"Yes, can't wait. I'll see you then."

"And remember, the theme is to bring an appetizer or dessert that starts with the first letter of your name. And that would be with an O." Danielle smiled and smoothed out her dress.

"Yep. O. Got it. I can bring oranges or Oreos."

"Well, um, you could. But most of the other book clubbers tend to…" and she whispered this part, "bring something homemade."

"Of course, I was just kidding," Olivia replied.

"Oh, ha ha, you are so funny." Danielle looked relieved as she turned toward her home, her long hair swinging as she walked like the sidewalk was something between a catwalk and an ad for a luxury beach house.

"I will never forgive you." Olivia glared at Marven. He wagged his tail, unbothered by her look. "Well, we need to head back now because we are going to drive to the bookstore. Do you like rides?"

Without waiting for an answer, she picked Marven up. He looked pretty pleased to be carried. She ran into the house and grabbed her keys and purse, Marven still tucked under her arm. It wasn't much different from holding Samantha as an infant. On the way to the bookstore, she opened the window to see what Marven would do. He walked right up to the passenger side door, put his paws up, and stuck his head out the window. His ears, gums, and hair all flapped in the wind.

When Olivia pulled into the parking lot, she cracked all the windows. "Marven, I'll be quick. It's a beautiful crisp day. You just sit in the car until I get back." Olivia wasn't sure if someone walking past her car would think she was crazy or caring to be talking to a dog.

Olivia ran into the little bookshop and was greeted by the calm quiet of the rows of books. She ran her hand along the beautiful covers, bashfully walked over to the top sellers' section, and picked up the Alphabet Diaries with its big medallion on the cover that screamed Book Club Favorite. It was thicker than she thought it would be. She flipped through quickly and went to the last page: 523! Maybe she could read the beginning and end? She flipped through it again and noticed each chapter corresponded with a letter in the alphabet, then cursed the alphabet for being so long. Olivia looked over at the register. She noticed a cute, young literature-reading-looking guy, and suddenly felt sheepish about her purchase. She walked over to the poetry section and grabbed a classic poetry collection to smarten up her selection. To make herself feel less guilty about the extra purchase, she vowed to read them to Sammy. She hadn't read Sammy much poetry. She hid the alphabet book underneath.

"Hi, there." Olivia put the book down and took out her wallet. She glanced at the door to check on her car, where she could see Marven sitting in the front seat, staring at her. She smiled at Marven and then brought herself to look at the bookseller, handing him her card.

"Lots of people have been buying this one," he said as he held up the Alphabet Diaries.

Olivia blushed as she said, "Book club," and then felt about as suburbanite and lame as could be. Cute boy didn't even notice the poetry book.

Olivia took her bag and mumbled "thanks" as she made her way back to Marven, who, let's face it, was the only man besides her husband she needed to impress.

She opened the door and Marven started licking her face immediately as she slipped into the driver's seat. "Aw, I missed you too, Marven. We've got some reading to do."

When Olivia arrived home, she plopped down on the couch with Marven by her side and opened the book to chapter A. She read quickly, jumping over some words. By the time Samantha got home, she was only on letter D, for drama. Each chapter offered a unique perspective, and she had to admit the book was enjoyable. She hated herself for liking it so much.

"Damn you, Danielle," she said to herself.

"Hi, Mom. You didn't come to the bus stop," Sammy said, petting Marven as he jumped up and down to greet her.

"Sorry, got lost in this book. Trying to get it done for book club tonight."

"I was just hoping to see Marven."

Olivia peeked out from behind her book and gave a pretend frown.

"You know what I mean." Sammy came and sat right next to Olivia. Like right next to her. Not two feet away, but as close to on top of Olivia's arm and body as possible, so it was hard for Olivia to turn the page. Olivia normally didn't mind her child's invasion of her space, but she was feeling a little stressed trying to cram this book in before book club. Sammy shifted positions, jammed her elbow into Olivia's side, and put her head on Olivia's chest.

"Sammy, I love you, girl, but do you want to go get yourself a snack or something and come read with me? Or go play with Marven."

"Hmm. Maybe," Sammy said, but did not move an inch. Her hair tickled Olivia's nose.

Olivia hugged Sammy, hoping a little motherly love would do the trick to move her along so she could get her book read, but nope.

"Want to come out and play with Marven and me?" Sammy pushed her head into Olivia's chest, a small wedge of pain.

"Sammy. You're hurting me. I wanted to read more. What if I go outside and read while you play with Marven?"

"Will you make me a snack?"

"Yes." Olivia crinkled her forehead, but at least snack and outside meant she could have some space and read more. These were the times Olivia thought about having another kid, because Sammy could never keep herself occupied—she always needed Olivia or Steve nearby.

A cut apple, some cheese and crackers later, Olivia was finally delving back into chapter D. The chemistry between the two characters was pretty amazing. Olivia was just picturing the strong, swimming shoulders of the leading man when she heard, "Mom! Mom! Mom!"

With a sigh and an eyeroll, Olivia shouted, "Sammy, seriously, can't I have one minute?"

"It's just Marven did something really weird."

"What did he do?" Olivia asked while reading the next line in her book.

"I was running around with him and he ran right into something. And then he did it again. And now he just seems confused. He's just sitting and won't run."

Olivia put the book down and called his name. She saw his ears prick up. And he took a few tentative steps forward and barked. Olivia went up to him and petted his head, but he jerked away as if surprised.

"Marven, it's just me, boy." She continued to pet him slowly until he calmed down.

"Let's keep an eye on him. I agree he's not quite right. I'm going to call Jen and see if she thinks I should take him to the vet again."

Olivia went inside and was just dialing Jen's number when Sammy carried Marven in. "He was just on the deck and fell right off. Mom, he just walked right off."

"That solves it. Let's go; we're taking him to the vet. I'll call on the way." Olivia shoved her book inside her purse, grabbed an applesauce pouch for Sammy in case she got hungry, filled her water bottle, and they were on their way.

As Olivia drove, her hands shook as she turned on the radio. "Don't worry, sweetie, I'm sure it's just his eyes or something. He'll be okay." She glanced back at Sammy. She had her chin nestled into the top of Marven's head.

"Hi, Dr. Paulson. Hi. We're fostering Marven from Last Chance Rescue. Yep, the dog with the eye issues. That's him. Today he's not acting himself. He ran into some things and fell off the deck."

Olivia paused to steady her breath and voice as the vet told her he could see the dog right away. "Great. Because we're actually on our way to you right now. Thanks so much. I appreciate you fitting him in."

"Sammy, see, it's going to work out. They will look at him and let us know what's going on."

Olivia looked at the clock. 4:08. Book club was at eight. She could skim more while they waited at the vet, make something beginning with the letter O, and make it work.

They arrived in the waiting room at the vet's office where two people sat waiting with their large dogs. A lady with a cat in a carrier sat as far away from the two large dogs as possible. There was also a kid with a smaller carrier that held what looked like a bunny or a ferret.

Olivia carried Marven up to the counter. "Hi. We have Marven here. Dr. Paulson said he could fit us in."

"Ah yes, Marven is having trouble seeing. We'll get him checked out in no time. We have Marven on file already from the rescue. Just go wait over there, and we'll call you when the doctor is ready."

Olivia petted Marven while he sat next to Sammy. It was crazy how much she cared for the dog. She knew she should take out her book and read, but she couldn't. She just wanted to pet Marven and make him feel safe and loved. Olivia reached over and squeezed Sammy's hand.

"You're doing a great job keeping him calm." Sammy's eyes looked big and sad. "Don't worry, we'll get him through this. Part of the foster family's job is to love them through the good and hard times."

Olivia gave Sammy a reassuring smile, but it fell flat. As Olivia scanned the faces of everyone else in the waiting room, she tried to figure out what each person was there for. Before too long, she heard her name and "Marven." Marven stood straight up as if he knew what to do next. Sammy put him on the ground and they led him to the examining room. The vet tech bent down on the floor, gave Marven a quick look, and then asked a bunch of questions as she scribbled notes onto her pad.

"I'm going to take Marven back now to get some vitals checked, and then I'll bring him right back to you." Olivia was thankful for the vet tech's sweet tone and how she looked Samantha right in the eye when she talked.

Sammy paced the little room nervously. She saw the X-ray light box and turned it on and off.

"Sammy, I don't think we should touch anything," Olivia said. Sammy looked up at her and nodded in agreement.

Olivia considered taking her book out and reading, but Sammy needed her attention. "Do you want to play a game while we wait?"

Sammy shrugged her shoulders. "What game?"

"We could do A-Z, you pick the category."

"How about we do dogs?"

"Okay. A is for Australian shepherd."

"Oh, is that the dog with the cool blue eyes?" Sammy asked.

"Yep, now you go, you've got B," Olivia said as she glanced at the door, willing it to open with good news and a happy Marven.

"Hmmm. B. Oh, bark. Or beagle!"

"Nice. I'm C. My brain isn't thinking well. Can I do 'cute,' for dogs are cute?"

"Kinda lame. But fine." Sammy smiled, forgetting why they were there. "D is for dog!"

"Um, that's even lamer. What about dachshund or Doberman?"

"Yeah, those are better, but now you're stuck with E."

"E." Olivia pondered the letter while secretly worrying about Marven and wondering what could be wrong. And while also figuring out what she might have in her cupboard to bring as an O dessert for book club.

"English spaniel!" Olivia shouted as she shook her head, trying to get her brain to focus on Sammy instead of thinking how she should just skip book club rather than pretend she got further than D in the book. Stupid list, making her try too hard.

Just then the door opened, but there was no Marven; only a very concerned-looking vet. He came over and shook both their hands.

"Hi, I'm Dr. Paulson. We talked on the phone." He leaned against the metal exam table as if it were comfortable and made of pillows.

"How is Marven?" Olivia blurted.

"Well, I'm glad you brought him in." The vet looked over at Samantha and then back to Olivia. "Do you want to talk privately?"

"No, Mommy I want to hear about Marven," Samantha said.

Olivia scanned the vet's face to figure out what he was going to say and whether she should hear it first. But Samantha rarely spoke up for herself with adults, so Olivia knew it was important to her.

"It's okay. You can tell us both."

The vet smiled weakly and chose his next words carefully. "As you know, Marven's life before he met you wasn't great. He suffered from years of neglect. The matted hair around his eyes turned into an eye infection that hadn't been treated for a very long time. And although we have been working hard to reduce the damage, sometimes there's just not much you can do when it's gone on for so long. And well, unfortunately, I did some tests back there and Marven is…"

Olivia held her breath, waiting for the word.

"Blind." And there it was. A word that crashed hard in the room.

"Poor Marven." Samantha wiped tears into her shirt.

"There are things we can do to help him live more comfortably. You should know that some blind dogs get so stressed from their lack of sight that they go through major behavioral differences, so this isn't something to take lightly. A blind dog who doesn't know it's being approached, for example, could bite when it's never bitten before." The vet looked over at Samantha as if to indicate she would be the one bitten.

"What can we do to help Marven?" Olivia asked.

"Well, for one, use your voice before you do anything with him, so he knows you are around. It's been shown that a dog's hearing can be a suitable replacement for sight. Make sure you keep your house the same so he can learn where the chairs are and not bump into them. You can make one area a safe zone so he can play without the fear of banging into anything. Look through your home for sharp edges, close off stairways, anything that could hurt Marven."

"So, like baby-proofing," Olivia said. She rubbed her head, suddenly feeling overwhelmed by all the small steps and hard edges in her house.

"Yes, dog-proofing isn't much different. For a blind dog, you'd want to keep his water bowl and food in the same place so he knows where his spot is for feeding. Anytime someone comes to your house or when you are out for a walk, let them know your dog is blind so they speak before touching Marven. Those are the basics. I can write down some excellent websites for you to check out that can help."

"We can do this. We can do this." Olivia said this more for herself than anyone else in the room.

"There's one more thing we need to discuss. We will need to keep doing the eye drops for the infection, but there is a chance Marven will need enucleation."

"What's that?" Sammy asked, looking at her mom for a sign of how bad that word was.

Olivia shrugged her shoulders because she had no idea what enunc-whatever was.

The vet lowered his voice and said, "Sometimes we need to do an operation where we remove the dog's eyes if he's in pain. We stitch his eyelids closed. It sounds worse than it is, and sometimes it's more comfortable for the dog."

The vet tech brought in Marven. "Hi boy," Olivia whispered. *Who is going to adopt you now?* She slowly petted Marven's ear. He turned his head into her hand, implying that it felt just right. "We will do whatever is best for you."

"Well for now, it's eye drops. And we'll see how he adapts. Call the office if you have questions or if anything changes."

"How will we know if he's in pain?" Sammy asked. It was a good question.

"He might stop eating. He could lie down more often. Some dogs paw at their faces or scratch their ears more. Shaking, too. These are all signs that the dog is experiencing discomfort."

Sammy bent down and gave Marven smooth pats on his back. "We'll take good care of you. Don't be afraid."

Olivia's eyes welled up.

"Doctor, thanks so much. Come on, Sammy, do you want to lead Marven out?"

Samantha took the leash and the three of them walked out of the clinic, feeling more overwhelmed than when they'd walked in.

Olivia called Steve on the way home, filled him in on the Marven news, and asked him to pick up a baguette and olive tapenade. Olivia knew Steve felt bad for Marven because he didn't even jokingly call him sausage.

The clock read 6:30 by the time they got home. Olivia started a pot of water for pasta. Screw book club and their homemade stress. Who was going to argue she didn't make a tapenade? It's just chopped-up olives and shit. Still, Olivia knew she should look at the ingredients when Steve brought the jar home. Just in case someone asked. In her entire life, Olivia had never made a tapenade.

Marven snuggled on the carpet next to Sammy, who hadn't left his side. Olivia grabbed her book and, as she approached him, said, "Marven, I'm going to sit with you too." Marven picked up his chin and then rested it back on the floor. Olivia skipped to the letter O in her book because she was suddenly paranoid that Danielle would make them each speak about their chapter. For the four hundredth time, she considered not going to book club. And she had almost convinced herself not to go and to gorge on the bread and tapenade herself, when Sammy said, "I think a book club sounds cool. Maybe you and me and Marven can start one. I bet he'd love to be read to now that he can't see. We can read books that have dogs in them!"

Olivia nodded her head and heard a million children's articles in her head, all telling her how important it is that kids read for twenty minutes every day. This would be a good way to ensure she read to Sammy more and damn, this meant she needed to go to book club so Sammy didn't lose her enthusiasm.

Steve walked through the door at 7:25 with groceries and wine. Olivia gave him a big hug for thinking of wine, because she had forgotten she was supposed to bring some.

"It was for me," Steve pouted.

"Just be happy you saved the day. I think we have a beer in the fridge."

Olivia immediately began cutting the baguette into round slices. She picked up the jar to read the ingredients and that's when she realized it wasn't tapenade. It was a red pepper spread.

"Oh yeah, I couldn't find the tapenade stuff. But I asked the guy, and he said this stuff is close."

"It needs to be an O."

"What?"

"Nothing. Crap." Olivia scanned the ingredients. There was olive oil. She grabbed some more olive oil and drizzled it on top. Olive oil and roasted red peppers it was. She remembered she had some pecorino cheese and grated that on top for good measure. It was going to have to do, and if anyone said anything, she would shove down their throat the story of her blind dog.

Does everyone feel this aggressive going to book club? She ran upstairs to change into her good jeans and a silky black tank top. She put on her black flats and looked in the mirror. She smoothed down her hair and ran some lipstick across her mouth. "It's as good as it's going to get," she told the mirror.

Olivia hurried back downstairs. She hugged Sammy and gave Steve a peck on the cheek. "I'm going to head over now."

She held her plate of less-than-homemade appetizer in one hand and a bottle of wine in the other. Her book was shoved under her arm. Steven ran to the door to open it, keenly aware that if Olivia used one of her hands, something may shift and fall. And he wanted that wine to survive the night and possibly make it back home.

"Have fun, Mom." Sammy waved.

"Fun," Olivia murmured to herself. This was supposed to be fun, and it had forced her to read at least part of a book. She would do better next month and read more of the next book when things were less crazy.

As Olivia walked up to Danielle's house, a twinge in her stomach reminded her that groups of women did not bring out her self-confidence. She pressed the doorbell.

Danielle did not disappoint. She opened the door with a welcoming hostess smile and wearing another dress. It was casually chic with a blue and black print that made her ready to go to fancy brunch or a bridal shower if one should suddenly pop up. Olivia saw Suzanne from around the cul-de-sac in the kitchen. Also in a dress. Was there a dress code memo Olivia didn't get?

"Hey, so excited we finally got you here." Suzanne took a sip of wine and cheered her glass in Olivia's direction.

"Excited to be here." Olivia scanned the countertop and saw delectable goodies—stuffed mushrooms, tartlets, breaded tofu skewers with cilantro dipping sauce. And holy shit, was that homemade baklava?

"I just brought veggies and hummus," said a woman next to Olivia with long brown hair and deep brown skin. She pointed to her snack and smiled. Olivia liked her immediately.

"I love veggies and hummus," Olivia said, putting her plate right next to her dish and away from the fancier ones.

"My name is Diya."

"Oh, like the light," said Olivia, then quickly blushed in case her memory had been wrong. She had read a book about Diwali and other Indian holidays to Samantha.

"Yes," Diya answered warmly. "This is my first time here. I work with Suzanne."

"Ah, yeah, me too. First timer. I'm Olivia. I live around the corner from Danielle."

Olivia glanced around the kitchen and took in the shiny white tile behind the stove. The delicately arched kitchen faucet was probably picked from a design catalog and not from a big box store. Olivia's brain instantly compared Danielle's kitchen with her own. She tried persuading herself to ignore these tiny bits of life information that truly didn't matter.

Danielle came and put a wine glass in Olivia's hand. "Red or white?"

Olivia looked at Diya and noticed she had red, so she said, "Red would be great. Thanks so much." Quickly, Danielle filled her glass and moved on.

All the food stayed on the counter, untouched. Olivia glanced at it, wanting something because in her rush she had eaten only a few bites of dinner. How was no one eating? Especially the baklava with the nuts and glistening honey.

Diya leaned over and whispered, "I came here right from work. Do you think if we start eating, they'll eat too?"

Bonded already through their appetizer choice and desire to eat, Olivia said, "Let's do it." They each filled their plate with just enough to make it interesting, leaving a little white on the plate so as not to look too greedy.

As Olivia crunched on a carrot full of hummus, Diya whispered, "Did you finish the book?"

Olivia shook her head.

"I tried to listen to the audiobook, but I only got to your letter. O was hilarious, though. That orangutan scene was so well done." Olivia smiled, realizing she was screwed and probably not going to add much to this book club banter. "I'm kidding about the orangutan." Diya bumped her on the shoulder to show she was just teasing.

"You just scared the shit out of me. I only got to D and read a few pages of O."

Diya laughed. "I only made it to L. I should eat a Linzer torte in honor of my achievement." She turned to the food and put a slice of torte on her plate.

By now, all the women were buzzing around the food. Grabbing a bite here and there. Commenting on what was delicious. Olivia's pepper crostinis were not touched yet. Each baguette piece sat there like a little circle of non-culinary shame.

"Shall we move to the living room? Are you guys ready to discuss?"

With a wave of her arm, Danielle herded the book clubbers into her living room. A light grey couch, patterned armchairs, and a rug brought just the right level of sophistication. A blue and white urn sat on the mantel next to a modern mirror.

"How do we want to do this?" Danielle asked as she unfolded a piece of paper that listed book club questions. When none of the women spoke up, Danielle spoke slowly, as if she was addressing a classroom of third graders. "Well, I figured since we had appetizers and such with our name and letter, it might be a great icebreaker for everyone to say their name and their favorite or least favorite part about the chapter that went with their name's letter."

Suzanne clapped her hands excitedly. "What a great idea, because I know we have some new people here tonight." She side-winked at Olivia. Olivia willed her own body to sink into the sofa and disappear. But sadly, she still existed.

Abby, the cool, earthy mom who looked like she had just come from a hike or a Patagonia store, went first. She gave a subdued wave and said, "Hi, everyone. I'm Abby. I brought the avocado toast."

Danielle interrupted eagerly with, "It was so yummy. What was that on top?"

"Chia seeds, pumpkin seeds, and hemp seeds."

Danielle's eyes widened at the mention of hemp.

"For protein," Abby answered to no one's specific question.

Suzanne nodded as if she was in on the protein's importance.

"My favorite scene was definitely the antelope in the forest. I love how it represented her connection with nature. I felt like the writing was so beautiful there. And reminded me how in the quiet of trees you can really find yourself."

"Do you really think that's what it represented?" Diya asked. Her tone wasn't confrontational, but more investigative.

"Do you have a different perspective, Diya?" Danielle quickly interjected, always the appropriate host, ready to smooth out any verbal display.

"Oh, it's just interesting, because I thought it was there to show the opposite. That ever since Candice moved to the city, she had no connection to anything natural. So, the antelope represented how far removed she was from anything natural?"

"Hmmm. Interesting." Abby shrugged.

"I also thought her boyfriend in the first chapter was a total dick. I knew they were going to break up," Diya said. Olivia started laughing, which made a few of the other women lighten up and laugh.

"When he told her that her ice cream scoop should be put in a different drawer, I was hoping she would hit him with it," Olivia added. More women laughed, and the room got a little more comfortable.

"Total control freak," Abby agreed.

By the time L for Laura was up, Danielle had refilled the wine glasses and moved the snacks onto the coffee table for easy grabbing. Olivia was enjoying herself now and found some of the women's insightful comments interesting. She'd forgotten how much she enjoyed digging into a book. And then suddenly, there were no Ms, no Ns, and it was O time. Her time to talk.

She took a sip of her wine and said, "My name is Olivia. I live down the street. And…" She looked around the room and couldn't make eye contact. She decided to be honest. "Even though I enjoyed the book, I didn't get to my chapter because well, I'm fostering a dog and it turns out he's going blind so I had to take him to the vet today instead of reading the rest of the book."

She looked up and, instead of judgment, she saw compassion, empathy, and worry. And then an onslaught of comments:

"Is he okay?"

"Oh my gosh, that sounds so awful."

"I'm so glad you still came."

"I didn't finish the book and I have no excuse."

Olivia smiled and told them all about Marven and what rough shape he had been in. Abby even vowed to donate to the rescue. By the end of the evening, Olivia's plate still had some baguette pieces on it, but she brought it home feeling good. And when she said, "See you at the next book club," she almost meant it. Well, depending on what book they chose.

CHAPTER 12
WHITE FLAG

Now that Olivia had conquered book club, she knew she needed to conquer the three letters that brought her little comfort: MOM.

It had been so long since they'd talked. Would she pick up?

No. It went to voicemail. But today, Olivia wasn't going to take no for an answer. She called again. It rang and rang. She was tired of her mother avoiding her unless she needed something. Olivia was not going to be ignored.

She called again. Her mind flooded with questions with every ring. Where is she? Does she see that it's me calling? Is she sober? What if I needed her and this was an emergency?

Voicemail. No, not good enough. She called again and wondered if anyone had a normal relationship with their mother. Would Samantha have a normal relationship with her? Or would Olivia turn into someone she didn't even want to call? One more time she pressed the call button. Screw her mother for ignoring her. Screw Patricia for being so perfectly polished when Olivia's life was so perfectly not. She closed her eyes, deep sighed, and pressed. It rang twice and Olivia's nerves were screaming just hang up, but she waited to leave a voicemail.

"Olivia!"

"Mom." Just saying that made Olivia feel like a child.

"And to what do I owe this pleasure?" Her voice sounded upbeat, as if Olivia hadn't just called her multiple times in a row. Olivia tried to discern whether it was normal upbeat, or I've been day drinking upbeat.

"Mothers and daughters often talk, Mom. You know, not just when they need money. I wanted to see how you were doing."

"Well, if you visited me, you would know how I'm doing." Her mom's voice lost all its sweetness.

"Yes, well..." Olivia wanted to scream, I haven't visited because last time you were drunk, and you scared Samantha. Instead, she said, "Well, you could visit me too you know. And your granddaughter. Remember her?"

Olivia tried to calm her breathing. She had not called her mom to yell at her. Even though she deserved that and more. She called her because she wanted her life to not always have this rip—where her mother was on one side and Steve was on the other. And alcohol was in the middle.

It's why she put her mom on her Me List. Because the truth was that Olivia couldn't erase her mom from her life. Even when she wasn't around, she was still stressed about her. Because even a shitty mom was still her mom. And she hadn't figured out how to let go of her yet, even though Steve and her therapist had both pushed her to.

Maybe this time it would go better? Maybe this time Steve could see that her mother wasn't all bad? Olivia pulled at the ends of her hair as she said, "I was thinking you could come over for dinner. At our house. I'll cook. You can see Samantha." Maybe she shouldn't tell Steve about the money lending until after her mom's visit?

"Oh." It was obvious her mother did not know what to do with that nicety. They had already come to the part of the conversation where talking normally turned to screaming and past grievances were thrown at each other like snowballs of hate.

"When? I have cards on Thursday with Jan." Her voice was even—not kind, not mean.

"How about Sunday? Six? Or at five? You could spend time with Samantha while I get dinner ready."

Silence. Then her mother quietly said, "I could do that."

They both knew what would come next. The gauntlet that divided Olivia from her mother. The choice that always lay like a path with two roads: one that led her mother to her granddaughter, and one that turned and led her to a bar or her liquor cabinet.

"But Mom, you can't drink before you come here. You cannot drink while you are here. Do you understand?"

"Yes, I understand!" her mom shrieked. Olivia could hear her mother tapping the table out of nervousness.

"Sammy has been asking about you. But there are rules. I'm not going to…" Olivia stopped herself because she needed to get out of this conversation with a hope of success. If she let her frustration with her mother get in the way, there would be no path forward. She was giving her mother one more chance. Not just because Olivia needed it, but because Sammy did. And Olivia could protect Sammy, but by letting just enough of her mother into their lives, maybe they'd both get something out of it.

Oh, there it was again. That glimmer of hope Olivia thought was dead. She smashed it back down in her stomach. She had no grandiose thoughts about her mother finally kicking this habit because a relationship with Samantha would show her the way. No. No. No. But yes, yes, yes, it was there, and Olivia couldn't quiet it. How do you give up hope on your mother?

Olivia reiterated their plans. "Okay, then. This Sunday. Five o'clock."

"I'll bring dessert." Her mother's voice remained equanimous.

"Great." Olivia's whole body released its tension. "And Mom, don't mention the money stuff to Steve."

"See you Sunday."

No "I love you." No "Thanks for the cash and for saving my butt once again." But at least the call was done. She had finally picked up.

And there it was, in the air all around Olivia. A door that had been shut for a long time opened a sliver of a crack. She knew she couldn't completely repair her relationship with her mother. No, there was too much to unpack. But she did want to live with it in a better way. She stood up and walked to the edge of the deck. Marven walked over. She petted his ears slowly, methodically, calming him and herself.

"Well, I did it, Marven. I called her and invited her here." The two sat there not moving, finding solace in each other, as they let the weight of the day surround them. *We should thank dogs more,* thought Olivia, because she was so grateful she had Marven there with her. Her little friend of fur and love.

That night, her conversation with Steve didn't go well. She couldn't even imagine how mad he'd be if he knew about the money, too. He stormed around the kitchen as he tersely said, "What do you mean, dinner? Here? In our house?"

"Yes. In our house. It'll be fine. I told her no drinking."

"You told her that last time." Steve cleaned the counter—more like angrily scrubbed it with a sponge.

"Look. Avoiding her isn't working for me. I need to figure out if there's a way she can be in my life."

"You always get hurt." He focused on one spot of dried food and furrowed his brow.

"I'm not the same girl I was. I know what I'm getting into. I know she's not going to change. That's the difference. I waited my whole life for her to pick me over alcohol. But what I'm hoping is that for an hour or two here or there, she can spend a little time with Sammy so she doesn't have the same gaping hole I do."

Olivia went over to Steve and put her hand on his forearm. "I would never let my mother hurt Sammy. You know that. Never." She said each word forcefully.

"I know that. But you let her hurt you. Don't you get that? And I'm never going to be okay with that." He walked over and hugged her. She buried her face in his shoulder and tried to breathe in the security.

Olivia knew Steve would never understand why she put her mother on her Me List. But that was exactly why it was called a Me List. Steve had two parents. Good ones. Olivia had an absent father, who last she heard was in Italy somewhere. And for better or worse, she had her mom. And she needed to give it one last try before she crossed their relationship off her list forever.

CHAPTER 13
HOT DOGS

It was 4:45 p.m. on Sunday. The microwave clock blinked at Olivia with each passing minute, causing her stomach to get tighter and tighter. Olivia cut a watermelon into nice, neat squares, even though her relationship with her mother was not neat. No, it was more like the watermelon juice that was slowly oozing across her counter. The knife felt good in her hand. Each cut made her feel in control. She popped a piece into her mouth. It was sweet, tasting like summer's promise.

"Sam!" Olivia called. "Sam!" Olivia called louder. Then finally screamed at top volume, "Sammy! Can you put this watermelon on the table outside?"

"What?" Sammy poked her head out from the next room, as if her mother had said absolutely nothing to her.

Sammy walked slowly over to her with her hands down. "Put this out on the table." Olivia thrust the bowl at Sammy, forcing her hands to reach up for it.

"Why are you so…" Sammy stopped herself and grumbled under her breath, "intense?"

"I'm not." Olivia tried to relax her shoulders, but they were stiff and uncomfortable.

She followed Sammy outside and looked at their deck. A pot of petunias sat in the middle of the table. Red plates and cups. Watermelon. Cheese and crackers. A pitcher of lemonade. It screamed cook-out. But the tension inside Olivia made her feel like she was the one getting cooked.

She heard Marven's bark, and she knew the time. "Sammy, come with me to greet your grandmother," Olivia said. It was a request that felt more like a security blanket.

Sammy bounded happily towards the door. She opened the door just as Olivia scooped up Marven.

"Hi." As Sammy opened the door, her enthusiasm turned to shyness.

Olivia's mom came in like a herd of rhinos. Her voice rang loud and high to overcome her nervousness.

"My granddaughter. Look at you! I brought you this." She shoved a large pink gift bag into Sammy's arms.

Sammy smiled and asked, "Oh, Mom, can I open it?"

"Let's let Grandma come in first before we open it." Olivia gave her mom a stilted hug, barely pressing her body into hers, and whispered, "Don't forget, no money talk."

Her mother nodded her head and asked, "Where's Steve?" Her judgmental tone was turned up to her normal high.

"He's outside, grilling." Olivia smiled, trying to add positivity to the fact that he was cooking for them all.

"Mhmm," was all her mom said.

"Here. Let's go sit outside and Sammy can open her gift." Olivia escorted her mom forward. Her mom was dressed in her usual poorly fitted jeans with a navy fabric top that looked more itchy than comfortable. And more dirty than clean.

Olivia opened the door to outside and said, "Honey, look who is here," with more sunshine to her voice than she felt.

Steve closed the grill and turned. "Rose, so nice to see you again."

Olivia's mother, Rose, did not move a step toward him. Instead, she pulled out the chair in front of her and said with glee, "Sammy, why don't you open what Grandma gave you?"

Sammy set the bag down and pulled out the pink tissue paper, throwing it to the ground. Marven came up and sniffed it.

"What's this creature?" Rose inquired.

"That's Marven. Our foster pup. If you want to pet him, say his name first because he can't see well. Isn't he adorable?" Sammy gushed.

"He's ummm..." but Rose did not appreciate any animal so she could only muster, "He looks well-loved."

Sammy pulled out a large arts and crafts kit from the bag. The type that has pencils, crayons, and watercolors all in one plastic organizer. *It was probably something she grabbed on the way to their house from the grocery store, but at least it's useful,* thought Olivia.

"Thanks, Grandma. I'll make you a picture."

Thank goodness for Sammy, thought Olivia. Her joy could make any awkwardness feel better.

"Why don't you bring some paper and sit and color next to Grandma?" Olivia suggested. She wanted to make sure her mother and Sammy spent time together. As soon as Sammy ran inside to get paper, Olivia was left alone with her mother, and a lifetime of angst sat between them and the lemonade.

"Want some?" Olivia poured herself a glass.

"Sure," Rose answered, looking around the yard. Marven sniffed her leg, and she looked down at him. "Nothing to see here, dog. Just an old lady." Her leg moved back and forth. A nervous rhythm Olivia had seen her whole life. As if shaking her limbs fast enough would quell her inner beast from wanting a drink.

"Marven is blind, Mom, so be careful with your leg. You all right?" Olivia asked as she felt the coolness of the cup against her hand.

"Yep. Doing just dandy," Rose answered and looked again around the yard, searching for something to say. "You use pesticides on that lawn, Steve?"

Steve, who had been staring at the grill as if every hot dog and hamburger needed his vital attention, turned, and said, "Nope, that's just Mother Nature."

Thankfully, Sammy returned with a few pieces of paper.

"What are you going to draw me?" Rose asked.

"Do you like dogs or cats?" Sammy asked.

"Ha. Neither," Rose answered. "Draw me whatever you want."

"You never had a pet?"

"Not really. We had a few outside cats your mother fed occasionally. Mangy ones."

"Really?" Sammy smiled because she enjoyed hearing stories about her mom as a kid.

"Grandma thinks everything is mangy." Olivia rolled her eyes. "Yep, my mom wouldn't let me have any pets, so I had to love the neighbor's pets," Olivia teased, her nerves finally settling enough so she could take a sip of her lemonade.

"Oh, here's where it starts. My mom was the worst." Rose bit her bottom lip, clearly trying to control what she was going to say.

Right at that moment, Steve said, "Hot dogs and hamburgers are ready."

He had been around Rose long enough to know when she was about to make Olivia feel bad about her childhood. As if Olivia had been the adult, as if she could have helped more than she did. Steve tried to put his hackles down, but he loved his wife and it was his shoulder she cried on, over and over, every time Rose let her down. Or got drunk and ruined an event. Or didn't show up. Or called when she was angry. Or called when she was not angry and begged for forgiveness or money, promising to change. The cycle was unending. And it was up to Olivia to end it.

"What would you like, Rose?"

"Oh, anything will do," Rose responded, which made it more difficult than if she had just said hot dog or hamburger.

"I want a hot dog," said Samantha. Steve winked at her to show that he knew her hot dog-loving heart.

"I'm the veggie burger," said Olivia.

"Oh, are you still doing that?" asked Rose, with an emphasis on *that*. As if being a vegetarian was some passing phase of Olivia's, even though it had been over a decade.

"Yep. Still eating healthy." Olivia smiled, internally reminding herself to stay calm and not get annoyed at her mother.

Steve passed a hamburger to Rose, a hot dog to Samantha, and a veggie burger to Olivia. He looked with dread at the chair that awaited him. "I love my wife. I love my wife," he repeated silently, willing himself to sit down.

Rose, never one to look past someone's awkwardness, said, "Steve, sit down. All that grilling probably has you famished."

Steve pulled out his chair and sat down, having accepted his fate.

Sammy smiled and skewered her whole hot dog on her fork, nibbling at the end.

Rose looked alarmed. "Samantha, I think your mom should cut that for you. Hot dogs are very dangerous for young kids."

Steve gave her a look. Rose added as if she had done research, "They choke. Number one choking hazard for kids."

"Sammy isn't that young, Mom. But yeah, when she was younger, we cut them up." Olivia picked at the bun of her sandwich, trying to ignore that her mother was giving her parenting advice. Should she remind her how many days she made her own peanut butter and jelly sandwiches when she was little, because her mother was passed out somewhere? Who was worried about her choking then? No. Today was about moving forward.

Rose took the fork out of Sammy's hand and started cutting the hot dog for her. "Mom, Sammy is fine."

Sammy, not used to an adult snatching her fork, sat there in shock.

Rose cut the hot dog vigorously, her shaky hands causing hot dog pieces to fly off the plate.

"Mom. Stop. She's fine." Olivia put her hand on her mother's wrist to try to put an end to the hot dog-cutting mania. But Rose pulled her arm back so violently, the fork and hot dog went flying and hit Sammy in the eye.

"Ow. My eye!" Sammy cried.

Olivia jumped out of her chair and went to Sammy with a napkin. "Oh, my goodness, are you okay?"

"I'm bleeding," Sammy cried as she wiped her cheek. Seeing the red drip on her finger made her cry harder.

"No, baby. It's just ketchup. It's just ketchup."

"Number one hazard for kids, huh?" Steve mumbled under his breath.

"I was just trying to help." Rose looked down at her plate and folded her arms. Her face was a mixture of scowl, resentment, and frown. "I've been a mother a lot longer than you, you know. It wouldn't hurt you to listen to me once in a while." She looked at Olivia and Sammy but did not apologize for any of the processed meat shenanigans.

"Yes, you had a child. But I've been a mother longer than you," Olivia said quietly as she kissed Sammy's head. She couldn't help herself. The words came and hit hard.

"I think it's time for me to go." Rose stood up and said, "Samantha, it was nice to see you again," before making her way swiftly to the door.

Sammy ran after her. "Grandma don't go. We didn't finish coloring."

Olivia got up quickly to go after her daughter. She reached her near the front door and put her hand on top of Sammy's shoulders. "It's okay, Sammy." And then added a lie to soften the goodbye. "Grandma told me she couldn't stay long."

Sammy gave a small, sad wave, incapable of understanding that the hot dog in the eye had been the least painful stab at that table.

"Thank you for coming, Mother," Olivia said, trying to add a dash of something positive to the moment.

Her mother nodded, let out a small disagreeable noise that was not quite a word, and closed the door behind her.

"Mom, Grandma didn't mean to hurt me with a hot dog," Sammy said.

Olivia gave her a big hug and said, "I know Sammy," and then lied again. "Like I said. Grandma told us she couldn't stay long. She had an appointment today, a very important one."

They walked back to the outside table. Olivia gave Steve a knowing glance. Steve, a grilling magician, produced a new hot dog for Sammy and the family ate quietly together. Sammy ate her hot dog without choking. Olivia ate her veggie burger and choked back years of memories of her mom not being there for her when she was a child. Why couldn't she just accept her mother couldn't be here for her now either? Olivia looked at Steve and wondered if he was imagining choking Rose.

Marven waited patiently under the table, hoping more bits of hot dog would drop to the ground.

That night, Olivia tossed and turned. Steve lay in bed next to her, reading his phone. After the third very loud sigh, he put his phone down and asked, "Do you want to talk?"

"No." Olivia huffed and turned her body over, trying to adjust her pillow to become more comfortable. She smashed her pillow so violently that if it had a pulse, it would no longer be alive.

Steve looked back at his phone, and Olivia flipped back over.

"It's just…why does she make me feel so bad? Shouldn't she be feeling bad? But now here I am, somehow feeling bad that she feels bad, or I don't even know. It's all bad."

Steve went to say something, opened his mouth and closed it, deciding on the insightful word, "Mmmhmm."

"I just want a mom who can come over and eat a hamburger and smile at my daughter. Is that too much to ask?"

"No. But Olivia, hon, your mom isn't that mom. She never has been."

"At least she wasn't drunk."

Steve put his arm around his wife.

"What did your therapist say about your mom?" Steve paused but didn't wait for her answer because they had repeated the mantra many times throughout their marriage. "You can change your feelings, you can change yourself, but you can't change your mom. She needs to do that."

"I just want a mom. I want a grandma for Sammy."

"You have my parents," Steve smiled.

"I do. And they are great. It's just lately, I feel like I have room for her. It's why I put her on my list. I thought maybe making some room is better than what I've been doing, which is to not include her. Because even when I don't include her, she's still in my life but in a negative way because I feel guilty. Basically, there's no way to live with my mother." Olivia smashed the pillow over her face, hiding under it. She peeked up and said, "I'm going to make an appointment with my therapist. Fucking moms. Making therapists money for years."

"Love you, honey." Steve patted the pillow and said, "Any chance you'd want to take out your anger and…"

"No." Olivia pulled the pillow back over her head.

"I figured. Just thought I'd try." Steve picked up his phone and rolled over.

CHAPTER 14
BRANCHES

Olivia woke up groggy and annoyed at her mother. Marven woke up with a slight film on his eye. Olivia did just what the vet had written in his instructions. She got a warm washcloth, wiped his eyes gently, and then put in the drops. She spoke gently to him while she did it, as if he could understand her every word. Marven grumbled, but overall did great.

Olivia heard her phone buzz and wondered if it was her mother texting to apologize. But it was Patricia. She was in no mood for her.

Check outside your door, then check your email.

Olivia opened the door a crack and peered out, half expecting to see something frightening or a large pile of something that needed to be done. Instead, she saw a cappuccino maker, a paycheck, and a note:

I can't thank you enough for all the help you've given me. I wanted to thank you with this gift which I know is on your list.

And then it just said "Patricia." No from, love, or sincerely. Olivia picked up the box and looked at all the features. It was nicer than the one she had scoped out online. She pulled the machine out of the box and found a place for it on the counter. It looked serious, like one that would be found in a small café in Paris. Damn, Olivia was hoping to be grouchy and obsess about her shitty mom all day, and now here was Patricia, making her day better.

She took a picture and sent it to Patricia with the text, *It's perfect. Thank you so much.* Olivia had taken out the instruction book and started skimming when Patricia wrote back, *I figured it'd make my emails easier.*

In all the gloom and drama from her mom's visit, and then with the excitement and promise of frothed milk, Olivia hadn't checked her email yet. Olivia went to her computer and hit refresh. Patricia's name was at the top three times. She opened email one:

Olivia, forgive the scattered nature of this email. My mother has slipped and broken her hip. I'm sending you a spreadsheet with the newest listings that all need For Sale signs. Please get the signs from Donna at the office and drive to each house and put them up. Thanks so much. I'll have my cell if you need me, Patricia.

What is it about mothers this week causing havoc? Olivia wondered. Okay, that wasn't bad. Certainly not worthy of a cappuccino maker. But there were two more emails to go.

Just heard back about the Worthington house. There's a showing today at 1:00. I'm going to go early to scope it out. I want you to be there with me in case I need some last-minute prep. Come early (12:30) but please stop at David's to get fresh flowers on your way over. I put in the order already. Attached is a detailed list of features of the house if you want to check it out. It's a real stunner, as you know.

Last thing, Kelly was complaining loudly at the office that she's so overworked, so I offered that you'd do her For Sale signs too. And I gave her your email in case you want to take on more work in the next few weeks. Sorry! Feel free to tell her no! Her list is attached. Donna has Kelly's signs ready for you. Hoping the coffee maker will give you extra energy.

Olivia opened up the doc that was named Kelly. Fifteen houses. Ugh. It was going to be a day of driving around and driving signs in yards. She looked at the next doc that said Worthington house. The house was 1.5 million dollars. The typical realtor fee was six percent, split between the broker and the real estate agent. That was a lot of money.

Still one more email. Olivia was afraid to open it. What other surprises awaited?

Olivia. Make that 12:30 for the house showing, so 12:00 for us to meet there (with the flowers). You can do signs tomorrow. I'm still in a meeting with my mother's medical team and I need your assistance NOW. I almost forgot to mention the wife is visually impaired. She might be wearing sunglasses, but I wanted to alert you so you can be sensitive to that. Please look through the details of the house with safety in mind and email me any features ASAP you think might be helpful. There is an elevator. Main bedroom is on the first floor, etc. Zero entry pool—not sure if that's good or bad? Please do some thorough research to find out what other features I should highlight that could assist. Also, they've looked at about ten other houses already. My mother's health stuff is coming at the absolute worst time. Any research you do will be so helpful and deserving of a bonus if I sell it! Thank you!

Olivia closed the email and stared over at her espresso maker. Now it was shining as a total guilt purchase. Patricia was dumping a big crazy morning on her. And Kelly.

Olivia wondered how much Patricia would give her as a bonus. Either way, it would probably be more than Olivia's hourly rate. And she could put it towards the vacation account that she still hadn't told Steve about. It had been so long that now it just seemed easier not to tell him and pay it back. Especially after yesterday's disaster with her mom.

Olivia clicked and looked at the Worthington house again. How do you sell a house this gorgeous to a person who might not be able to see its grandness?

Just then, Marven barked. She smiled at him and said, "Marven, let's go outside." No, a blind dog was not the same as a person. But Olivia was now more aware of how a crack in a sidewalk or a slippery floor could make it harder for Marven, so she was learning more about how to be sensitive to the world around her. Because, before that, she had never thought about it. Olivia wasn't thoughtless, but her life hadn't exposed her to such things.

Olivia opened her web browser, typed in *home modification for the visually impaired*, and started writing a list of features to look out for. She took notes: safe flooring—non-slip, warning textures in front of things like doorways or steps, contrasting colors on walls. By the time she looked up, her notepad was full, and she had written a few more items to flag, like removing loose area rugs. She typed up the list and sent it to Patricia.

She grabbed her keys to go pick up the flowers. But then she stopped, looked down at herself, and decided to go change. She had never been with Patricia in such a fancy house before. And even though Olivia knew her job was to assist Patricia with any last-minute requests before the buyers got there, she still felt like she should be dressed more nicely than in a sweatshirt. She decided on simple slacks and low heels. Anything higher and she might trip on a good day, let alone a day where so much money was on the line. Would Patricia forgive her if she tripped and bled out on the carpet?

She went downstairs to put Marven away. "Sorry, Marven, it's nap time for you." She gave him a treat that he took happily and crawled into his crate. "Wish me luck, buddy." Marven crunched his bone.

Olivia put her notebook into her purse and entered the address into her phone. The house was fifteen minutes away. She stopped by David's Flower Shop and picked up the bouquet without a hitch, except that she had sweated through her shirt. With no time to stop back home, she continued to the Worthington house, turned the air conditioner up high, and aimed the vents directly at her armpits.

As Olivia pulled into the beautifully manicured circle driveway, she saw Patricia already at the door punching the code in the lockbox. Patricia waved and went inside.

Olivia walked up to the door. It was such a beautiful door. Handcrafted wood. Iron trim around the window. The right combination of rustic yet gorgeous. When Olivia walked in, she noticed a phone entry system on the wall next to the door. Perfect; the buyer could speak to whoever was at the front door instead of looking. She stopped and looked down and noticed the natural tile. It was smooth, but not slippery. The kitchen had a huge island. No surprise. Olivia put the vase of flowers down. And told Patricia all the features she had noticed already. Patricia looked more stressed than normal. A few hair strands were out of place and her sweater looked wrinkly. Olivia wondered if it was the stress of the house or her mother's health issues.

"Look at this gorgeous Viking stove." Patricia lightly touched the knobs.

"It has cast-iron grates, which are great because I read flat top stoves can be a burning hazard for visually impaired people."

Olivia felt like an A-plus student. Do people in 1.5 million-dollar homes cook for themselves? She shook her head. This was not the time to be judging. This was the time to be learning and looking and helping Patricia. She looked at the marble countertops. She looked at the freshly-painted walls—neutral grays, soothing blues, natural tans. Everything was so clean. Olivia couldn't help but think of her walls and dirty baseboards. Mental note: she should paint her house. Or at least wipe down her baseboards so they looked white again.

"Can you go upstairs and make sure everything is in order?" Patricia asked. "I have a few more things I want to do down here."

The most beautiful feature of the house surprised Olivia when she walked upstairs. The biggest window overlooked the pool and beyond that was a stunning old oak tree, its trunk thick, its huge branches stretching out like ladders leading toward the sky. It looked like a staircase made of bark, perfect for a child to climb. Olivia imagined how much fun Samantha would have on those branches. She could imagine a carefree childhood, not like the one Olivia had grown up with. Olivia shook her head from side to side as if it could get thoughts of her mother out of it.

A knock at the door made Olivia look down at her watch. The buyers were early. She hurried down to see if Patricia wanted her to leave or if she needed anything else. But she couldn't find Patricia anywhere. She could hear Patricia's voice coming from the bathroom.

Olivia knocked gently. "Patricia, they are here."

Patricia opened the door, and her face was flushed. She pulled her cell phone away from her ear and her voice wavered. "My mother." It was all she could say. She cleared her throat and said, "Welcome the buyers and let them know I'll be in out in a minute."

Olivia felt bad for spending the morning wanting to kill her own mother off while Patricia was upset by her mother being so sick.

When Olivia opened the door, a nice-looking couple greeted her. The man was slightly older. He was wearing a gray suit. The woman wore sunglasses and a casual loose shirt and jeans that looked expensive. And cute navy flats. But what surprised Olivia the most was the additional guest. A brown and reddish-haired guide dog. She stopped herself from petting it.

"Welcome, I'm Patricia's assistant," she said, more to the dog than the couple. The man laughed. "You can give him a quick pet if you'd like."

"Sorry, I confess I'm a dog lover. In fact, I just…" And then Olivia stopped, suddenly aware that her Marven story might not be the best story. Or maybe it would be. Oh, she was overthinking everything already. Was she being overly sensitive, or not sensitive enough? The couple smiled at her graciously and broke her inner mental tornado. She gave the dog a pat. "I recently started fostering a dog." His tail wagged back and forth.

"Yeah, Rigley here is on loan right now," the husband said. "My name is Mark."

"I'm Sherri." The woman stuck out her hand for a firm handshake.

"I'm Olivia. And Patricia is just finishing up a critical phone call. Her mother had a fall this morning and is in the hospital." Olivia took a huge breath in and kept talking to fill the quiet and space until Patricia appeared. "This house is amazing. I've been walking through it."

"Sorry to hear about Patricia's mom," said Sherri.

Mark put his hand out and said, "Take us to your favorite feature."

"Oh, technically I can't. I'm not a licensed real estate agent." The window came to mind. Olivia ignored that idea and said, "Why don't you just start down here and I'll go check in on Patricia? I know she can't wait to show you the house."

"Is your favorite feature down here?" the woman asked, more straightforward than brash, although Olivia's neck grew hot from her direct tone.

"We've seen a lot of houses," Mark added to explain his wife's bluntness. "They all start to look the same."

Olivia swallowed. Her mouth was suddenly dry. She decided to trust her gut.

"My favorite feature is outside."

"Great. Let's go see it. Come on, Rigley," Sherri said.

Olivia walked in front of them, commenting quietly as they walked through the house. She knew she wasn't a real estate agent but, as an assistant, she could say what she noticed out loud, right?

"This flooring is natural tile. Makes for a non-slippery walk." Sherri nodded her head with a slight smile.

As they passed through the kitchen, Olivia pointed to the Viking stove. "Not a flat-top," was all she said. Inside, she was screaming for Patricia to finish her phone call. Olivia hoped her mother wasn't dying or dead, but she also didn't want to kill this house sale.

"Ha. My mom is always worried about stoves." Sherri held up her hands and said, "I haven't burned one of them yet. She burns hers all the time from baking. I should be worried about her."

Olivia opened the French doors to the patio and said, "Here is my favorite feature. But again, I'm not a realtor, just an assistant."

Mark dictated what they were seeing. "It's a nice pool, Sherri."

Olivia quickly added, "Ah yes, a zero-entry, so no steps. But that's not my favorite. It's right beyond that. The oak tree. It's something out of a picture book. It's stunning. If this were my house, I'd spend time in its shade. And with perfect branches to climb, my daughter would be up there in a second. I saw it and I could almost hear her laughing and squealing like a monkey."

The couple was quiet. Only Rigley wagged his tail. Suddenly, Olivia felt so stupid. A million-dollar house and she just showed them an ancient oak tree.

She heard Mark whisper, "Are you okay?" He held Sherri's hand.

Before Olivia could say anything else, she heard the throaty sound of an "ahem," and Patricia smiling nervously. "Sorry I'm late. This is a fabulous backyard. But I can't wait to show you the amazing one-of-a-kind walk-in shower-tub in the main bedroom. The past owner had some mobility issues, so it's a perfect blend of luxury and safety."

"Oh wow, that sounds amazing. We haven't gone upstairs yet," Mark said as he squeezed his wife's hand.

As they walked ahead, Patricia pulled Olivia to the side and said in a terse voice, "Trees can be planted anywhere. A top-of-the-line bathroom that meets her safety needs can't. Thank you for filling in, but I think I can handle it from here." Patricia kept walking and didn't turn around. Olivia stood there, stunned. Patricia's mood had gone from a cappuccino to Frappuccino so quickly. What good was a nice gift if Patricia's words were scalding?

Olivia felt her eyes sting with tears. She knew Patricia was stressed about her mother. But Olivia was trying her best. Of course Patricia had to come just when she pointed out that stupid old tree. Olivia ran to her car, turned it on, and was at least three blocks away before she let herself release her tears. She banged the steering wheel with her fist.

"It's just a job. It's just a job," she repeated to herself. As she drove farther away from the beautiful houses, she realized she was crying, not just because of Patricia. She was also crying because at that moment she thought she had shown the potential for that house to become a home. And now she just felt stupid. She wiped her snotty nose on her arm. A home was something Olivia valued more than anything. It wasn't about the beautiful throw pillows or fancy sink faucet. It was about how a home made you feel safe. Growing up with her mother and father fighting, her home never felt like a secure place to live. Her damn mother. Olivia had already counted on the bonus money from the house sale to help repay their vacation fund. And now it was all a mess.

Olivia opened her glove compartment and pulled out a napkin. She always shoved extra napkins in there for Samantha from whatever drive-through they went to. She was tired of being alone with her emotions, so she called her husband.

"I'm quitting," she said as soon as he picked up.

"Well, hello to you too. What's going on? Do you need me to kill Patricia?" Steve's voice sounded concerned.

"No, don't kill her yet. I'm just driving home from a disaster of a showing. And what do I have waiting for me at home? Ten piles of laundry I haven't done. I need to go grocery shopping. We're almost out of milk. And for what? Just to get paid while Patricia makes me feel like an idiot?

"Look. We've made it this long on one salary. If it's making you miserable, just quit."

"No. It's more than that. It's just…"

Olivia wanted to confess everything at that moment. How her mother had ghosted her after she gave her the money. How Olivia wasn't the amazing balancing act. She had been pretending. She was more of a slowly drowning act. But it annoyed her that Steve had been so fast to think she should quit. Hadn't he noticed the changes in her? How she was feeling more confident about herself?

"Shouldn't you be trying to build me up? Telling me you believe in me? Not just telling me to quit?"

Steve got quiet. "Look, you're upset. You never like anything I say when you are upset. I want you to do whatever will make you happy. If you are happier not working for Patricia, then quit. Find something else. Or don't. I support you being happy."

"I wasn't happy before."

"What?"

"I wasn't happy. Do you know I went like five months with my hair in a wet ponytail? I would go days without talking with anyone but Sammy. And then when she started school, I'd have to force myself to leave the house. I was basically in a relationship with Netflix. For God's sake, I don't even own tweezers anymore."

"Sweetie, take a deep breath. I don't know what you want me to say."

"I want you to want me to own tweezers." Olivia pulled down the sun visor and quickly glanced in the mirror at the tiny forest of eyebrow hair. Each stray hair was a symbol of her self-care neglect.

"I can buy you tweezers."

"It's not about the tweezers," Olivia yelled. And then, in a softer voice, said, "I want you to want me to care about myself."

"Of course I want you to care about yourself. I love you. But can we finish talking about this when I get home tonight? I have a meeting that I can't miss."

"You always have a meeting you can't miss," Olivia said grumpily. Although she was madder at Patricia and herself than Steve.

"Sweetie, I'm sorry you are having a bad day. I can pick up milk on the way home if that helps a little. And tweezers."

Olivia felt like a deflated balloon. "Yeah, pick up milk. Don't worry about the tweezers. I'll get them sometime. There's more I want to tell you. But we'll talk later." She drove home listening to the radio but not hearing any of the music.

When she got home, she let Marven out of his cage and sat on the floor so his happy little body could jump on hers. After a few wiggles, he bent down for a long stretch, during which Olivia couldn't help but say, "Ohhhh good stretch," as if her words helped his body stretch even longer. "Marven, today sucked. I know it's silly. I just wanted to…" She couldn't quite find the words, and Marven seemed to be ready for the bathroom and not a confession. So instead, Olivia said, "Let's go outside in the back, Marven. You can pee."

While Marven sniffed the grass, Olivia stared out at the yard. Her pocket vibrated. She didn't even look at her phone as she answered it. She figured it was Steve checking back in on her after that emotional dump fest. But it wasn't Steve.

"Hi, Olivia." Patricia's voice had never sounded more irritating and Olivia had never hated the sound of her own name more than right now. Olivia wanted to yell "I quit" and throw her phone across the yard. Her face got red as her humiliation boiled inside her.

"I wanted to let you know they made an offer on the house." Patricia's voice was curt mixed with a touch of "I was rude and I know it, but I'm not going to say it."

"That's wonderful. Was it the tub?" Olivia said tub with as much venom as one can make a three-letter word have. And before Olivia could get the words "I quit" out, Patricia said the words, "It was the tree." Patricia spoke so quietly that Olivia wondered if the phone had been disconnected.

Olivia couldn't believe what she had heard. Surely it was a mistake. "Patricia, what did you say?"

"Sherri is pregnant with a girl. So your little story of your daughter happily playing in the tree stuck with her. She mentioned it to me. And I'm sure the walk-in tub helped too, of course."

Patricia tried to sound breezy, but Olivia could tell every word of that statement was like eating a big pointy verbal cactus.

"That's wonderful," Olivia said enthusiastically, because the love of her own daughter made her truly excited for the couple.

"We will talk about next steps tomorrow. I need to go to the hospital to be with my mother. I will make sure to give you a bonus from the sale like I said."

Patricia hung up the phone before Olivia could be a decent human and ask Patricia more about her mother. And before Olivia could utter the words about quitting.

Olivia smiled. She did it. Maybe with the bonus, she could repay her vacation account and put this stressful lie to rest. She was tired of always having to juggle her mother's bad decisions with Steve's opinions. It was like an angry teeter-totter inside her heart. And she was done with it.

CHAPTER 15
SHARDS

Eight chairs. All with honey-oak wood and brown cushions. Olivia waited in her therapist's reception area and looked at the uncomfortable chairs that were arranged in two rows. Nobody talked or looked at each other while they were waiting. What would they say? Which therapist do you see? What are you here for? Do you hate your mom or dad? Anxiety or depression? Olivia kept her mind busy by counting things. Eight chairs, three spidery green plants that looked fake, twenty-four squares on the ceiling, and wait, there it was, her name being called out. Olivia stood up and made her way to the door, leaving the rest of the patients and their worries behind.

Olivia walked into her therapist's office and sank into the big leather couch. Next to her was an essential oil mister that smelled like a blend of bergamot and lavender. A big spiky tree sat to her right. She'd spent many a session staring at that tree. Her therapist, Laura, smiled. Olivia wondered if someone trained therapists on how to have a welcoming, non-judgmental smile.

"I like your sweater," Olivia said, because she did. It was light blue and looked soft, a color Olivia would never have chosen for herself because she always tended to go more neutral. *She probably thinks I'm sucking up to her and I don't actually like her sweater.*

"Thanks. What brings you in today?" Laura asked, pausing as therapists do to indicate you should start talking.

"My mother." Olivia dropped the word "mother" into the room with a loud, crisis-bearing thud.

"Mmm. Go on."

Laura had been Olivia's therapist since Samantha was born. Once Sammy came along, she knew she had to work on her past to be a better mom. Anger bubbled up in her throat every time she had wonderful moments with Sammy. It was like her past and future couldn't stop colliding. When Sammy touched her face, Olivia's heart would flutter, but then a beat later she would wonder why her mother hadn't felt this way about her. Now that Olivia knew a mother's love, the failure of her own mother's love felt oppressive.

"I've been working on myself lately. I have a job. A new friend. I have this list of things I want to do this year to become a better me."

"That all sounds positive," Laura encouraged. She wrote something down in her notebook and nodded her head yes, so Olivia kept talking.

"And one of the biggest obstacles for me is my mom. I want a mom. I want Samantha to have a grandma. It's just hard because, well, my mom just isn't that type of mom, so I thought if I included her in something she could fit into our lives in a tiny way. Because not having her in my life hasn't felt great."

"And do you remember why you came to that decision? To not have her in your life?" Laura posed it as a question, but they had spent a very long year together, working towards that decision.

"Because she's toxic. She's a drunk. She's not dependable. And she makes me feel bad about myself." Olivia sighed and slumped back onto the couch. She knew in her head what came next. Why would she want a toxic, drunk, irresponsible person around her daughter? Why? Because our hearts are not logical. And Olivia's heart was formed wanting love, but instead got a big hole of disappointment that her mother had never filled. Her husband and daughter filled it and that should have been enough, but it wasn't. Olivia would give anything to fill that hole and quiet her desire for normalcy.

"Why do you think you put your mom on your list?" Laura asked a question that Olivia hadn't yet asked herself.

Olivia was quiet for a minute as she picked at the rim of the couch with her fingers. "I wanted to pick things that would improve me, make me happy, make me face my fears. I even went on a ropes course with my daughter, high in the air. And well, my mom is something that holds me back from being happy."

She said it. It was true. Hearing those words floating in the room didn't make them any easier. Her relationship with her mother was always in her way. Even when she avoided it. Even when she stuffed it down deep. It was there. She was there. A symbol of need and love that could never be extinguished.

"So, I invited her over." Olivia moved her hand to the thread of her jeans and smoothed over a piece that had come out over her knee.

"And how did it go?" Laura asked and smiled, even though her widening eyes revealed she knew how it went.

"It started out not terrible. I was nervous. She brought Sammy a gift, which was nice. But she started judging me as a mother when she wasn't even a mother at all. And then she left early. Sammy was crushed." Olivia frowned and stared at the good old prickly tree like always. She imagined the leafy hands saying, "It's okay." One of the tree's leaves was brown, so Olivia knew it was a real tree. This brought her some peace. She didn't want to give her feelings away to a fake tree.

"How did you feel when she left?" Laura changed positions in her chair but presented the question with the same simple clarity that seemed to open the room to more air, where Olivia could ponder.

"Terrible. Frustrated. Confused. Sad."

"Hmm."

"I know. It was silly for me to invite her. But I just thought if I could be different, she could be. And then maybe Steve could see that she wasn't all bad. And then I could tell him about the money I lent her without him jumping down my throat."

Laura opened her mouth, but Olivia stopped her. "I know what you're going to say about my circle of control."

Laura smiled. "Yes. I'm glad. What you can control is you. What you can't control is your mother."

"Is it stupid I keep wanting her?" The question brought tears to Olivia's eyes. Not the tears of a thirty-something woman, but the tears of an eight-year-old who waited on her bed, hoping for a bedtime story and wondering if she'd get tucked in only to sneak downstairs to find her mom asleep at the kitchen table next to a bottle of wine.

"Mother-daughter relationships are complicated. It's normal to want that and to mourn that. Olivia, your relationship with your mother isn't normal, because your mom is an alcoholic. That's not your fault."

Olivia's chest tightened; she could never accept those words, "It's not your fault." Once again, her tears betrayed her and showed Laura how much those words hurt.

"Say it with me, Olivia. My mom is an alcoholic, and it's not my fault."

Olivia whispered, "It's not my fault." Olivia ran her hands through her hair, scratched at her scalp, and asked, "But how do I get past this? How can I let go? How can I accept she doesn't love me like she should? She can't just swoop in and make me feel this way and leave. I want closure. I want..."

"Olivia, I wish I could tell you that you could have a talk with your mom and you would get all those things. You've asked her to come here and to work through it, but she's never accepted that invitation. We need to work on moving past your relationship with her, but it's you we need to work with." She paused before continuing, "It's almost time for our appointment to end. But I have a homework assignment for you. Write a letter to your mom telling her everything you are feeling and what you want. Don't mail it. Make another appointment with me and bring it."

"Okay." Olivia stood up and stretched. That was one comfy leather couch. She didn't feel much better, but at least she had a plan to help her work through her emotions.

On the drive home, Olivia wracked her brain, trying to figure out why she couldn't move on from her mom and let their relationship go. Wouldn't that be so much easier and better for her than holding out hope, only to be disappointed? Remembering her graduation, she was aware of how her mind seemed to bring up all the past examples of total defeat. What mother doesn't show up to her daughter's graduation ceremony? How many daughters spend half of their graduation celebration looking for their mothers among all the family pictures, flowers, and hugs, only to realize she's not there? How many daughters get a message hours later saying, "Something came up. I'll make it up to you." As if you can repeat a life moment like graduation. Olivia pulled up to her house and noticed two cars in Patricia's driveway.

She ran into the house and let Marven out of his crate. "Hey buddy, want to go for a walk with me? I could use some fresh air." Marven wagged his tail in agreement. The great thing about dogs was they rarely said no. As Olivia passed Patricia's house, she heard screaming and then a loud crash. Olivia stopped in her tracks and her heart skipped once or twice. She scooped Marven into her arms and walked up Patricia's manicured front path. She knocked loudly on the door, hoping to break up whatever was happening inside. If Patricia was in trouble, Olivia should help. She heard another crash. Flooded with a sudden rush of adrenaline and worry, she opened the door without stopping to worry about what she'd find inside.

Broken glass and blue and white vase shards were scattered over the floor—triangular pieces of ceramic like a puzzle that could not be put back together. Dirt swirls on the cream Persian carpet. Water on the hardwood. And a very angry Paul, about five feet away from Patricia.

Olivia stepped carefully and said, "You all right? I heard noises. Do you need help?" she asked as she took out her cell phone, ready to call 911. She added a little angry side-eye at Paul to make sure he knew she'd make the call.

"I'm fine," Patricia said as she straightened her clothes and fixed her messed-up hair. And with a small, forced laugh, she added, "Just your normal divorce discussions."

Olivia petted Marven and held his little body tight. He was shaking from agitation.

"Nothing about my ex-wife is normal," Paul seethed. "But it's nice to know she finally decided to embrace the neighbor next door. What is it you used to laugh about, Pat? How she was always dressed to go nowhere? What was that nickname you called her?"

"Paul, shut up," Patricia said, the words terse.

"O-no-life. Olivi-not? What was it? Instead of Olivia. Yeah, Pat, you were always so good at making up stuff to tear other people down. Remember when you'd just call her sweatpants? Did sweatpants make it for her walk today? Oh, that was a good one."

Patricia looked up at Olivia and opened her mouth but said nothing. Her eyes revealed shame and regret, but they did nothing to help the sting of Paul's words.

But Paul was not done. And Olivia started to back up as his anger fueled more words. "And you can say that I'm the reason for the divorce. But we all know that when you gave up on Chris was when we really split."

"I did not give up on my son." Patricia's face turned red, her mouth tight with anger.

"Where is your son, Patricia?" If Paul's glare could light Patricia's face on fire, it would instantly blow up in flames with the hate he was throwing at her.

"He's getting the help he needs." Patricia stared back with ice-cold eyes that squelched his look.

"Why don't you tell your friendly neighbor where your son is? Oh, right. You don't talk about it. You hide it and pretend like everything is just fine. Maybe that's why our son had an overdose. On our front step."

"Get out!" Patricia screamed. "Get out!"

Marven barked loudly at the screaming. Paul turned around, ran out and slammed the door. Olivia heard the rev of an engine and the squeal of tires as he backed down the driveway.

Olivia's feet didn't know if they should go forward or back up.

"I love my son," Patricia said quietly, looking over at the shards of the vase.

Olivia bent down, placed Marven by the door, and said, "Stay." She started stacking the shards of vase to help clean up. "Of course, you do."

Patricia whispered, "Addiction is so…" but then stared at her shaky hands.

"Destructive," Olivia answered and gave her a knowing glance.

Olivia wanted to tell her how her whole life had been colored by addiction. She wanted to tell her how watching her mother relapse time and time again almost killed her, and how she couldn't imagine watching her child go through it. Olivia wanted to say that she had seen Patricia's son that day the police came. She could tell it was serious, and she had judged her, but now that she knew, she knew Patricia had done the right thing. Because her mother had wasted her whole life struggling. And what Olivia really wanted to say was Olivia's mother had wasted Olivia's life with her struggle, too.

But the sting of Paul's words still soured Olivia's mouth. She stood up and her foot caught the edge of a piece of vase. She reached down to get it.

Patricia politely said, "I can finish this up. You can get going."

And even though her insides twisted with emotion, Olivia handed her the shard of vase and said, "Marven probably needs to go to the bathroom." She took the dog's leash in her hand. "I'll check in with you later." Olivia paused and added, "About work." She closed the door and heard it click behind her.

When Olivia was halfway down the street, she thought about going back, but then she remembered the ridicule on Paul's face and what he had said about the nicknames. Clearly, she had been the butt of many jokes. Her life. Or lack thereof. Patricia had judged her for being a stay-at-home mom. It made her sick. She knew which sweatpants he was referring to. She had gained a lot of weight during her pregnancy and after she had Samantha, losing it took a long time. Her gray sweatpants were the only ones that had fit. But every day she would put them on and take Samantha for a walk because she had to, or her home would close in on her. Her baby blues had crushed her. Those walks were all that kept her sane. And to think Patricia had mocked her when all Olivia needed at that time was a friend. Someone to tell her it'd be okay. That she would sleep. That her hormones would calm down and she'd stop crying. Those walks were damn near impossible some days, but she pushed through the depression, got her ass into those sweatpants, and got herself outside. Those walks were a symbol of her being a warrior. And the sweatpants slowly became less needed. But she still kept them in a closet—a secret symbol that she could push through hard things.

And if only Patricia had opened up about her son. Olivia was the one person who understood the terrible roller coaster of hope and dismay that comes with watching someone you love choose a drink over you. How addiction became this other person in your family, always hovering, always ready to destroy. A silent weight you carry.

CHAPTER 16
GLITTER

Olivia was still on edge when Sammy arrived home from school. And as the day turned into night, Olivia's nagging frustration about Patricia turned into complete and utter agitation. It didn't help that Steve came home late from a work meeting that had turned contentious.

Dinner was nothing more than "Pass the potatoes," or "Here's more salad." Sammy finished the meal off with the words parents hate most. "I have a school project due tomorrow."

"What? Why didn't you tell me earlier?"

"I did, Mom." Sammy fidgeted and put her hands under her butt on the chair. "It's my hundred-day assignment. Do we have any poster board?"

Olivia put her head in her hands. Sammy had told her last week. But between Patricia and her mother and life being a never-ending list inside her head of all the 400 things she was supposed to remember every day, she had forgotten.

"No, we don't have any poster board. I need to buy poster board for us to actually have poster board." Olivia felt like the Eeyore of her daughter's creative possibilities.

Steve looked at them and tried to smooth out the situation with, "Can't you just use four pieces of paper taped together? We have lots of paper."

"Fine." Sammy's eyebrows tightened into a grumpy zigzag.

"Don't say fine. I'm trying to help." Steve hit his fists on the table and stood up.

Olivia went to the closet where they kept their craft supplies and opened it. Tape and a random coloring book fell out.

"Our house is always a mess. No one puts anything away neatly," Olivia said under her breath, even though she also never put anything away neatly. Every closet in their house overflowed with unfolded towels or crammed toys. She scanned the shelves and pulled out some paper, which made some other papers take flight and land on the ground.

"Ugh. I hate this house," Olivia said as she grabbed glue, tape, and random coloring crayons and markers. She brought them over to Sammy and asked, "Is this enough? What else do you need?"

"I need my one hundred things. What do we have a hundred of?"

Olivia looked at her daughter. "Pennies?"

Steve said, "I have a hundred nails."

"Really." Olivia shook her head. "Her hundred-day project can't be a weapon she takes to school."

"It was just an idea." Steve shrugged.

"A bad one." Sammy glared. Steve said nothing but shot her a disapproving look.

"Jennifer made a heart with candy. It was pink and purple and so pretty. Plus, she had glitter," Sammy added with a look of total jealousy on her face. "It had a cool design and there's no way I can do better than that."

"Well, that's not a good way to think about something. Whatever you do will be great, because it's yours." Olivia found their big jar of pennies. "There's probably a hundred in here."

"I don't want pennies. It's stupid." Sammy looked down at the table and picked at a piece of dried-on food.

"Well, go look around the house and see what you can find. Or, if you want to brainstorm, I'm happy to help you. But you can't just sit there shooting down all our ideas when you haven't said anything." Olivia folded her arms to show Sammy she had had enough.

"Greg did Legos in a bag. It was lame."

Olivia got up and went to the craft closet. "Hmmm. A hundred is a lot. We have stickers."

"Lame!" Sammy yelled.

"It's your assignment. You look." Olivia went to the kitchen, pulled out Sammy's chair, and angled it so she slid off. "Seriously, get up and go look for stuff. Enough."

Steve was in the cabinet and held up the bag of mini marshmallows to Sammy.

"I don't want any."

"No. I was showing them to you for one hundred things."

"Oh. That might work."

Olivia frowned. She was hoping to have Sammy look and not have Steve solve it for her. Steve chucked the bag to Sammy.

Sammy ripped open the bag and spilled a few on the ground.

"Sammy, careful. You don't have to open it like a monster." Olivia rushed over and bent down to get the marshmallows before Marven came running. Her knees cracked on the way down. She put the handful of marshmallows on the table.

"Eww. I don't want those. They fell on the floor." Sammy hit them with her hand.

"Seriously? You're being a brat. You don't need to eat them." Steve sat down at the table next to her and took out his phone to read the news, which was like being present physically but not mentally, and not much help to anyone.

Olivia stayed calm and said, "You need a hundred, and I don't know how many are in there."

"Maybe I should count them?" Sammy asked.

"Go for it." Olivia went over to the sink to wash her hands as Sammy made ten groups of ten marshmallow families. One by one, she began gluing them on her paper.

Olivia soaped her hands and made them very sudsy with her lavender soap. Lavender was supposed to be calming, right? She closed her eyes, trying to push away thoughts of Patricia from this morning. As Sammy glued quietly, Olivia grabbed her phone to check. No text. No email. Nothing. No apology. No work list. Just silence.

"Mom, these aren't sticking."

Olivia could hear in Sammy's voice that she was on the edge of frustration, tears, or both. Olivia glanced over at Steve and gave him the "put down your phone and pay attention look."

"You need to put less glue," Steve interjected over his scan of sports tweets.

"But the paper keeps moving. If we just had poster board like Jen had, it would work better." Sammy's whole face was red and scrunched up with frustration. Glue dripped from her little fingers.

"Well, Jen probably reminded her parents about the project before the day it was due," Steve said without looking up. "And Jen's mom doesn't work. She spends her day at Starbucks sending PTA emails."

"I don't want to do this stupid project anyway." Sammy pushed the paper, glue, and mini marshmallows out of her way and towards Steve.

As a cascade of white glue and sugar came his way, Steve backed up and scolded her. "That is not okay. We are trying to help you. You're being rude. Go upstairs."

"Fine. You weren't helping. I hate you." Sammy ran with heavy footsteps that pounded with anger up every single one of the stairs for emphasis. And then a slam of the door to seal the point.

Olivia stared at the mess of glue and sugar on the kitchen table and looked over at Steve.

"Really?"

"She was being a brat." He got up, grabbed his keys, and started walking away.

"You were being a brat too. PTA emails? Where are you going?" Olivia asked as she shook her head, trying to keep her internal rage down.

"To the store to get poster board and more mini marshmallows. And better glue. That glue sucked. And if there's glitter, I'm getting her glitter. Because fuck Jen and her overbearing mom." And without asking if they needed anything else, he walked out the door.

Men always get to leave, Olivia thought. It's not fair. She could hear Sammy crying loudly upstairs, and of course Olivia was left to deal with it. She stared at the mess on the table. A better mom would probably make Sammy clean up with paper towels, but Olivia didn't feel like being the better mom tonight. She wanted to clean it up and go calm Sammy down so she'd finish her assignment.

Olivia sprayed cleaner on the table over and over, more than she needed, turning the little white marshmallows blue. She was trying to clean up the whole not-so-good day with the spray. She wiped it up with paper towels as she listened to Sammy's howls get louder. She walked upstairs and Sammy was on her bed sideways, crying and playing with Legos at the same time. Marven was at the edge of her bed with his head down.

"Your dad went to get you poster board and more marshmallows," Olivia said quietly as she sat on the bed and rubbed Sammy's back lightly. With a slightly positive uptick in her voice, she added, "And he even said he'd look for glitter."

"I don't want to do the project."

"I know. I know you're frustrated. But that's not an option. Schoolwork will always get done in this house. Do you understand?"

Sammy cried more and threw her Legos. "You're being mean." Sammy pouted.

"Ha. This is not mean. You don't know what mean is, Sammy. Do you know how many times my mom helped me with a school project, or even asked about one?"

Sammy looked up curiously.

"Zero. Zero times. No one was ever getting me poster board. I made do with what I had. So you better change your attitude because your dad and I were trying to be nice. That doesn't mean we are going to do the project for you. I've been to school already. I don't need to do the project; you do."

Olivia sat staring at Sammy. Sammy didn't budge. Olivia didn't budge. Between them sat the whole night of frustration and probably space for more than a million mini marshmallows.

Finally, Olivia edged forward, opened her arms, said "Here," and Sammy instinctively buried her face in her mom's stomach. Olivia held her as she cried and said nothing. She sat there reminding herself to say nothing and to provide comfort, because Sammy needed her arms more than her words. They sat there for a long time saying nothing, letting love talk until they heard the door.

"I'm back," Steve called from downstairs.

"Sammy, let's go see what Dad got. It'll be okay." Olivia took Sammy's hand and Sammy let herself be led down the stairs, their hands linked together making it all feel better.

On the table were two poster boards, glue, a bag of mini marshmallows, and a bag of Smarties candy. And a big thing of silver glitter.

"Oh, Smarties! That's way better than marshmallows." Sammy's eyes lit up. "Can I eat them too?" She quieted her voice while she fidgeted and said, "While I do my project."

"Sure," Steve answered and then looked at Olivia to make sure that sugar was okay.

She said in a terse mom voice, "Just one packet."

Sammy quickly unrolled a wrapper and popped some in her mouth while Steve opened the glue.

Olivia grabbed a bowl, unwrapped more of them, and put the candies in the bowl. "It'll be easier for you to grab." She looked at the clock: 7:15. Getting close to bedtime. She tried not to let her stress snowball by thinking about how tired Sammy would be tomorrow if she didn't get to bed on time tonight.

Sammy was all concentration, her little tongue sticking out of her mouth as she glued, glued, glued smarties one by one into a big circle. Her parents sat at the table, trying to control the urge to help her glue and instead hurrying her on with words of encouragement.

"Looking good, Sammy," Steve said.

Sammy smiled. "Now for the finishing touch." She opened the glitter and Olivia's insides screamed, "OH GOD NOT GLITTER! IT'LL GET EVERYWHERE. GLITTER IS EVIL." But on the outside, Olivia just smiled as Sammy shook the glitter all over the poster board to add a ton of sparkle.

"We'll let it dry on the table, Sammy. I can drive you to school tomorrow so you don't have to carry it on the bus." Olivia was already thinking about letting Sammy sleep in so she wouldn't be a disaster of anger and mood in the morning.

It was 8:30. Sammy had glued her last Smarties and was starting to look like a puddle of a child.

"Come on, kiddo, let's get you to bed." And because Olivia had just read a book on positive parenting, she made sure to praise Sammy's effort. "I really liked how you didn't give up and kept working." As Olivia trudged up the stairs next to Sammy, she felt the weight and exhaustion of being a parent.

"Brush your teeth and go to the bathroom." Olivia pointed, as if Sammy didn't know where her bathroom was. "I'll get out PJs for you."

Like a little zombie, Sammy made her way to bed. Instinctively, she raised her hands, allowing Olivia to slide off her shirt and pull a nightgown over her head.

"You can leave your leggings on if you want," Olivia said.

Sammy nodded her head and crawled into bed. Olivia lay down next to her because she was tired too.

"Why don't I tell you a quick story while you close your eyes?"

Sammy snuggled her body into Olivia's heart and Olivia tried to breathe it all in. These were the moments she tried to hold onto, these quiet times where she was nothing more than Sammy's mom. Knowing her body could create a world of comfort for her little daughter meant so much to Olivia. It was a world of comfort her mother had never shown her. And so she started talking, telling stories of unicorns and friendship. Before she knew it, she had closed her eyes and had fallen asleep too.

When Olivia woke up, the house was dark. She had no idea what time it was, but she quietly made it to her own bed, where Marven was happily stretched out. She pulled up the cover a little to roll his furry body over and make space for herself. He begrudgingly went down to the bottom of the bed and circled, finally plopping down with his head on her foot.

In the darkness, Olivia felt the swirl and pull of her thoughts. She was annoyed Patricia hadn't reached out. She was frustrated at Steve for letting his stress into dinner and his parenting. She wished she had a mom she could call to talk to. Loneliness filled every millimeter of darkness, wrapping around her body and pulling her down into depression.

In her head, she thought of the email she wanted to write to Patricia. Telling her how hard she had worked. And how she had trusted her. And that she had judged her too. For not wearing sweatpants and for always being an uptight bitch. God, how she wished she could call Patricia a bitch, even though she knew she wouldn't.

Olivia never told people how they hurt her. Isn't that how she got here? Isn't that her problem with her mother? Oh how Patricia and her mother twirled together like a tornado of feelings in her head. Olivia also felt guilty when she thought about Patricia's son. She did not judge her for that. She was probably the one person Patricia could talk to about it. Olivia tossed and turned. Marven growled and stretched out his body away from her. Olivia couldn't fall back to sleep. Her little nap in Sammy's bed had thrown off her pattern, so she decided to give in to her thoughts and go downstairs. Marven picked up his head and listened as she left the room and then stole her warm spot.

Downstairs, Olivia turned on the kitchen light. She saw Sammy's poster on the table. The extra candies were still in the bowl. The table shining with glitter and glue. Really? Steve didn't clean up? She wiped up the table as best she could, the many paper towels shimmering silver every time. No matter how hard she wiped, tiny pieces of square glitter stared back at her. Finally, she gave up. She took out a piece of paper and pen and sat next to the bowl of Smarties. She took one candy and let it dissolve slowly in her mouth. Who should she write to? Patricia? Or her mom, as her therapist had instructed?

Olivia wrote on the white paper. She made the D in dear swirly with her blue pen.

Dear Patricia,

I trusted you. I didn't want to even like you. I was proud of my job. Now I hate everything. Oh, and by the way, my mom is an addict.

Sincerely, Olivia.

Olivia looked at her words, then crumpled up the letter. She felt better. Lighter. She popped another candy in her mouth. This one was harder. The words didn't flow. She stared at the paper. Where to start? Where to end?

Dear Mom,

I want a mom. I don't know why. Maybe because in movies and TV shows, they always help. I could use help. I could use a friend. But you've never been there for me. You've never shown up. Remember my dance recital? My graduation? And yet I always invite you in. I can't help wanting to invite you in. I'm writing this letter because my therapist told me I should. I know she wants me to tell you to get out of my life. That I deserve better. That by keeping space for you, I'm keeping space for a wound that I pick. I wonder, do you think of me? Do you feel me not there? Or do you just fill your glass and drink away my space? Do you not miss Dad? Do you not miss our family? When we had a family? I have a family now. I love my daughter so dearly. I don't understand why you didn't love me. I feel my soul in every inch of her skin. Did you not look at my skin and love me? Did you not want to protect me? You didn't protect me. You did the opposite. You created a home of hell and you numbed yourself to it. I learned how to wash my hair and brush the tangles. I learned to make mac and cheese. I learned how to sign your name. I learned everything by myself. Without a net to fall on. And it got old. It made me hard. But I'm not going to be hard like you. Samantha deserves better. I did too. I gave you so many chances, Mom. Why didn't you take a chance on me? Why didn't you love me? I need to close my wound to you. I need to close my heart to you. I need to choose me. This is me saying I can't anymore. This is me saying goodbye.

Olivia paused but wrote the word that came naturally and signed: *Love, Olivia.* This letter she did not crumple up. This letter she stared at, folded into a neat square, and put in her purse. She looked at the clock and knew it was time to go back to bed. She had tucked her thoughts in for the night and was ready for sleep. There was glitter all over her hand.

CHAPTER 17
LIVER

There was something about the first cup of coffee in the morning that made it taste like heaven and hope. Olivia sipped it and checked her email. Still nothing from Patricia. Should she write to her? Make sure she was okay?

A combination of pride and embarrassment held her back. Instead, Olivia walked to the stairs and called up to Sammy, who was brushing her teeth.

"Sammy, want a bowl of raisin bran? I'll get it ready for you." She heard Sammy grunt, which in the morning was about as good as it got for an answer.

Olivia fixed a bowl for Sammy and a bowl for herself. Olivia drank her coffee fast. She'd bring the second cup with her on the drive to school. Planning her coffee drinks was like planning pleasure. Olivia needed it lately to get her through the day.

Sammy came trudging down the stairs but lit up when she saw her poster dried and on the counter.

"It looks good, Mom." She touched each piece of candy to make sure they'd stay put.

"Yeah, I checked them too." Olivia winked at her. "I put a roll of Smarties in your lunch."

"Really?!" Sammy's face burst open with a big toothy grin that only the promise of sugar could create.

"Yep. I figured you deserved it since you worked so hard and didn't give up when your first idea didn't work out. You're just like an engineer."

Was it too early for growth mindset parenting? Olivia always managed to fit her new parental reading in somewhere.

"Engineers work on many revisions to get things right, so failure is part of their job and considered progress." Olivia smiled at Sammy, hoping her words weren't too heavy-handed.

Sammy scooped some raisin bran into her mouth, dribbling little milk spots on the table. "Sylvie is going to be jealous cause her mom wouldn't let her do anything with sugar."

"Well, everyone does different things. That's what makes the hundred-day project interesting, right? To see what everyone thinks of."

"I guess so." Sammy stared into her bowl.

Olivia looked at the clock. "We have five minutes until we need to be in the car."

"Mom, I hate when you rush me." Sammy rapidly shoved spoonful after spoonful of cereal into her mouth.

"Woah, woah, woah. Wasn't trying to rush you. Just wanted to let you know what to expect."

Olivia got up to pour another cup of coffee and added some creamer to her cup. She went to the closet, grabbed a baseball hat, took out their shoes and placed Sammy's by her feet.

"Put them on, so you're ready." She put on her sneakers and shoved her hair into a baseball hat, so she looked more prepared for the day than she was. She always worried about school drop-off, that today would be the day the principal or a teacher would ask her to get out of the car, revealing that even though she had on a shirt and baseball hat, she wore pajama bottoms.

No one stopped her today at drop-off, but Olivia was grateful to the teacher who helped Sammy out of the car and oozed excitement about her poster.

"Wow, that looks like a great poster. Is that for One Hundred Days? Nice work."

Olivia watched Sammy beam with pride as she walked into school. She didn't even turn around for a wave.

Olivia turned on the radio, reveling in the moment after Sammy left the car. She sipped her coffee alone, feeling like the car and the day were hers. She heard her phone ring but ignored it, figuring it was Steve apologizing for being an ass the day before. Let him sit with that for a bit. Olivia was feeling her coffee and the music.

When she got home, she heard her phone buzz with a message. She took it out and saw it wasn't Steve's name. It was the three-lettered name that meant stress: Mom. With a simple message: *Call me.*

This might be a three-cup-of-coffee kind of morning, thought Olivia. Her finger hovered above the contact and pressed it. Her mom answered breathlessly. "Olivia, is that you?"

"Yeah, Mom, I got your message."

"Do you think...?" Rose paused and then rushed her next words. "Can you come to a doctor's appointment with me today?"

Olivia steadied herself as she tried to remain calm and not let her mother's usual hypochondria get the best of her. "Yes. What's going on?"

"My stomach has been acting up. And I can't get rid of these bruises, so I finally went to the doctor. I've been living with Hep C forever, you know. But the doctor made me do a bunch of blood tests and now he wants to meet in person. And, well..." Rose got quiet.

Olivia could feel her mother's anxiety, and it ignited her internal battle. She's your mother, Olivia. She needs you. But she'll probably wind up hurting you. But she's sick. Olivia squashed the rest of the buts in her head and said, "Of course. What time?"

"Could you pick me up in an hour and we'll go together?"

Olivia looked at her watch and said, "Yep. That works. See you then." She contemplated calling Steve to tell him, but she didn't want to talk to him yet. Plus, he'd just say it was another one of her mom's scams. And she hadn't even confessed to the last scam, which cost her a few thousand dollars.

Olivia typed an email to Patricia that was short but pragmatic:

My mother is sick and I must take her to the doctor. I won't be available until later today if you need my assistance.

She hit send and felt nervous. But it was on Patricia now to respond. Before Olivia could stand up, she heard the ping of her email.

Hope your mother feels better. I do not need your assistance today.

Sincerely, Patricia.

Olivia stared at the email. It felt cold. But so did her email. She hated this. How could she be a house away from Patricia with things feeling so weird? Olivia shook her head to get the thoughts of Patricia out of it and got ready to pick up her mother. The ride to the doctor's office was quiet; neither Olivia nor Rose wanted to say too much. A few obligatory comments about the weather, a story about Samantha and her poster, and they'd arrived.

Rose approached the receptionist while Olivia glanced around the waiting room. Doctor's offices were strange things. They didn't try to be homey. The chairs were never comfortable. There was always a stack of magazines—a germy editorial offering to the bored.

Olivia sat down next to an open chair and watched her mother existing in this space. Just like any other patient. Saying her name to the receptionist. Rose walked over, sat down next to Olivia, and immediately grabbed a magazine.

"They say she's cheating on him." She pointed to the cover of a celebrity couple.

"Oh, yeah?" Olivia feigned interest, even though she didn't know much about either actor.

Before the conversation could lead to anything substantial, Rose's name was called.

The doctor's promptness made Olivia nervous. *Bad news comes quickly,* she thought.

Olivia and Rose sat down in front of the doctor like a normal mother and daughter, even though they were not. Olivia wanted to hold Rose's hand, but that wasn't something they did. The doctor opened Rose's file and skimmed it, but Olivia could tell it was just for effect. He knew what he was going to say. She could tell by the serious lines of his mouth.

"Last time you were in, your blood work showed that your AFP levels were elevated, so we did an MRI."

Olivia did not know her mother had gone for an MRI.

"The MRI showed several spots on your liver, so we did a biopsy."

Olivia tried to hide the surprise in her face, but she felt like the doctor could tell this was all news to her.

"I'm sorry to say the results of the biopsy show that you have liver cancer. Because of the size of the tumors, surgery is not an option. The cirrhosis in your liver makes this a tricky case. We could proceed with chemotherapy and radiation, but there are some lifestyle changes we'd have to discuss."

Olivia knew this was the nice way to say, "You can't be an alcoholic."

"I have some pamphlets that talk about the effects of chemotherapy and what support you would need. We also have a nurse support hotline that can help with symptom management. This is your daughter, yes?"

"Yes."

"At this stage, your mother's cancer isn't curable, but it is treatable. She will need support."

"Of course." Olivia cast her eyes down, not wanting the doctor's gaze to enter the internal dialogue that was ping-ponging between stress and guilt and sadness.

"What if I decide I don't want chemo?" Rose's voice sounded small.

"Mom!" Olivia stared at her mother, shocked that she wouldn't fight for her life.

"Olivia, my friend Berta went through chemo. It was awful, and she still died. I don't know if that's how I want to go. And you say treatable, not curable. What if I put myself through all this for nothing? And I've only ever made it a few months without..."

"Drinking," Olivia said in her head.

"Refusing treatment is an option. An option with consequences." The doctor searched their eyes for where the conversation would go next. Rose nodded her head.

"Without treatment, and with cases like yours that are so advanced and include multiple other considerations—your Hepatitis C, cirrhosis, and history of..." his voice quieted as he said, "alcohol consumption." After another pause, he went on. "The survival time could be less than four months. But every case is different." The doctor tried his best to add enthusiasm to his tone. "Also, you should know that chemotherapy has come a long way and many patients respond to it with minimal side effects."

Rose was quiet.

"Thank you, doctor. What are the next steps?" Olivia asked.

"I've made an appointment for Rose on Thursday to meet with a specialist. He can discuss the treatment plan in more detail and answer questions."

"I can go with you on Thursday," Olivia said to her mother, who nodded with a slight smile. But she still looked like she had just seen an alien. Her whole life had changed.

On the way out, Rose went to the bathroom and Olivia quickly texted Steve to arrange for him to leave work early so she could stay with her mom.

Of course, was his answer, which warmed Olivia's heart.

They drove to her mom's apartment in complete silence. When they got to the door, her mother's hands shook as she put in the key. Olivia hadn't been inside her mother's apartment in a long time. This was the apartment her mother needed money for. This was what she was so desperate not to lose. When they walked in, Olivia glanced around. A few of Samantha's pictures were on her fridge. A round table for two, under a light. A brown, worn couch. A TV on a metal stand. A small table next to the couch with a few empty glasses. The apartment did not smell clean. It smelled sad. Like garbage that had been there too long. Counters that hadn't been wiped. Like too many microwave meals for one.

"Want me to make you tea?" Olivia asked. Her mother settled down on the couch, instinctively picked up the remote, and turned on the TV.

"Hmmm. Sure. I might have some bags above the mugs."

Olivia searched the cupboard and found some individually-wrapped tea bags with Chinese letters on them that were probably left over from a takeout order.

She heated the water and brought her mom a cup.

Her mom looked up and tried to grab the mug from her, but it was too hot. Olivia turned the mug outward to her mom so she could take the handle, but Rose didn't think to put the remote down, so it was awkward. Olivia put the mug down on the table and took the old glasses to the sink. She couldn't even hand her mother a mug of tea. They were that out of sync. What made her think she could take care of her?

Olivia sat next to her mother and watched the game show she had on. "Nowhere to go."

"What?"

"That's the answer. Nowhere to go."

Rose looked at the board of letters on Wheel of Fortune and said, "You're good. You should go on it."

"Ha. I'd probably freeze if I was on it."

"You were always good with words." Rose smiled and picked up her tea.

Olivia felt thankful for the small conversation and thought maybe they could get through this diagnosis together.

"I don't really love tea. You want it?" Rose handed the mug over.

Olivia took it and put it in the sink. She needed her heart to steady, instead of rocking from side to side like a boat. "I'm going to call Steve and check in. Do you mind if I go into your bedroom?"

Rose waved her hand in the direction of her room and said, "Nah, it's a mess. But no problem. He'll be delighted to know I'm going to kick the bucket."

"Mom. That is not true."

"What? That I'm not going to die, or that Steve won't be happy?"

"Neither."

Rose glanced back at the TV. "You were right. It was nowhere to go."

Olivia nodded and went into her mother's bedroom. Three empty wine bottles sat next to her bed. A bottle of vodka, half-full. The bed was unmade. The sheets tan. The cover an old, crocheted blanket. Olivia wished she had a comforter or something to make this bedroom feel like her mother slept there instead of just drinking there.

She sat on the edge of the bed, but then reconsidered and stood while she called Steve. He picked up right away.

"You doing okay? I'm so sorry about your mom. How is she handling it?"

"She's watching TV."

"Denial?"

"I don't know. We're not really best buddies. She hasn't said much."

"It's nice that you're with her."

"I wish it felt nice."

"I know. I'm sorry. But you're doing the right thing. I know this isn't easy."

Olivia didn't say anything. She wanted to feel the comfortable silence between them. She just wanted to feel something normal.

From the other room Olivia heard her mom say, "Do you have any gum?"

"Yep. It's in my purse."

Rose rifled around Olivia's purse looking for gum but instead found a folded piece of paper, which she opened. She read the letter quickly, and then folded it up and carefully put it back in the purse.

When Olivia came out, Rose was staring at the TV, not chewing gum.

"Olivia, I'm really tired. I'm just going to go to sleep."

"Do you want me to stay? Get you dinner?"

"No. I'm fine. I'll call you later or tomorrow."

Olivia grabbed her mother's hand, wishing her hand could speak for her, but also feeling relieved to get out of the apartment.

"I'll come tomorrow. We'll go for a walk."

Rose nodded and walked Olivia to the door.

"Mom." Olivia tried once more to find words.

"Don't. It's fine. Thank you for coming." Rose gave her a half hug, and Olivia did her best to accept her body into hers. She was already stressing over the half-bottle of vodka and worrying her mom was going to put that into her body instead of sleep. Olivia thought about making an excuse, going back to her mom's bedroom, and pouring it down the drain. She walked out the door instead.

As Olivia turned the car onto her street, she saw Steve and Sammy walking Marven. The three of them making their way down the sidewalk made her smile. Her family. It was just what she needed. She rolled down the window and shouted, "I'll park the car and meet you. I could use a little walk." Marven's tail wagged at her voice. As Olivia pulled into their driveway, she noticed one big change. The sign in front of Patricia's house now said *Sold*.

CHAPTER 18
MUG

When Olivia got Patricia's "We need to talk" email, she was in no mood to either meet or talk. She responded with the truth:

I'm meeting my mother this morning. I don't know how long I'll be. Will text you when I return so we can find a time to talk.

She wrote *Sincerely, Olivia.* And then deleted it. And then wrote it again. The formality felt more obvious than sticking her tongue out. Olivia grabbed the biggest travel mug she could find. Today was going to require a big cup of coffee. Full strength. She eyed a pitcher. That might be taking the caffeine too far. She decided on her thermos for camping. Only quantity could power her through a day that involved taking care of her mother and dealing with the fallout from that awkward conversation between Patricia and her ex.

Olivia thought the day needed coffee, but when she opened the door to her mother's apartment, she quickly realized nothing was strong enough for what she was about to find.

"Mom?" Olivia called out and moved instinctively to the quietness of the bedroom. Her mother often slept late. Her bed was unmade, but she was not in it. She knocked on the bathroom door expecting a "Be out in a minute." But what she got was a door that slowly creaked open.

As she turned around, she noticed that her mother's drawers were open, and they were empty.

Dread washed over Olivia. Her pulse raced. She turned around and shouted, "Mom?" But she knew in her heart the answer would be silence. She went back to the kitchen and on the table was a folded piece of lined notebook paper with one word on the front: *Olivia.*

Her tears started sliding down her cheeks before she read a word. Past abandonment whispered to her over her shoulder, reminding her disappointment was always part of her relationship with her mother. How could she be so foolish?

Her mother's letter was written with shaky penmanship:

Olivia,

I've decided that doctors and treatment aren't for me. I'm going to visit a friend for a while. Thanks for your help.

A few words were scratched out. And then the words: *I love you, Mom.*

Olivia held the letter up to the light and could see the words that were written before: *I'm sorry.*

Olivia picked up her phone and dialed her mother, even though she knew what she'd hear. Instant mailbox. She thought about leaving a message, but her mouth wouldn't form words. Instead, she sat down on the hard kitchen chair with her pain.

She banged the table hard with her fist. She flung the napkins off the table. She ripped up the pieces of the note. It didn't quell her anger. It enraged her that her mother had chosen to run. But she was even more pissed off at herself and her heart for always leaving a spot for her mother to creep back into before she napalmed it into pieces. Her stomach felt hollow, as if the hole her mother had left was creating a tunnel of ulcers and bile.

She looked around her mother's apartment. Did the money she lent her even matter now? Would she be back for any of her stuff? Or would she just leave it all behind? Olivia stared at the lone mug in the sink. She was nothing more than that. A dirty cup left behind for someone else to take care of. She walked over to the sink, lovingly filled the mug with soap, and washed it like a small child, while tears fell down her face. She opened the cupboard and put it next to the few other glasses. Olivia left the apartment and slammed the door behind her. She stopped mid-step to go back and made sure it was locked.

Olivia drove home feeling the rage of every slow driver in her way. She just wanted to be home with her dog and not think. To not think her mother was going to die before she ever saw her again. To not think why her mother had to leave her with just a note. She pulled into the driveway and did not look to her right. She did not notice Patricia waving at her. Olivia stormed into the house and let Marven out of his cage. As she opened the back door to let him go out, the front doorbell rang.

Olivia opened the door in a huff and said "What?" before her eyes had time to realize it was Patricia. Patricia took a step back and put something she was holding in her arm behind her back.

"Oh, I'm sorry. I saw your car pull up, and I figured this might be an easy time to talk."

Olivia felt the enormity of everything she had dealt with at her mother's apartment on her shoulders. She stared straight at Patricia while inside she was on her knees, crying and banging her hands on the floor, ripping the wood into splinters. She blinked back tears.

"It's not a great time, actually." Olivia avoided Patricia's eyes and stared at the grass outside. She tried to focus on just one blade of grass. If she could keep her mind focused, she could get through this conversation without unraveling. She wasn't going to let Patricia know anything. She didn't deserve to know anything.

"Oh, it's just I don't have much time." Patricia took another step back.

"No, it's fine. You're here. So, let's talk. What did you need?" Olivia's voice was curt and to the point.

"I came to give you this. It's a check, your bonus from the Worthington house, and a little something else to say thank you. You can open it later. And well, I wanted to say goodbye. I'm actually leaving for Belize tomorrow."

"Oh. Wow. That happened quickly."

"Yeah, it's sort of a whirlwind." Patricia spun her hand in the air and laughed nervously. "After that fight with Paul, I just realized I need to move on. To get away. Packers can do the rest. Feels a bit crazy, but it's going to be an adventure."

The thought of Patricia realizing her dream made Olivia want to, well, cry. She was not happy for her no-longer friend. She was mad. Mad that she was dealing with her runaway dying mother while Patricia went from escaping divorce to escaping the world in a beautiful bungalow by the sea. Mad because after all the time they'd spent together, Olivia felt like she was saying goodbye to someone she was getting to know but never really knew at all. Some people get to leave. Some people have to stay.

Olivia couldn't hide her tears from Patricia. She found herself awkwardly hugged and shoved into Patricia's shoulder and onto her luxurious, silky-smooth shirt. Olivia tried to stop her tears and snot so she wouldn't ruin it.

Olivia wiped at her eyes in an attempt to remove some of the wetness and shame from her face. She didn't want to talk. She didn't want to share any of what she was feeling with Patricia. Her heart was not a house, and it was not for sale.

"Olivia, I'm sorry. The last few days have been a mess. And I wanted to come talk to you after my husband..." Patricia paused and cleared her throat with an angry twitch. "I mean ex-husband...said those awful things. About me. About you. About my son."

"You could have told me about your son. I would have understood." Olivia's tone was harsh, even though she didn't mean for it to sound that way. She wanted to say more. She wanted to open up. But Patricia had put the wall up again. And she no longer felt the need to overcome it.

"The thing is, Olivia, I've been unhappy for so long. With him. With my life. My awful words were more about me than you." Patricia looked at Olivia hopefully, but Olivia's eyes left no room for her to enter them.

"These tears aren't for you." The words came out coldly from Olivia's mouth.

"What?" Patricia looked at her, sympathetic and confused.

"My mother is dying. I went over to be with her this morning." Olivia left out the part about her mother leaving. Patricia wasn't her friend. She didn't get to know those details anymore.

"Oh, I'm so sorry. You said this was a bad time. I should have walked away. Can I do anything?"

Olivia tried her best to ignore Patricia's look of genuine concern because she did not want to be warmed by any kindness.

"It's fine. I just need time to deal with it all."

"I understand," Patricia said. "You have my email if you need anything. Even though I won't be next door, I do care, Olivia." Patricia searched her eyes.

The two not-quite friends, who had shared so much the past few weeks, couldn't even share the space between them without both of them awkwardly moving their feet and shifting their weight.

Patricia broke the silence with fake enthusiasm, "Oh, next week Michael will reach out to you. There are about five different people clamoring for you at the office. If you want to keep working, there's opportunity. Ted even said he'd pay for school if you wanted to get your realtor's license. The Worthington house deal might have been shared around the office." Patricia winked at her and held her hand out to shake.

Really? They were ending this all with a handshake? Patricia added, "I'm sorry Olivia, I really am," as she shook her hand and put her other hand on top just for a second, to make the gesture less formal.

Olivia didn't know if she was sorry for their failed friendship or her mom, but it didn't matter. She gave Patricia a half-hearted wave and said, "Good luck." She had more to say, but no energy to say it. Instead, she closed the door, put the check and envelope on the counter, sat down on the couch, and let her tears flow.

Marven came in from outside and reached his paws up on the couch so that Olivia could lift him and plop his plump body on the couch next to her. He turned around three times, then lay down and put his head in her lap. She patted his head instinctively, running her hand gently over his ears. Marven's little body let out a happy sigh as his breathing relaxed.

"I don't know Marven. I'm just so sad. I feel like I've lost her for good this time."

And for a moment, her mind knew she was talking about her mother, but her heart also felt the sorrow of losing Patricia. The truth was, she had enjoyed working with her. She had enjoyed finding herself again, even if she hated Patricia just a bit. Somehow that hate had driven her to push herself in ways she hadn't in a long time, and that's why, within those bands of hate, there were also feelings of something more complicated. There was gratitude mixed with friendship and empowerment, and Olivia hated how confused that made her feel.

Marven pushed his nose into her hand so that Olivia would keep petting him. Olivia obliged, looked at him, and said, "I know I should be mad. I am mad. That somehow, Mom gets me to care. Every time. She reels me in like a fish. And here I am. And now she's going to die. She's going to die and there's nothing I can do. And I'm just supposed to sit here and accept it."

Marven rolled onto his side to expose his belly. Olivia scratched back and forth on his tummy, watching as it became spotted with water as Olivia's tears dropped onto Marven's beautiful round sausage of a tummy. "Why do I care? She's just a snobby woman who used me as her assistant and pretended we were friends. Nothing more. Nothing less."

Olivia realized she was no longer talking about her mother, but Patricia. And the snowball of confusion made her stop petting Marven.

Olivia got her phone and tried to call her mother again, but it went right to voicemail. This time she left a message, "I love you, Mom. Please call me." She then called her therapist's office to schedule an appointment. She deliberated over calling Steve. But she'd rather pick at her emotions like a scab. She made tea in her favorite mug and sat next to the one man who wouldn't judge her. So what if that man was a dog?

CHAPTER 19
POPPY SEEDS

Olivia's phone buzzed and her heart lurched. But it wasn't her mother. Or Patricia. It was Steve.

"Hey, I'm picking up Sammy from school today. She and I have a little surprise. Please go do something nice for yourself and return home at 6:00 p.m. Don't ask questions."

Olivia read the text again. And cried more. She hadn't even told him about her shit day and here was this unexpected gift—time? Olivia thought about the five million things on her to-do list. Maybe she could do a combination of things—something she needed to get done and something for herself. Or maybe she'd sit on the couch and sulk for a little longer? No. Patricia didn't sulk. She left. Just like Olivia's mother left.

"Marven, want to go to the woods for a walk?" Marven wagged his tail at the W-word. "Then we can run to Target and pick up a few things on our list. Won't be long. You can wait in the car." Marven continued to wag his tail excitedly, even though he only understood "walk."

Olivia drove to the woods by her house and parked. The path was quiet but familiar. She used to take Sammy to the woods all the time when she was a baby. She loved watching her little body amble up to a pinecone and pick it up with curiosity. They would stop at fallen trees and count the rings.

Marven's little body moved down the path slowly, stopping to sniff at every fern and pee on every tiny, budding evergreen tree. It made Olivia happy that his lack of sight didn't stop him from enjoying the woods.

The air felt good in Olivia's lungs. The tall limbs of the trees looked like arms, inviting her into the forest to get lost for a while. These trees had been born before her and would outlive her. These trees were supported by strong roots that she envied. Olivia's roots were as shallow as her mother's weak promises. But Olivia would build something better for her family. With each step forward, she searched the forest for inspiration. She wanted to walk away from the pain that her mother had caused her. She did not feel sturdy like an oak. She felt like a young sapling, unsure that a future storm wouldn't knock her over. But Olivia could feel herself growing within all these strained relationships. In the relationship with her mother. In trying so hard for Patricia and then being let down by her unkind words.

Olivia turned down a path near a river with trees poking out at awkward angles along the slope. Growth was all around her. It wasn't always straight. It was crooked and weird like the bent tree that grew sideways. It was risky like the tree that had fallen halfway and been caught by another tree's branches. As she picked up Marven and stepped over the large tree limb, she was reminded that growth sometimes was also failure and hurt.

Olivia glanced at her watch. Forty minutes had gone by and they'd probably walked far enough for Marven's tiny legs. And to be honest, her legs were tired too.

"Let's go back, Marven," Olivia said. Marven followed her. She didn't feel alone in the woods with Marven. That was the beauty of the silent companionship of a dog—it could transform any path.

Olivia pulled into the drive-through at Starbucks and ordered a "puppuccino" for Marven, who licked it up happily. She ordered a chai latte for herself. The walk and the tea felt like self-care. She ran into

Target and grabbed milk, eggs, bread, some rosemary and mint hand soap, just because. When she pulled up to her house, Steve's car was already there.

Olivia opened the door and yelled "Hello!" Marven rushed past her to do his job of greeting his family with enthusiasm.

Sammy came bounding around the corner. Out of breath, she said, "Mom, you can't go in the kitchen. Here." Sammy shoved a bath bomb into Olivia's hand. "Go upstairs and take a bath. I picked it out. It has real flowers in it! I'll come get you when we are ready."

"Yes, ma'am. But I have a few groceries for the fridge. Can I bring them into the kitchen?"

"No. I'll take them." Sammy put the bags around her wrist, the weight of the milk pulling her little arm down.

"You sure you don't want help?" Olivia smiled.

"I'm good," Sammy said with gritted teeth, as she walked shakily away with too many bags.

"Going to take my bath then," Olivia said loudly, so Steve could hear her too.

Steve yelled from somewhere in the kitchen. "We love you, honey. Everything is under control. Go take a bath."

Whenever Olivia heard that everything was under control, she knew that was fair warning everything was surely not under control. But she started the bath anyway and tried not to think about what surprise—or mess—awaited her in the kitchen. Steve was notorious for causing trouble in the kitchen. He tried hard, but he used a lot of pots. Created a lot of mess. And something always seemed to go wrong. Like the time he used the wrong end of the leeks and made a very crunchy but interesting sauce. Or the time he tried to recreate their favorite Italian meal and attempted homemade gnocchi, which had a very rock-like texture.

The bathroom grew balmy from the warm water in the tub. Olivia dropped the bath bomb in the tub and watched it fizz. She couldn't remember the last time she had taken a bath. She slid her body into it and tried to soak away the morning. Her mother. Patricia. And to just accept her family trying to love her and do something kind for her. She needed love. Their trying soothed her more than the lavender in her bath. She closed her eyes and breathed in the steamy air. She imagined getting the call that her mother was dead. Her hands covered her eyes as she tried to control her sobs. Love surrounded her and all she could think about was the one person who didn't love her but should. Her shoulders shook and made ripples in the tub water as she let out her sadness. Olivia heard Sammy's big stomps on the stairs and quickly tried to dry her eyes with her wet and bubbly hands.

"Mommy, we are ready for you," Sammy shouted happily.

Sammy's voice reminded Olivia that she was different than her own mother. Everything about her daughter and her relationship with Steve was a fuck-you to the past and Olivia's childhood. Sammy was a future of love. Olivia was ready to embrace whatever today's future held.

She called to Sammy. "Can you hand me the towel, sweet pea?" Sammy walked in and grabbed the blue towel. "I'll be right down. Just let me get dressed."

"I'll go tell Dad," Sammy beamed, giddy with excitement for whatever their plan was.

Olivia smiled while she pulled on jeans and reached for her favorite hoodie, but stopped and instead picked out a nicer top. And then took off her jeans and put on a skirt. She knew Sammy's smile would be so big.

Olivia came down the stairs and was greeted with the smell of potatoes and herbs. Sammy walked up to her and said, "Welcome to Sam's restaurant. Can I show you to your table?" Then Sammy whispered in her ear, "You look pretty, Mommy."

"Oh, how nice. Yes, that would be lovely." Olivia slipped her hand into Sammy's as she led her to their kitchen table, which now was adorned with a vase full of flowers and a red tablecloth.

"I picked out the flowers and tablecloth myself," Sammy beamed.

"They are so pretty."

"I wanted it to look like a real restaurant," Sammy said.

Steve came to the table with two glasses of wine and two salad plates. "Appetizers are served." He winked at her.

"Sammy, you going to have salad too?" Olivia asked, knowing she hadn't seen her daughter eat anything green or healthy in a few months.

"Oh, don't worry. I've eaten. I'll be back for dessert." Sammy smiled and ran upstairs.

"What's that about?" Olivia asked as she sipped her wine.

"Your daughter wanted us to go on a date. She saw your list. I tried getting a babysitter, but Cassie canceled and so Sammy came up with this idea instead." He held up his glass and clinked hers.

"Aww. She is a pretty great daughter, isn't she?"

"You deserve it."

"Also, Cassie always flakes out. You shouldn't use her."

"I thought she was the one we liked?"

"She used to be. But then she got a boyfriend and now is never available."

"She's not the one with long brown hair?"

"No. That's Cassandra."

"This is why you handle the babysitters." Steve shook his head.

"But I appreciate the effort," Olivia said, as she took a bigger sip of wine. The deep fruity flavor tasted so good. She was trying to pace herself, but she wanted to gulp it down. "A date at Sam's restaurant is perfect. It's nice to be home after the morning I had."

"Yeah, how is your mom?"

With Steve's casual words, the dam that Olivia had been holding inside broke a little. It took Steve a moment to realize Olivia was hiding her face in her hands, crying softly.

"Gone," Olivia said. As she said those words, sadness filled her body as if every vein pumped heartache and abandonment instead of blood.

"What do you mean, gone?" Steve asked as he came over and put his arm around her.

"I went to her apartment this morning to help her. And she wasn't there." Olivia poked her head out from beneath her hands, grabbed the wine bottle, and refilled their glasses.

"Maybe she just needed some space to process everything?" Steve offered.

"Well, she's getting a whole state of space and maybe even more, because without treatment…" Olivia stopped. She couldn't say the words.

Steve reached out and held her hand.

"I didn't realize. I thought this would be a good idea because of dealing with your mother. Is this not what you need right now?"

Olivia cried harder. "No, I love this. I was just waiting until you got home to talk. It's been such an odd day. Then Patricia cornered me as I came home and we had this awkward goodbye."

"Patricia. Always the busybody."

"No, it wasn't that. I don't know. Oh, and she gave me this." Olivia stood up and grabbed the letter off the counter. She waved the check back and forth. "A check."

Olivia opened the letter. Her eyes scanned the words and her expression fell. Steve asked, "Everything okay?"

"No. Yes. I don't know. I was sort of an ass to Patricia earlier because she was an ass to me. But this letter is just so…" Olivia shook her head. She lifted her hand to reveal three airline tickets.

"What's that?"

"Airline tickets."

"To where?"

"Belize. To stay with her. To accomplish our vacation goal."

"That's great."

"I can't accept them."

"Why? It's an amazing gesture. She probably wanted to do something positive with the money she got from her divorce."

"Because we aren't friends."

"Clearly, she thinks you are."

"Yes, she expresses that in this letter." Olivia read Patricia's words out loud.

"The past year was one of the hardest of my life. I don't know what I would have done without your help, but also your friendship. I'm not the woman I was when I said those awful words about you. I leave tomorrow and there is so much I'm happy to leave behind. But your friendship is something I want to carry forward. Please accept these plane tickets and come visit Belize. Just knowing I'm going to have friends visiting me in my new life makes me feel stronger. I haven't had many friends like you."

It was signed *Patricia* in her official signature, with a capital P. She didn't have a less formal signature. Now, when Olivia looked at her penmanship, she could see that the tightness of her letters held pain, not perfectionism.

"Liv." Steve grabbed Olivia's hand. "I'm the first to call Patricia pretentious and uppity. But I've also seen you change the last few months. You've been more yourself. Happier. Proud. I don't know. But Patricia has been good to you, good for you."

"So, you're telling me you want to visit Patricia in Belize?"

"I'm telling you that you should consider it. Maybe we stay at a hotel not too close to her house, though."

"I don't know." Olivia sipped her wine and tried to imagine a world where Patricia was her friend and she went to Belize. But all she could think about were Patricia's husband's words. The tickets felt like charity to make Patricia feel less guilty about what she had said. And Olivia was done with complicated relationships. Plus, thanks to the check, Olivia could refill her vacation fund and go wherever she wanted.

Olivia looked up at Steve as her thoughts bounced around in her head. She really looked at him. The creases in his eyes. The scar on his cheek from when he had fallen off his bike as a kid. She was so lucky to be able to look at him and know who he was. Patricia didn't have that.

"Would you mind if I excuse myself to the ladies' room? Plus, I want to go peek in on Sammy. What did you buy her to occupy her so quietly?" Olivia gave him a sly look.

"Who said I bought her anything?" Steve put his hands up to make himself appear less guilty, which meant he did buy her something and it was probably electronic.

"Go ahead. It'll give me time to fix…I mean, get our main course ready."

"Oh no. What happened?" Olivia feigned a worried face.

"Nothing I can't fix."

"Steve?"

"Let's just say poppy seeds and pepper look similar."

Olivia started laughing. The laughter felt good to her body. She was tired of holding in her emotions. Olivia took a tiny sip of wine and said, "I'll be back." She waved as Steve rinsed off some very black and speckled carrots.

Olivia sneaked upstairs and peeked at Sammy, who was playing with a new toy that made her repeat a pattern to get a high score. It wasn't the worst thing Steve could have bought for her. Sammy looked up.

"Is it dessert time already?"

"Nope. Just wanted to stop in and say thanks and give you a kiss." Olivia sat down on the bed and kissed Sammy's head. "Thanks for all this. It's a pretty great date. And you are a pretty awesome kid. Do I tell you that enough? I love being your mom."

"Mom," Sammy moaned playfully, "I know."

"Good." Olivia smiled. "I'll go back to dinner. You go back to your game."

Without looking up, Sammy said, "Love you, Mom."

Without looking up, Olivia said, "I know. Love you too."

Olivia went back to the kitchen table to find a plate full of food and a husband who appeared a little dejected.

"Good news. Bad news," Steve said. "Good news. I could rinse the poppy seeds off the carrots. Bad news. I used pepper in every recipe. So, there are poppy seeds in the mashed potatoes and the coated tofu."

"I'm sure it'll be awesome." Olivia took a bite of mashed potatoes and smiled through the tiny crunch of seeds on her teeth.

"I can handle that kind of bad news."

Olivia yummed her way through the tofu while trying to secretly scrape off a few poppy seeds. Talking about her feelings concerning her mother with Steve didn't make it better, but it did help. It made Olivia realize it was time to tell Steve about how she was going to use the check she got from Patricia to repay what she had given to her mother. But before she could, Sammy appeared.

"How's your date going?"

"Best date I've ever been on," said Olivia, as she pulled Sammy in for a hug.

"It's not over yet." Sammy went into the kitchen and came back with a plate of brownies. "I made these all by myself."

"I'm so glad," Olivia said. Then whispered into Sammy's ear, "This means there's no chance for poppy seeds in them."

"I heard that," said Steve.

Sammy jumped into Olivia's lap, and they ate a yummy fudgy brownie together. Patricia could go to Belize. Olivia had her own island full of love right here in her kitchen.

CHAPTER 20
BRIDGES

It was a night of dinner, chocolate dessert, and too much wine. It was a night of family, and that was just what Olivia needed.

The next morning, Sammy happily crossed off date night from Olivia's Me List, which was hanging on the fridge. Steve pointed to Number 9, "vacation," and gave Olivia a knowing look. He smiled mischievously and said, "I'd be happy to take care of Number 10 for you."

Olivia laughed. "You've taken care of date night. Leave the last one to me," she said and winked at him.

Once her family left for school and work, the house was quiet. Marven was asleep on the couch. The entire house seemed to be waiting for the family to return. Olivia could feel the silence in the pillows neatly arranged on the couch. She could feel the nothing to do staring back at her from every wall. She felt a pang of sadness. Her house hadn't been this quiet in a long time because Patricia had always been right next door with something that needed to get done.

Patricia's presence had transformed her house from a building where she waited for school to end to a place where Olivia lived and worked. Olivia hadn't appreciated it enough, but now that the feeling was gone, she realized how much joy it had brought her.

A car beeping next door interrupted Olivia's thoughts. She heard a knock at the front door and opened it to Patricia, who stood holding a bowl with a plant in it.

"Sorry. One more thing before I go. I bought this for myself, but I thought you would like to take care of it."

Olivia regarded the beautiful pink and yellow flower. "It's a lotus."

"Yes. I bought one after you told me what they meant. It was on my Me List." Patricia looked down sheepishly.

Olivia didn't say a word. She just stepped forward and took the lotus out of Patricia's hands.

"I know the tickets are a bit much," Patricia said. "But I couldn't just leave. I couldn't start this whole life on my own. I thought somehow knowing you might come might make it feel like home. I don't have that many people in my life. I don't have anyone. And my son…" Patricia looked down as if her lips didn't work, hoping the silence would talk for her.

In a voice that was more quiet than strong Patricia said, "Will you come?"

Olivia said, "I don't know. It would be…" She looked at Patricia's face. A few months ago, Olivia had thought of Patricia as a woman who had everything and no room for her. Now she realized Patricia had almost nothing, leaving more than enough space for Olivia.

Patricia's face tightened as if she wasn't sure what words were going to come out of her mouth. And before Olivia could stop it, her heart answered for her. "It would be amazing."

Patricia's relief showed all over her face. The driver in the car beeped the horn again as a reminder that Patricia had a plane to catch.

Olivia still wasn't sure if she should accept the tickets, even after her admission that it would be amazing. Olivia's lips couldn't quite form a smile. She ran her hands through her hair and said, "I still have to think about the trip, Patricia."

"Just consider it." Patricia looked up at Olivia and this time she didn't look confident. She looked like a normal person. A person who had been hurt and been through a lot. Patricia turned to leave. Olivia shifted her feet and out came the words, "Wait. One thing. Before you leave."

Olivia wanted to tell Patricia about how quiet her house was this morning and how awful it had felt, but instead she said, "Thank you. Thank you for trusting me, empowering me, and helping me take my first step back into work."

"We were a good team, weren't we?"

"Better than a team. We were…"

Now it was Olivia's turn to not finish her words. She couldn't say "friends" out loud because Patricia's ex-husband's words filled her with self-doubt and were still too loud in her head. But it was more than that. The weight of her mother's abandonment and insecurity hung on Olivia like an anchor, causing her to close herself off to friends and preventing her from moving forward.

It was in that quiet space that Olivia left room for their friendship. She wasn't going to take a step forward. She waited for Patricia to take the next step, to replace that distance with a kind hand or gentle smile. The world would be a better place if more people built bridges in that emptiness. But today was not a day for building bridges; it was a day for saying goodbye.

After a moment or two, Patricia said "Must go" and walked back to the waiting car. Before stepping into the car, she looked toward her old house, then at Olivia and gave her a wave. Not a formal pageant wave, but a genuine, slightly goofy, I'm really going to miss you wave.

Olivia managed a small wave back as her other hand clutched the lotus plant. Her heart was used to this. Used to seeing people leave her behind. When Patricia's car was no more than a speck down the street, Olivia realized she had secretly hoped Patricia was going to be a person who stayed.

CHAPTER 21
BAGGAGE

When Diya wrote the next week and asked Olivia if she would be interested in joining a weekly hiking club, Olivia knew she should say yes. But part of her wanted to hide under the covers from the world and from friends. Luckily, Diya didn't take no for an answer.

"Why are we here, again?" Olivia asked Diya, as they let the rest of the women walk in front of them. Women who had nicer leggings and more eager feet.

"Accountability. And I've been on a Cheetos kick and feeling guilty," Diya answered.

"Ah, makes sense." Olivia laughed as she huffed and puffed up the trail, careful not to trip on the rocks and roots.

"Easier than reading books?" Diya paused at the top of the path to catch her breath.

"We'll see. Damn, these ladies walk fast." Olivia looked at the five women ahead, all moving with pace and purpose.

"Hey, when do the new neighbors move in?" Diya asked casually. Olivia's entire body grew tense at those words, because to think about new neighbors meant thinking about Patricia. And she had been trying hard not to think of Patricia.

"Don't know. My guess is probably a month?" Olivia put her hand on a tree and used its sturdiness to prevent her from slipping on the trail. She looked up at the women ahead to make sure she and Diya were keeping up with them.

"Hope they are nicer than your last neighbor," Diya added.

"Oh, she wasn't that bad." Olivia felt protective of Patricia. "I mean, she did help me get a job."

"Yeah, that's cool. For some reason, because you complained about her A LOT, I thought you hated her." Diya smiled, aware of Olivia's shift in temperament.

Olivia concentrated on each step forward.

"She moved where again?" Diya asked.

"Belize."

"Holy shit. That's nice."

"Yeah, she gave me tickets to visit."

"What? Why don't any of the people I hate move to exotic places and hook me up? Guess she didn't hate you."

"Guess not. It's weird. I probably won't go. I mean, we're not even friends. It's complicated."

"Wow, plane tickets," Diya said again. Olivia said nothing. She let the sound of sneakers on dirt and the chatter of the other women in the group fill her silence.

Maybe it was the adrenaline from the walk, but when Olivia got home, she felt good. She responded to a few emails and set up some interviews at the office for the following week.

Patricia hadn't lied. Opportunities were lined up for Olivia. Marven slept at her feet, looking adorable. Olivia picked up her phone and carefully snapped a picture of him. She hovered over Patricia's name. Put her phone down. And then picked it back up and sent the picture with the text: *Wrote Donna today to set up interviews. Thanks. Marven is hard at work, as always.*

She put the phone down and felt good about herself. There. She had done it. By writing to Patricia, Olivia was above it all. Or so she thought. Because when her phone rang and she saw Patricia's name, her hand shook and her stomach felt like she had eaten one too many olives. Should she put her straight to voicemail? No, she couldn't do that—she had just texted her the photo. It'd be too obvious. Her cell rang again. Olivia had never noticed how annoying its ringtone was. She'd have to change that.

"Hello." Olivia wished her voice sounded more sure of itself.

"Olivia, oh thank God you picked up. I need help." Patricia's voice sounded out of breath and upset.

Olivia's mind went into overdrive. She pictured Patricia alone in some Belizean rainforest, being chased by someone. "Patricia, are you all right? Are you being attacked?"

"What? No. Nothing like that. But I desperately need your help and…" Patricia paused. Her voice shook with vulnerability. "There's no one else I can ask to do this for me." Patricia sighed from the weight of her words.

Olivia's leg shook with anticipation of the uncertainty of the conversation and the emotion in Patricia's voice. "What? What do you need me to do?"

"I need you to go to my son's rehab and drive him to the airport and make sure he gets on the plane. My ex was supposed to do it, but he went away and didn't tell me. He was just going to send a car to pick him up. But Olivia, I just don't trust…" Patricia's voice got quiet as she found the words. "Chris gets released tomorrow from rehab and he's supposed to come and stay with me. And well, last time…last time, things spiraled out of control so quickly. I can't lose him again. The first flight home wouldn't get me there in time and Chris doesn't want to stay one more day longer than he has to. And I just…"

It took Olivia a few seconds to realize Patricia was crying. Her sobs made her sound more like a strange bird than a mother worried about her son.

How many times had Olivia wished she could help her mother overcome her addiction? How many times was she hurt when she slid back to the bottle? She couldn't help her mother. But she could help Patricia.

"Patricia. I will do this for you. I understand what a big deal this is." And even though Patricia's words and outreach stirred Olivia's heart, she wasn't ready to open up about her mother. "I will make sure he gets on the plane safely. Just tell me the details."

Patricia's voice snapped back to Patricia with a perfect P as she read the address of the rehab, the instructions, and the airport time.

"I'll make sure he gets to you."

"Thank you, Olivia. Thank you. I'm going to call him and let him know."

The next morning, after taking Sammy to school, Olivia made her way to Sun Light rehab. She may as well have been picking up a package of explosives, she was so nervous. For Olivia, that's what addiction felt like. Never feeling sure. Always worrying that your mother, or in this case Patricia's son, could blow up your world and there was no way of stopping it. But Olivia was going to make sure this exploding package made its way safely to Patricia. After that, it was in Patricia's hands. Olivia didn't envy the road Patricia had ahead of her.

Olivia found her way to the receptionist's desk like she was at a hotel, even though she knew the guests here weren't really guests. The place smelled funny. A mixture of Clorox, old shoes, and fake flowers.

When Chris came out, he didn't look nervous. He was bright-eyed as he walked up to Olivia and hugged her tightly. She did not expect it. Her whole body went limp for a second in his big embrace. A laugh escaped her as she said, "I guess you're glad your dad is not picking you up?"

"Yeah, I hate that prick." Chris's smile didn't waver, even though his words were less than kind.

"I'm just glad to be walking out those doors and not in." Chris walked toward the door and gave the middle finger to the receptionist. "I'd say see you later, but I hope I never see you again."

Olivia mouthed, "Sorry and thank you" to the receptionist, while she hurried to follow Chris out of the rehab center.

As they walked to the car, Olivia looked down at the grass and tried to make small talk. "So, I guess your mom told you I'll be taking you to the airport."

"Yes. Sort of. I mean, I screened her call. But she left a message, so I knew my dad bagged out on me. I'd like to say I'm surprised. But I'm not. If I had a dime for every time my dad disappointed me, I'd be in rehab." Chris chuckled as he tucked his hair behind his ear.

Olivia did not laugh. Instead, she stood up straighter and clutched her keys nervously.

"Relax, it's a rehab joke."

"Funny." Olivia opened the door to her car for Chris, as if she was a valet. He chucked his red duffel bag in the back. The bag had the name of a school on it with a basketball in the middle. Olivia wondered if Chris still played basketball. Or if addiction killed that too.

Olivia looked up at the sky and, confirming her belief that her ride was going to be total awkward shit, the sky went from sunshine to doomsday clouds. This was not going to be easy. She sensed Chris was like a spooked stallion who was unsure which way to run.

But then she thought of her mother—how many times had she walked this path with her? How many miles would she have walked if it meant getting her to the other side? Chris was as close as he would ever be to getting past his addiction. Sobriety felt like inches, but each inch forward was still an inch forward. Olivia could do this.

As she got into her side of the car and turned it on, Chris cranked the music and shouted, "So you're my mother's assistant?"

Olivia scrunched her nose at the word assistant. She had been assisting Patricia. But it made her feel like some low-level helper who got coffee. She turned down the music a little and said, "Yes. I worked with your mom. She taught me a lot, actually." Olivia tried to brighten the mood with a little positivity.

"Let me guess; she taught you how to listen to everything she says. And make you feel like you're doing everything wrong. It's cool, I know my mom's a bitch. You don't have to pretend you are friends or anything. I bet she's paying you to take me to the airport. How much does a ride with her loser son pay these days?"

"First of all, we are friends. And she's not paying me. And second of all, didn't your fancy rehab have any family therapy for you?"

"Ha ha, touché." Chris's face relaxed as she laughed. He pulled the string on his sweatshirt and said, "Yeah, hours of therapy. But they can't change my mother. Or my prick father."

"Hey, at least your mom is sending you to Belize. It could be worse." Olivia looked at the clock. They had plenty of time to get to the airport.

"What could be worse than being a twenty-three-year-old addict who needs to be babysat by his mother?"

"She could live in New Jersey."

Chris laughed and made a little snorting sound.

Olivia shuffled in her seat, pleased she managed to help him to relax a little.

"Have you ever been to Belize?" Chris asked.

"Nope. But your mom's house looks really beautiful."

"I went there once. I think that's when I knew my parents were going to get a divorce."

"How old were you?" Olivia took a sip from her water bottle and stared at the traffic ahead. Come on traffic, keep moving this kid towards the airport.

"Eight."

"Eight!" Olivia spit out a little water. "Sorry, that was gross. I just didn't expect that answer."

"Let me guess, my mom painted a wonderful portrait of a loving family?"

"No. Not really. I guess I just assumed it."

"Well, how's this picture? My strongest memory of Belize was my mom taking me on a boat ride to go snorkeling. We woke up early. She was super secretive, like it was an adventure just for us, and I felt so special. I can remember tiptoeing through the house so we didn't wake my dad."

"What's so wrong with that memory? It sounds sweet."

"Well, when we got home later, my dad started screaming at us. Before we even made it into the house. Before I could even tell him about all the fish we'd seen." Chris rubbed his hands on the knees of his jeans as if rubbing them would help coax out the rest of his words.

"And that's when I realized that special trip was a game. I was a pawn. I was being used to hurt my dad. They had gotten into a fight the night before. He was supposed to be with us. Time with me was just a weapon they used against each other." Chris shrugged his shoulders and looked out the window.

Raindrops streaked the windows of the car. Olivia turned on the wipers. She didn't say anything. She just let the sound of the rain mix with the radio to create a soothing music of its own.

Traffic slowed. Olivia watched Chris fidget as he stared straight ahead. Her mommy heart opened for him.

"I don't know your mom that well. But I know what I'd say if you were my daughter."

Chris looked up at her and gave a slight nod to show he was listening.

"I'd tell her I was sorry for what I put her through. That I loved her. More than she could ever imagine. And that I couldn't change the past, but I'd be there for her every day in her future."

Chris made a "hmm" sound and went back to looking out the window.

Maybe silence wasn't a bad thing, Olivia's brain told itself. Olivia's heart, on the other hand, went back to hating Patricia just a little bit.

CHAPTER 22
FLIGHT

As Olivia pulled up to the airport, traffic slowed as she flicked on her left turn signal to enter the short-term parking lot. Before she knew what was happening, Chris was grabbing his bag, opening the door, and jumping out of her car into the traffic. He shouted, "I'm good. Save your money for parking. Thanks for the ride." Her mouth slightly agape, she watched him dodge cars as he made his way toward the terminal.

Olivia couldn't get out of the parking line, so she pulled into a parking space to exhale. She dug out her phone to text Patricia. But what should she write? Could she say she got her son safely to the airport? Texting *Hey, got your son safely to the airport, but he jumped out of the car* certainly wasn't going to work.

Olivia's gut said no to that text. Before Olivia could stop herself, she'd grabbed her purse and headed into the terminal. She needed to see Chris at least get through security.

As she walked into the building, she saw Chris walking out in the opposite direction. Olivia tried to hide behind a little old couple so Chris didn't see her, as if she was in a spy movie. But Olivia was feeling nervous, not suave or sly, so she accidentally stepped on the heel of the lady's brown shoe. The little lady let out a howl as if Olivia had just broken her in two.

"I'm so sorry," Olivia said as she looked up to make sure Chris was still on the bench. He had his earbuds in and was listening to music, staring straight ahead.

"Watch where you are walking." The old lady glared at her while the gentleman next to her added, "People are too much in a rush these days."

"It wasn't that. I'm so sorry. It's just..." Olivia looked up and saw the bus rounding the corner. "I'm sorry. I need to go." She ran outside to where Chris was sitting as she heard the old couple grumbling behind her.

Chris was lost in his music. Olivia could have made a huge ruckus and he would never have noticed. She didn't have to be a spy after all. She sat right next to him and he didn't even look over. She pulled out one of his earbuds and Chris looked shocked as he said, "Hey, what are you doing..." and then his face changed to the oh-shit-I'm-in-trouble look.

"I didn't know planes take off from here," Olivia said sarcastically.

"Just getting some air."

"Oh, really? You weren't about to get on this bus instead of going to Belize?"

"What's it to you? My mom said to get me to the airport. You got me to the airport. Your job is done."

"This isn't just about your mom," Olivia said so loudly that a few people turned around.

She stared straight ahead and whispered, "It's about my mom, too."

"My mom is your mother?" Chris looked appalled. "How is that, like, even possible?" He looked Olivia up and down like she was an old decrepit child of Satan.

"No. Your mother is not my mother. Thanks." She tightened her ponytail and took a deep breath. "My mom is an addict. Alcohol mainly. And I spent my whole life watching her run away from me when I needed her most. I will not let you do it to your mother."

"Look, your mommy issues have nothing to do with me." He crossed his arms and looked annoyed.

"Maybe they don't. Or maybe they do. Maybe I know how it feels to be on the other side when someone doesn't show up. It sucks. It's hell. And your mom might be a…" Olivia quieted her voice and said, "bitch. But she doesn't deserve that."

"So what do you want from me?" Chris said as he scanned his phone for his next music choice.

Olivia reached around and pulled out his other earbud.

"Hey. That's private property. I could have you arrested."

"Really, kid? That's what you're going with?"

"I don't know. It sounded good."

"Here's what we're going to do. We are going in there. And I'm going to help you check in. You are going to go through security. And you are getting on that plane."

Olivia felt like Marven when he heard the neighbor weed whacking—her hackles were up and she was ready to fight.

"Fine." Chris grabbed his bag and stood up. "Give me back my earbuds though." Chris stretched his hand towards Olivia.

"Fine." Olivia dropped them in his hand. They walked into the terminal, both looking exhausted from dealing with the other.

"You know what? Change of plans. Come with me." Olivia walked up to the ticket counter while Chris put his earbuds back into his ears and zoned out. She quickly texted her husband, then grabbed Chris's arm and positioned him so she could see him as she talked to the ticket agent. Chris rolled his eyes at her.

"Are there any seats left on the flight to Belize?" Olivia asked.

"Hold on. Let me check." Olivia watched the ticket agent's fingers clickety-clack on the keyboard.

"Yes. Looks like it is not a full flight."

"Great. I have a voucher for a flight. If I give you that information, can I use it today?"

"I don't see why not." It took more than a few minutes for Olivia to give her name, social security number, and a bunch more information to get a ticket. The seat next to Chris was open on the flight. Olivia wasn't sure if he'd think that was as lucky as she did. Chris stood next to her, oblivious, listening to his music.

Finally, Olivia nudged him to get his attention. "We're done."

"Oh, cool."

Olivia walked up to security and Chris said, "Well, thanks for the talk. And I'll be sure to have my mom send you a fruit basket at Christmas."

"Not so fast." Olivia put her arm up to block Chris.

"What now?" If looks could kill, Chris's eyes held knives packed with bigger knives packed with poison.

"I'm going with you." Olivia gestured to the security line.

"What?" Chris pulled his sweatshirt hood over his face. "Nooooo."

"Come on, it won't be all bad. I'll buy you some good snacks and candy. We don't have to talk. I'll buy a magazine. It'll be relaxing." Olivia pulled Chris into the line with her and people started to queue behind them.

"This is bullshit."

Olivia had just given up her ticket to her vacation to make sure this kid got home to his mother, even if it was a vacation she hadn't yet agreed to take. She had no patience for his anger. He was the one who tried to run away. She was doing the right thing. She knew it.

"This *is* bullshit," she said. "You're bullshit. And guess what? Deal with it, because I'm hand-delivering you to your mother. You can either pout about it or realize I'm giving you an opportunity to stop running from your past and face it. You want to heal and move forward? It starts with dealing with your mother. I will not let you ghost her. I will not let you run away from yourself. It gets you nowhere and one day you'll find yourself old and still running away from the people who love you."

"Me going to Belize isn't going to bring your mother back, you know."

"I know. But it will bring you back to your mother. And she deserves that more than worrying about where you are."

"Are you, like, in love with my mother or something?"

Olivia laughed. Relieving the frustration felt good. She couldn't stop laughing.

"Honestly, kid, I don't even know if I like your mother some days. But I know how I feel not knowing where my mom is. And I don't wish that on anyone. Even your mother. I'm not letting you become some shadow she worries about. You deserve more than that, too."

Olivia didn't know what was going on inside Chris's brain, but he kept moving forward in the security line, which she took as a positive sign. They approached the conveyor belt, and Chris dropped his phone and earbuds in the tray. He took off his shoes and mumbled something under his breath.

"Did you say something?" Olivia asked as she put her purse on a tray next to his.

"I said I want Twizzlers."

Olivia smiled. "I love Twizzlers. We'll get two bags 'cause I don't like to share."

As she walked through the X-ray scanner, she realized she was doing this. Her husband was amazing for saying yes to her text. There was a flight back tonight. It was really just a few hours and a lost plane ticket to make sure Patricia's son didn't disappear. She'd give anything to know where her mother was. Anything.

Finally through security, Olivia and Chris loaded up on Twizzlers. Olivia also bought herself two cheesy women's magazines that she'd never let Samantha see her read, but that would pass the time during the flight. And besides, learning what her favorite color said about her love life and the top twenty-five sexual positions might come in handy.

As they sat waiting at their gate, Olivia mulled over what she should say before composing a text to Patricia. She didn't want to lie, but she didn't want to tell the truth either. It wouldn't do any good to cause Patricia to feel stressed or guilty about what Olivia was doing. Olivia texted most of the truth: *Chris is through security and on his way to you.*

Patricia texted back instantly: *I can't thank you enough.*

Olivia wondered what Patricia was going to say when she discovered the whole truth. And then she shook her head. It's not important. What's important is Chris is going to Belize, where he can start working on himself and his relationship with Patricia.

Olivia texted her husband: *Thank you for understanding why I need to do this. I love you. I'll call you when I land once I've spoken with Patricia. And then my flight back is tonight!*

Steve wrote back a thumbs-up emoji with the words: *I love you.*

The boarding announcement came over the muffled speaker. Chris and Olivia made their way onto the plane. They shuffled through the narrow path and found their seats together. Chris kept his earbuds in, and Olivia could hear the loud music from where she was sitting. But at least he looked content. Two magazines and a plane ride later, they'd be in Belize.

Olivia flipped open her magazine and she felt Chris lean over, reading over her shoulder. Weirdly cozy, but fine. When she got to the page about sex positions, she skipped over it quickly. She was not going to read that with Patricia's son.

"Hey, you want my other magazine?"

"What?" Chris pulled out his earbuds.

"You want to read this one?" Olivia handed over the second magazine she'd bought.

"Oh yeah, sure." Chris instantly began flipping through it.

Olivia felt more relieved without Chris reading over her shoulder and flipped back to the sex positions article. Maybe some of these should be on her Me List for next year.

Olivia was lost in her magazine when she noticed Chris fidgeting. First, a jumpy leg. Then he scratched his jeans on his kneecap over and over.

"You doing all right?" she whispered. Chris didn't respond. Olivia could hear the music from his earbuds. He started picking more aggressively at his jeans. And then he put his head and arms down on his lap like he was folding himself up.

Olivia rubbed his back and took out his earbud just a little. He didn't flinch or change positions or look up.

"You okay?" Olivia went into mother mode and worried Chris was about to be sick. She kept awkwardly patting his back in an attempt to calm them both.

Chris looked up, saying nothing, before putting his head back down on his lap. Olivia rubbed his back in a circular motion like she did for Samantha when she was having trouble falling asleep. Was it a good sign that Chris was letting her comfort him? She knew what her mom looked like when she desperately was jonesing for a drink. Was this addiction, nervousness, or plane sickness? Was this any of her business? Yes. It became her business when he tried to leave on a bus and when she jumped on a plane with him.

Chris put his head in his hands and sat up a little. He started rocking back and forth. Olivia removed her hand from his back. She glanced at him and mouthed the word *okay*?

She saw the flight attendant and asked her for a cup of cold water. Hydration never hurts.

The flight attendant brought the water, and Olivia handed it to Chris. She was trying to give him privacy, as much as possible in a cramped airplane.

He took the cup and drank it in silence.

Olivia didn't know when she felt more nervous—when she'd thought Chris was going to run away, or now when she had no idea what was happening inside his body and head. Suddenly, she too felt overwhelmed. She didn't know this kid. She barely knew Patricia. And now here she was, smack dab in the middle of both their lives. And at about 35,000 feet.

"Thanks."

"No problem." Olivia smiled at him to encourage him to keep talking.

"Sorry about that."

"Does that happen a lot?" Olivia tried to look calm and non-judgmental.

"Yeah. It's just like…life is ahead of me, you know." He rubbed his neck, trying to regain his composure.

"Yeah," Olivia said even though she didn't actually know, but she knew she didn't want him to feel alone in his thoughts.

"Belize is ahead of you," she whispered.

Chris repeated the words, but when he said them, they sounded like they weighed 500 pounds. "Belize. Yes, with my mother." His whole body tensed as he asked, "What are you going to tell her?" His voice sounded panicked.

"I'm going to let you tell her. Good news is my flight back is tonight, so I won't have a lot of time to chat." She winked at Chris. "But it's more important that you talk to her. Be honest with her. The good and the bad."

Chris nodded. But didn't speak.

"Belize looks like a beautiful place. Maybe you can figure out some things there. Enjoy the ocean."

"Mhm," Chris said, as he slowly picked at a string on his jeans.

"You know what I think?" Olivia asked.

"No. But I think you're going to tell me." Chris smirked. Olivia felt relieved. She could work with a smirk.

"My daughter tells me I talk too much. But I've got one more thing to say and then we can eat Twizzlers and finish reading our trashy magazines."

"What?" Chris looked at her. Really looked at her. Made eye contact and everything. And in that moment, Olivia didn't see an addict or a punk. She saw a kid. A lost kid.

"I think your mom picked Belize because she remembered that time you woke up early and went snorkeling, and it was the best day of her life. Because it was the day she realized even if life was total shit with your dad, she had you."

Chris shrugged his shoulders and popped his earbuds back in. And Olivia smiled because she knew somewhere within his music that thought was beating along too.

Olivia pretended to read her magazine, but her mind was elsewhere. Why was it so easy for her to see Patricia's love for Chris? Did her mother love her more than she was giving her credit for? For Olivia, staying was love. But maybe for her mother, leaving was love?

The pilot came on and announced they were preparing to land.

Olivia looked over at Chris. Was he ready for landing? Not just on a plane, but in real life? She hoped so.

CHAPTER 23
BROOD

Some people can open a present that is exactly what they don't want without betraying their true feelings. An itchy homemade scarf. A blouse with a terrible print. A new kitchen gadget for a cuisine they don't enjoy. Those people have a game face ready for whatever comes their way. It didn't surprise Olivia that Patricia's face could handle the joy of her son coming out of the gate, as well as the shock of Olivia being there as well.

Patricia hugged her son tightly, looked him over, and said, "Oh, look how long your hair has gotten. We can get you a haircut this week if you'd like." Chris just shrugged his shoulders and stood there like he was a dog getting judged at a dog show. As she inspected Chris, she peppered Olivia with questions. "Are you staying? Is this your vacation?" along with throwing some supportive barbs her way: "Of course, you can stay with me. And even though it's unexpected, it's wonderful." Olivia quieted her friend down. Because after you fly someone's son across the country, you need to admit to yourself, she is your friend.

"Patricia, this is my gift to you. I'm not staying. I'm actually on the next flight back. But Chris needed..." Olivia smiled and made eye contact with Chris. "Just a little extra support to make it to you and, well...I know how much you love your son."

Patricia gave her an enormous hug. It was squishy and wildly uncomfortable, so Olivia knew Patricia must have meant it.

"I do love my son. And I can't believe you are here." Patricia smiled at Chris with tears in her eyes, reinforcing to Olivia she had made the right decision. Patricia's tears were mixed with pain and heartache. Olivia recognized them well.

"Do we have time to take you around a bit before we return you for your flight home?" Patricia put her arm around her son. An arm, yes, but to Olivia, it looked like the start of a bridge between two people who could find family and love again.

"Oh, I don't know. I think you and Chris should get going. I've got magazines I can read."

"Nonsense. I'd love to show my two favorite people my new life. Let's go. You know I won't take no for an answer." Patricia smiled and ushered them to her parking space.

Olivia walked up to the car and whispered to Chris, "Are you cool with this?"

"Mm-hmm. Makes my life easier. My mom can't attack me with questions if you're here."

Olivia laughed. "Don't bet on it." She held her hands out and said, "You take the front seat."

Chris sat down and stared ahead. His body was stiff and uncomfortable. Not slouchy. No earbuds in. His face filled with dread, like he was about to go on trial.

There were no questions or cross-examination by Patricia but plenty of tour guide banter as they made the way down the road surrounded endlessly by trees. "My house is over an hour from here."

Chris let out a little moan. Patricia patted his leg. "I'm sure we have plenty to catch up on to keep us busy." Then she looked back at Olivia and said, "My home is not quite as far as Placencia. That's where Coppola's resort is. You might want to look into that when your family comes." Patricia winked at her.

Olivia had to admit that besides the annoying wink, Patricia looked good. She seemed energized and alive. She was wearing an island print dress, probably some fancy resort wear that Olivia had never heard of. Olivia tried to spy on Patricia's shoes to see if her sandals matched. But she couldn't quite get the right angle without giving away that she was looking.

Patricia pulled the car over.

"Everything okay?" Olivia asked, looking outside her window.

Patricia's voice got very quiet. "Yes, just look in that tree. Do you see it?"

Chris said, "There are lots of trees. Which tree?"

"That one there. Up top. Here, roll down your window and listen."

Olivia sat in the little blue car, staring at a tree, not knowing what was going to happen. But because it was Patricia, Olivia obeyed. She rolled down the window and was instantly hit with muggy air that smelled of forest mixed with dirt road and car exhaust.

And then she heard what sounded like an angry dinosaur.

"What is that?" Olivia looked around, expecting Jurassic Park to appear out of the wild jungle forest and T-Rexes to run over their tiny car.

"It's a group of howler monkeys. See them up at the top?"

"How does a monkey that size create a sound so ferocious? I always thought monkeys were cute." Olivia watched a monkey go from branch to branch, its mouth open wide. "Wow, this place is incredible." Olivia scanned the trees and all the various colors of green. It's like God used every color in the green crayon box to bring the rainforest to life.

"Wait until you see how big the iguanas are. You know, some people eat them."

"Gross," said Chris.

"I heard they taste like chicken," Patricia announced.

Olivia smiled. Monkeys and iguanas. Patricia sure was far away from her divorced husband. "New goals. By the time I visit, you need to eat an iguana and tell me if it tastes like chicken."

"Can't I stick to Twizzlers?" Chris asked.

Olivia laughed. "Nope. You're a new man. Got to try new things."

They drove around a little more until Olivia checked the time and said, "We should probably head back to the airport." She put her hand on Chris's shoulder and added, "The flight won't be quite as much fun without you."

"Well, hopefully Chris will still be here when you come back, Olivia." Patricia gave Chris a knowing glance.

Chris slumped back into the seat and put up his hood.

Patricia looked into the rear-view mirror and smiled nervously at Olivia. Sensing the mood shift in the car, Olivia did what she did best. She chattered on about anything she could think of. Her opportunities at Patricia's office. Marven. Sammy.

Before Olivia knew it, she heard the clicking of Patricia's turn signal and they were back at the airport. After the eventful day, Olivia was ready to head home. "Thank you for the tour, Patricia. It was nice to see how beautiful this place is. Gets me excited to come back in the summer."

"Let me get out and give you a proper send-off," said Patricia. She exited quickly and came around to Olivia's side.

Olivia stepped out of the car and said, "Bye, Chris. Good luck. I'm so glad we met." Chris peeked out of his hoodie, waved at her, and retreated back into his sweatshirt for solace.

Patricia closed her door for her. "I know we only have a few minutes, but obviously thank you for bringing him to me. But tell me what really happened." The all-business tone in Patricia's voice threw Olivia for a second.

Olivia tried to think of how to say it nicely but also so Patricia, as Chris's mother, knew what she needed to watch for.

"There's no easy way to say this. But Chris tried to run away at the airport."

"Run away? Why? Where?" Patricia's face reddened and she sounded flustered.

"I don't know. I saw him waiting for the bus."

"Didn't you drop him off?"

Olivia ignored Patricia's accusatory tone. She tried to keep herself calm by becoming interested in flattening the wrinkles on her pants.

"He jumped out of the car before I could park."

"Oh. So he didn't make it to the airport terminal. No wonder."

"No wonder what?"

"No wonder you felt the need to accompany him. To make up for your lack of duty."

"My lack of..." Olivia started shaking her head. "No. no. no. That's not what happened." Why was Patricia attacking her like this? Olivia had gone overboard to get him here. Didn't she understand how she'd almost lost him?

"I'm just trying to understand. I mean, he was just released from rehab, so he's dealing with a lot. That's why I wanted him to come here, so he could relax. I thought he would think of this as a vacation. Why wouldn't he want to come?"

"I think you and Chris can talk about that during your drive. He's got lots to share. Listen to him." As Olivia said those words, she could see Patricia's spine straighten by about five inches and that's when she knew she had gone too far.

"You spent one afternoon with my son and now you know more than me." Patricia's smile was not really a smile. It was smug and angry with curled-up lips.

"Patricia, I didn't mean to upset you. I did this for you. Look. I need to go. I just want you to understand your son is a flight risk. You need to keep a close eye on him. I know this sounds rude. But I'm not trying to be. I'm trying to look out for you and him. He needs you. But you need to know he's not out of the woods yet. He got out of rehab, but this might be the hardest part."

"Thank you, I'll keep that in mind," Patricia went from friendly tour guide to cold as ice.

Olivia tried one more time to get it right. "I know how much you love your son. That's why I made sure he got to you. Because I didn't want you to never see him again."

Patricia's tone turned intense. "I was nervous he'd be tempted to drink or something, but not run away. If I thought Chris wasn't going to board that plane, I would have never asked you."

"Addicts aren't predictable," Olivia said flatly.

"Thank you for judging my son. And thank you for bringing him, but now I think you need to go." The red in Patricia's face burned hot enough to light a thousand campfires. But with dignity and controlled wrath, she turned and walked away. Her steps were as hard as a soldier's and her glare even harder, like ammunition.

"Patricia," Olivia said. But Patricia opened the driver's door and only gave a glance in her direction. "Patricia," Olivia said more loudly. "For the record, I wasn't judging your son." But Patricia slammed the door before Olivia could say, "I was speaking about my mom."

The engine revved as Patricia drove off fast. Olivia huffed and went inside to find her plane. How did everything always go wrong with Patricia? Patricia was so damn unlikeable sometimes. It was off her back now. Olivia had done the right thing. And she knew, as a mom, it was difficult to hear tough things about your child. Especially after your divorced husband said worse things in the past.

Olivia stopped for a moment before she walked into the airport and looked at the blue sky. Would she come back? This friendship felt more like a bowling alley in her head. Was friendship supposed to feel like a wrecking ball? Olivia walked into the first shop she found and loaded up on chocolate. The flight back deserved better candy. She had earned it.

CHAPTER 24
DELICATES

Luckily for Olivia, the next day was a return to normal life. No howler monkeys. But Sammy sure seemed like a wild animal as Olivia got her ready for school, arms like an octopus as Olivia tried to help put her shirt on. Olivia was racing against the clock to get to her therapy appointment on time. But Sammy was in a mood, the kind where every single pair of pants she owned suddenly felt too scratchy. None of her favorite shirts were clean. And she wanted to wear a cape to school over a dress from last summer that was two sizes too small.

Somehow, Olivia convinced Sammy to wear a green sweater over a rainbow dress with rainbow leggings. Colorful and crazy, but it made Sammy happy. Before Olivia knew it, she was sitting comfortably on the uncomfortable couch and spilling her latest adventure to Belize to her therapist.

Patricia.

Her mom.

Chris.

They all felt so intertwined in Olivia's heart.

"Do you think it's important for Patricia to like you because you want your mom to like you?" Laura asked.

"Can I get water?" Olivia asked. "I'm super thirsty." She stood up, walked over to the water cooler, and took a paper cup, aware that her therapist could probably see through her hydration scheme. Olivia sat down on the couch, bouncier than she intended, overcompensating for her inner stress and spilling water on her pants.

"Great. Now it looks like I peed."

"Olivia, are you avoiding the question?"

Olivia tried not to make eye contact.

"I think my mom probably likes me. She's my mom. Patricia isn't my mother. I don't know what she is."

"But you flew to another country with her son. That was a big act of friendship for someone you aren't sure of."

"Yes. I know it was crazy."

"Do you think it was crazy?"

"No. I think I saved that boy's life." Olivia put her cup down. And wrung her hands. "Maybe to you, it seems crazy. But to me, it seemed like I had to do it."

Olivia could feel the emotion she had worked to push down make its way into her chest. An explosion of tears came out as she tried to get her words out.

"I just want to know if my mom is okay. It's killing me. I keep going on with my everyday wondering where my mom is. Knowing she is sick. And there's nothing I can do about it. And Patricia doesn't deserve to live like that."

"Do you think you deserve closure?"

Olivia grabbed the tissues on the table, dabbed her eyes, and blew her nose, sounding like a baby elephant. She shivered. The air in her therapist's office was always too chilly. She stared at the pot of flowers on the table. The slight smell of flowers did nothing to settle her nerves.

"It doesn't matter what I think. My mom thinks I deserve this." Olivia looked at the clock to see how much longer she had. Today it felt like she was being gutted like a fish.

"What do you think you deserve?"

"I think I deserve a mom who loves me. I think I deserve a friend who is thankful I've gone the extra mile to make sure her son was safe. I think I deserve better."

"Do you remember what you put in the letter you wrote to your mom?"

"I need to choose me."

"And how can you do that?"

"Put me at the top of my Me List." Olivia said those words more confidently than she felt them.

After therapy, she decided to put herself first by tackling a thing or two left on her Me List. She went to the fancy store in the mall she used to go to when she was in her twenties and her body bounced instead of sagged. But Olivia liked her figure these days. Not because it was shaped a certain way, but because she understood its power. It brought Samantha into this life. Surely that deserved appreciation and acceptance. And surely that body deserved new underwear.

She looked in the window at the silk nighties and see-through bras of lace. Did she even want a see-through bra now? She'd choose comfort over sexy these days. As she peeked in the store, she saw a for sale sign and teal panties that were a beautiful color. She walked right up to them. The fabric felt smooth. She looked at the price tag. On sale for $14. Pricey but pretty, and they looked like comfy, itty-bitty shorts.

"Can I ask you something?" Olivia heard a low voice and dropped the underwear.

"Sorry, didn't mean to scare you." A young guy in a baseball cap stood there, his face redder than the garment he was holding. "This store intimidates me."

Olivia laughed. "Me too."

"If you were like totally pissed at your boyfriend, would you want this?" He held up the red nightgown.

"It depends. What did you do?" Olivia looked at what he was holding. There wasn't much to it. Lace, spaghetti straps, a little silk.

"Talked to my ex-girlfriend."

"Just talked?"

"She liked something on my Instagram and then DM'd me. I shouldn't have responded."

"That doesn't seem too bad. Did you tell your girlfriend?"

"Well..." The guy held up the cute outfit. "Was gonna tell her tonight with this apology?"

"Oooh, apology with a defensive move; ready with a gift. Nicely played."

"I just don't want her feeling insecure. And the thing is, all it did was remind me that my ex is not for me."

"So why didn't you tell your girlfriend?"

"I don't know."

"Well, it's good you are being honest with her now. That's probably more important than whatever you pick out."

Olivia looked down at the table. She still hadn't been honest with Steve. Was it about the money or was it really about admitting she'd been wrong about her mother yet again and owning the fact that her mother created a wedge in her marriage? Olivia grabbed the turquoise underwear.

"Can I ask you something? Are boy shorts sexy?"

"I mean, you did just use the words boy and shorts. Are either of those words sexy to you?"

Olivia frowned and held up a pair of black lace underwear. Then she held up the boy shorts in her other hand to compare.

"Nah, I'm just messing with you. Guys are super easy. If you feel sexy in anything," the guy looked down at her hand and saw a ring, "your husband will be happy."

Olivia bought the turquoise for herself and the sexier black lace pair, too. On the way home, Olivia kept turning her therapist's words "what do I deserve" over and over in her head like pancakes. She was going to make some changes. Bigger changes than just her underwear. Her Me List had started her on this path of change, and now she was going to keep taking steps that got her closer to the happiness she deserved. She believed in her family. The one she created. And because of that love, she also believed in the power of a home. Not just a house with a pretty wreath and furniture, but a home with love and fights and wet socks. And toys all over the place. A home that held all the things that made life pretty and messy. She was going to get her realtor's license and help more families find that special place. But first, she had one more place to stop.

The bar was empty. She wrote down the song from 4 Non Blondes that she knew she wanted to sing. The song started, and it instantly brought her back to her childhood. A good day. Olivia and her mother dancing.

The words filled the screen with the first lyrics, but once again Olivia couldn't get her voice to come out. It was like her whole body was stuck in the memory. Her mother was two months sober, and it felt like this time she could do it. She had a job. Her mom brought home a little chocolate cake to celebrate her two months and all that was ahead of them. It all felt within reach.

Olivia held onto the microphone like it was her mother's hand. She could still hear her mother singing. Round and round they spun and danced and sang. They belted out the chorus so loudly that the neighbor banged on the floor from above. But they didn't care. They laughed and sang louder.

Olivia stood on the stage silently and gripped the microphone even tighter as she saw the words going by and the song kept playing without her. She thought about her mother's hands and how tightly she'd held them that day. Like if Olivia could hold on tightly enough, she could help her mother keep choosing sobriety. But now Olivia knew it didn't matter how tightly she held onto her mother. It was her mother's grip that slipped. It was always her grip. And it killed Olivia to feel that slip. Every time. It didn't matter how many books she read about addiction. She always took the slip personally. If she could just love her mother more. She. She. She. It didn't matter how many times her mother had failed, Olivia kept putting her hand back out.

Olivia gripped the microphone with hands wrapped in heartache and the words, "I try," escaped her lips.

And this time she kept singing. She could hear her own voice get louder along with the memory of her mother. She looked back at the beautiful memory full of hope and it didn't break her. Sometimes the good is harder to look at than the bad. The bad you can jab with a stick and understand. But the good is tricky because it involves your heart. Olivia didn't know what to do with it all swirling around her on that stage or in life. But she knew she had to figure out a way to let go.

When she finished the song, there was still no one there. Just the bartender cleaning some dishes. No one clapped. No one paid attention that the song was over. But deep down, Olivia knew that something inside herself was changing.

CHAPTER 25
BOMB

With her family's enthusiastic support, and backed by many of Patricia's colleagues, Olivia started her online courses to get her license. A sixty-hour course in Real Estate Fundamentals, plus a thirty-hour course in Real Estate Practices. Once she finished the courses, she would need to pass the broker's licensing exam, and then she'd be on her way to selling home sweet homes.

On her first day of studying, Olivia received her first postcard. Olivia stood in her kitchen looking over the postcard as she tapped her fingers nervously on the countertop.

The front of the postcard had a picture of Belize's ocean. The back contained only a few words: I'm sorry. Chris told me everything. And then, in her signature Patricia-big-P handwriting, her name with what looked like a small heart above it. Or a three with a line on it. Could perfect Patricia have trouble making a perfect heart? Olivia's body shook and her stomach went squishy at the sight of her handwriting.

Friendship should not make you feel panicky, she thought to herself. Olivia looked at the postcard again and said out loud, "I deserve better." She threw it in the trash.

The next day, as she was digging in to read about disclosures and contracts, she went to the mailbox and got another postcard with the picture of a Keel-Billed Toucan. Olivia smiled at its yellow face and canoe-shaped beak. But when she flipped over the postcard, she stopped. It wasn't Patricia's handwriting. It was Chris's, with the words: Thank you for all that you did. His name was written in a small scrawl. Olivia knew Patricia probably forced Chris to write this, and it felt ingenuine.

The next day, Olivia didn't go to the mailbox. She avoided it. She didn't open it when she walked Marven. She turned her head away from it when she brought Sammy home from the school bus. Olivia was not going to open that mailbox because she was not going to be controlled by Patricia.

Olivia had forgotten all about the mail by the time Sammy was helping her make dinner. Sammy loved baked potatoes, but mostly she loved stabbing them with a fork and getting ready to put them in the oven. It was her special job.

"Now stab this guy four times, and then let's salt and pepper him." Olivia held the potato, slightly scared she might get forked herself.

Sammy eagerly poked the potato four times by thrusting her fork into it hard.

"Good job." Olivia wrapped it in aluminum foil and said, "All right, let's do one more." Just then, she heard Marven bark. "Oh, I bet Dad's home."

Steve came in the door and instantly said, "What's this about?" as he walked into the kitchen.

"We're in here. Making potatoes," Olivia said, without looking up.

Steve put a stack of postcards fifty deep on the counter.

"What?!" Olivia looked at the pile and flipped one over. It just had the words: I'm sorry. She flipped over another: I'm sorry. Sammy picked up one with a tapir on the front.

"Can I have this one?"

Olivia peered at the back while Sammy was holding it and saw the words "I'm sorry" written again.

"I'm not sure if Patricia is sorry or psycho?" Steve said as he flipped over each postcard.

"Maybe she's both?" Olivia grabbed the postcard out of Steve's hand.

"Let's just keep making dinner." Olivia smiled at Sammy. "Last potato?"

As Sammy poked holes into its skin, she asked, "Why is Patricia so sorry? What did she do, Mommy? She's the lady who got you your job and made you want to sell houses?"

"Yes, baby. But it's just not that simple."

"That's a lot of postcards, though."

"That is a lot of postcards. Patricia likes to do things a little extra."

Olivia smirked as she saw Steve rolling his eyes in agreement.

"She must be a good friend if she sent you so many postcards." Sammy looked at Olivia inquiringly. "One time Betsy made me three pictures of rainbows at school."

"That's wonderful, honey. Betsy is nice."

"Is Patricia nice?"

"Patricia can be nice. But honestly, this feels more like love bombing to me."

"What's that?"

"Sometimes people go over the top with attention like this and it can feel more like manipulation."

"Potato talk is getting serious, isn't it, hon?" Steve came over and picked up Samantha and gave her a hug. "Wanna check in on Sausage and see how he's doing?"

"His name is Marven, Dad." Sammy smiled. "Yeah, I'll go see if he wants to play. But don't worry Mom, I won't love-bomb him." Olivia nodded as she pulled some broccoli from the fridge and washed it.

"Don't you think she's a little young for stories of manipulation and friendships gone wrong?" Steve asked once Samantha had left the room.

"I don't know. I wish I'd understood what a narcissist looked like from a young age. Maybe I would have dealt with my mother better."

Olivia looked at the pile of postcards. "I mean. What the hell am I supposed to do with this?"

"I don't know. Recycle them?" Steve looked at a few more postcards. "Sure does look like a pretty place."

"I didn't mean what should I do with the actual postcards. I meant with Patricia. With her messy friendship. With these grand gestures and the..."

"Plane tickets," Steve finished, looking at another beautiful picture of the rainforest with a pink exotic flower that looked bigger than his hand. "Accept she's a psycho, take the plane tickets and run."

"It's not that simple. I swear she makes friendship feel like a dirty word." Olivia wrung her hands together.

"Whatever you want. I don't envy your friendship." Steve looked at a beach photograph longingly before dumping the cards in the trash. And she could see his body let out a little sigh.

The next day, Olivia didn't get a postcard. No. She got a knock at the door and a vase full of flowers. Expensive ones. Not the ones filled with cheap carnations and filler. This vase had vibrant ranunculus of all different colors—oranges, pinks, whites, and deep burgundies. And what was that heavenly smell? Fragrant eucalyptus and lavender. Never in her life had Olivia been so furious at flora. She slammed the door on the delivery man. She carried the large vase into the kitchen and put it on her countertop.

She didn't have to look at the card. She knew who they were from. But she opened the stupid tiny card and read it anyway: Thanks again for all that you did. Patricia.

Olivia's whole body felt like a shaken bottle of bubbly water. She was ready to explode. Olivia picked up her phone and dialed Patricia.

Patricia answered in a sing-song voice. "Oh, you must have just gotten my flowers."

"Yes. I did."

"Are they gorgeous? I just learned about that floral shop. The owner is wonderful."

"Yes. They are beautiful."

"Oh, wonderful."

"No, Patricia. This isn't wonderful. You can't send me a bunch of postcards and flowers. That's not how friendship works."

"What's wrong with beautiful flowers?" Patricia's voice still sounded way too syrupy and fake.

"I don't want flowers. I want honesty." Olivia exhaled her frustration and blew her hair away from her face. Talking to Patricia felt like talking to an overly giving wall. But it was still a wall.

"Well, I honestly wanted to give you flowers. And I just thought I could show you all the great places you could see in Belize. I don't have many people to send postcards to. I thought it would make you excited. And after talking to Chris and him telling me about all that you've been through with your mother, I felt like I owed you an apology."

"Yes. See. That's friendship. Where we talk about things that matter. I wanted to mention my mom a hundred times. But…" Olivia stopped herself. Was this frustration worth it? Was Patricia worth putting herself out there? Did Olivia actually want a deep friendship, or would it be easier to have surface-level friends? Ones where you get coffee and talk about stupid things like who you hated from the school pickup line? Talking with Patricia felt like opening a vein.

Olivia concentrated on taking a slow breath in and out to calm herself like she had taught Samantha to do when she felt overwhelmed. "Thank you for the flowers. You didn't have to do that. And yes, I've spent my whole life watching my mother's addiction, and it's why I couldn't let Chris not board that plane."

Olivia paused, and her damn nose filled with the heavenly scent of the flowers and calmed her. How could her nostrils betray her like this? She breathed in deeply and asked, "How is Chris?"

Patricia's voice shifted. It no longer had a melody to it. "He's doing okay. I think. We've had some good talks. Angry talks. It seems this divorce hurt him more than I realized. But he started working at a local canoe place where they give tours. And I think that's been good."

"Oh, being outdoors and canoeing sounds like a wonderful opportunity." Olivia looked around her kitchen. The dirty counter. Her well-worn table. What would a change of scenery like canoeing feel like?

"Maybe Chris can take you when you come." Patricia put those words out there like a little test.

Olivia sighed again. Why did their friendship feel so weighted? Why did this trip make her feel like a pawn in a game of chess instead of like she was receiving a gift? Just when Olivia thought she knew her next move, Patricia added, "I have one more gift I'd like to give you. When Chris disappeared the first time, I hired a private detective to find him. I'd like to give you his name so you can find your mom. If you want."

Check. Mate. Sob. Olivia's relief at the prospect of finding out if her mother was alive caused an instant flow of tears. She put her hand over her phone so Patricia didn't hear her crying.

"Olivia? Olivia. Did you hear what I said? Did I make a mistake? Is that too much again? The truth is, I don't have many friends. Not real ones." Patricia got quiet.

Olivia wiped her eyes, steadied her voice, and said, "Thank you, Patricia. I would really like the name."

"Great. I'll send you the contact information. I took the liberty of giving him a heads-up that you'd be calling him. I hope that's okay. You helped bring my son back to me. I want to return the favor." Patricia said the words coolly, as if trading and locating lost, addicted family members was something everyone did. But for once, Olivia was fine with the breeziness. It was nice to think it was that easy to find out if her mother was okay.

This was a gift. If Olivia had a chessboard in front of her, she'd be throwing it across the table because all bets were off in this game. Patricia was going to help her find her mom. And for that, she couldn't hate her. Even a tiny bit.

"Well, let me know what you learn. I'm here for you, Olivia." Patricia's voice revealed her insecurity. Its humanity was like an open door with fresh air blowing through, keeping their friendship breathing. "I'll give you a call next week to check in," she added, "like friends do." Olivia could hear the shy smile in Patricia's words.

Olivia was still thinking about Patricia's newest gift as she cut vegetables for dinner. Another day, another meal. Sometimes it felt like all Olivia did was cook dinner for her family, do dishes, and repeat. That night over pasta and broccoli, both Sammy and Steve gushed over the pretty flowers. Sammy kept getting up from the table and jumping around while smelling the flowers.

"Sammy, why don't you go play in the backyard? I think you've got too much energy for dinner tonight."

"I'm going to play with my new jump rope!"

"Perfect."

As Sammy skipped away from having to clean up dinner, Steve pointed to the vase of flowers and said, "Patricia does have good taste in flowers. I noticed you didn't ditch them like the postcards."

"I didn't. But I did talk to her."

Steve raised his eyebrows. "How'd that go?"

"Honestly, I was going to tell her off, but then..." Olivia looked down and picked a piece of dried craft paint off their table.

"But then? What? This woman. I swear we've talked about Patricia more than anything else in our marriage lately."

"I know. It's funny. I realized today that I thought Patricia was crap at friendships, but then I realized so am I. I don't have that many female friends, you know?"

"You can probably thank your mother for that," Steve said flatly. He pulled out a slightly wilted flower. "Is a trip to Belize worth all this stress?"

"Yes, my therapist has pointed out the Patricia-mother connection more than once." Olivia pulled the flower out of Steve's hand. "I have a more important question for this flower."

Steve put his hand on hers and said, "Oh, don't worry, I love you. You don't need to ask it that."

She smirked at him, yanked the flower away and asked, "Should I find my mother or not?"

"You know where she is?"

"Patricia gave me the name of a detective."

"Of course she did. Because people like Patricia have private eyes."

"I think I want to do it. I want to find her. Just to find out if she's okay."

"And what if she's not?"

"I don't know. I hadn't thought of that. I just thought if I knew where she was, and if she's okay, I could be okay."

Steve let out an exasperated sigh. "Forget what I said earlier. Patricia isn't the one we waste time on in our marriage. Your mother holds that spot."

"That was a dick thing to say."

"Look. When it comes to your mom, it never ends well. Never. I love you. But I'm tired of you letting your mother into your life just to destroy you every time. And to be honest, I'm tired of talking about Patricia. Just break up with her. Ghost her. Whatever. Just get them both out of our marriage."

Olivia tried to get the next words out, but her tears moved faster than her mouth. Steve had already slammed the door behind him.

She put her head down on the table, tired from the verbal chess with Patricia, tired from having a mother that brought only complication, and tired that the one person she trusted most couldn't see why this was so important. Just then, she felt a familiar nuzzle on her ankle. She bent down and petted Marven slowly. Marven circled Olivia's leg and laid down on her foot—claiming her with his little body.

Olivia stroked Marven's head. "I won't let her hurt me. I just want to know if she's alive."

Olivia looked down at him. Marven looked up. His little eyes might not see well, but she knew they could see inside her soul and understand why she needed this. She didn't have a real mother, but she could find real answers, and that was her comfort. It wasn't the kind of comfort that made you soup when you were sick, but the kind that let you sleep more easily.

"This is something I have to do," she said out loud, as if saying the words made them a binding contract. She thought of her karaoke song and how she felt staring at the happy memory. Maybe this is how she could let go? From a distance.

The next day, Olivia called the detective and sent him pictures of her mother and all the contacts she could think of who might know where her mother was. The list was short. There was Susie down in Florida. A neighbor who had lived next door to them and later moved away. A few drinking buddies. Olivia didn't know her mother or her acquaintances well these days, but with every detail or picture she sent the detective, she felt the load on her shoulders become lighter. She might not know where her mom was, but she was trying. She was doing something.

She didn't need to tell Steve what she was doing. Just like the money-lending. This was something she needed to do. He wouldn't understand. He couldn't. He had a mom who cut his sandwiches when he was little and took pictures at every major life event. A mom who hugged him when he was sad and was there for him when he needed her. A mom who remembered birthdays and even celebrated half-birthdays with a cupcake. He had a mom who stayed.

CHAPTER 26
DOG TREATS

Two weeks had passed since the detective called with news of her mother. Rose had seen a few of her friends but then moved on. As Olivia drove, she pushed the thoughts of her mother out of her head. She also pushed away the fact that she was hiding all of this from her husband, but sharing it with Patricia.

Today wasn't about her mother or secrets. Today was about celebrating. She parked her car and made her way into Target, stopping to look at some scented hand soap in a colorful blue bottle that she most definitely did not need. Her phone rang. She glanced down to see the word, "Patricia." Olivia pushed the cart with one hand and talked with the other. "Hey there, I'm in your favorite place."

"Jeanette's salon?" Patricia answered.

"Okay, my favorite place. Of course your favorite place would be some fancy salon."

"Starbucks?"

"Close. Target. Just picking up a few things."

"Don't forget sunscreen," Patricia added.

"Got that already."

Patricia had been faithfully calling Olivia every week, just to talk or catch up. No big agenda. Sometimes Olivia would tell her about the detective, or school, or Samantha. Sometimes Patricia would tell her how Chris was doing.

"Well, I was just calling to tell you I can't wait to see you."

"Me too."

Silence. Not awkward. Comfortable. Olivia pushed her cart past a fluffy white pillow and touched it with her hand. She stopped in front of a cute little craft sign with letters you could use to make words. She picked it up and looked at the price tag. Right now, the sign said: LIVE LAUGH LOVE which made Olivia want to LIVE LAUGH VOMIT. She dropped the wooden sign in her cart anyway.

Patricia rattled off a few more things not to forget as Olivia strolled past the fancy hair products with rosemary and lavender. Past the bath bombs Sammy always begged her for. Past the organic chocolate bars with fun flower wrappers that called out to her. Instead, she walked to the aisle displaying things needed for the day's festivities.

"Patricia, I've got to go now. But really, I can't wait to hug you tomorrow. In person."

"Me too." Patricia's voice wasn't overly excited or high-pitched. But Olivia knew her well enough to know that was pure happiness.

"Bye!" Olivia hung up and smiled. She stared at all the wine labels. "Should I go for a cute label that always winds up being shit wine? Or an ugly label that winds up being decent?" she said out loud to no one. She decided on both—one label with a purple penguin and one boring black label with red writing.

She looked into her cart. Wine. Paper plates. And, of course, the treats Marven liked. She was ready.

When she drove back home, she could see Jen's car was parked in the driveway. Olivia ran into the house and Samantha greeted her happily. "Everyone's outside, Mom! Did you get the stuff?"

"Got it right here!" Olivia held up the Target bag as evidence.

She walked out to her deck where her family was gathered with Jen, Diya, and the big banner that said "Congratulations."

Steve held up his glass and said, "I'd like to take a moment before we get started to toast my wife. Not only did she get her realtor's license today, but this is also a big day for our family."

"Sausage." Steve looked down and smiled at Marven, who bumped into the chair. Steve cleared his throat and said, "Marven, welcome officially to the family."

Samantha clapped her hands. She bent carefully down and gave Marven a pet behind his right ear, which he loved so much that he tilted his head into her hand. When she stopped, he barked to make her keep going. Olivia laughed. Sammy said, "Don't worry, buddy. I won't ever stop."

Jen had brought over a printout of their official adoption papers, and Olivia signed them. Everyone cheered. It was a good day. No, it was a great day.

That night, Olivia surprised Steve by wearing the black underwear she had bought. Tomorrow was an even bigger day. Tomorrow, they were leaving to go to Belize. Steve laughed as Olivia climbed onto his lap and kissed him. "I like this new you," he said as he slid his hands over her black lace. Just then, her phone rang.

"Ignore it." Steve kissed her shoulder and slid down her bra strap as she fell back onto the bed. The phone rang again and Olivia grabbed it to see who was calling. She pushed Steve off and said, "I need to take this."

"Hi." Olivia stood up and walked to the other side of the room. "No, this is a fine time."

Steve sat on the bed and watched her.

"Oh. No, that's good. Did you give her the letter? Yeah, I understand. Thank you." Olivia stared straight ahead and hung up the phone.

Steve came up to her, looking confused. "What was that all about?"

"You'll be mad."

"For the record, I can never be mad when you are wearing black lace."

Olivia smiled at him, but it wasn't a real smile. She quickly buried her face in her hands. Her emotions were coming fast. "It was the detective."

"Oh." Steve pulled at his eyebrows, which he did when he was annoyed.

"It's fine. Everything's fine." Olivia's voice quickened when she saw Steve pull at his eyebrows. "I know you weren't on board with the detective thing, so I've just been keeping you out of the loop."

"Out of the loop," Steve repeated the words as if they would make more sense if he said them. They weren't a couple who kept each other out of the loop. They were in the loop kind of people.

"You know, I thought it was all the studying that had you acting weird. And your obsession with that Me List. But it was this. You were hiding shit from me."

"I'm sorry. It was so important to me and you didn't get it."

"What I don't get is why you let people like your mom or crazy Patricia walk all over you. You deserve better."

"Well, I thought I deserved answers." Olivia's voice got louder and her chest, neck, and face flushed pink.

Steve said nothing. He sat down on the edge of the bed and stared down at the floor.

Olivia kept talking. "He found my mom on the beach, stoned out of her mind with a friend. So, that's good."

"That's good?"

"I needed to know she was alive."

"What happens now?" He brought his hand to his other eyebrow and pulled it.

"Now we go to Belize. Marven gets to hang with Diya for a week."

"Oh, yeah. It's that simple."

"Yeah. I gave the detective a note to give her. If she wants to, she'll contact me. If not..."

"If not?" Steve glanced at her. Olivia looked back confidently to show she had finally accepted the possibility of "if not."

"The detective will keep tabs on her until I decide what to do next. The ball is in my court now, don't you see? If I want to let go, I can. It's on my terms."

"The ball is never in your court with your mom."

Olivia sat down on the bed and grabbed his hands. "Tomorrow, you, me, and Sammy are going on a real vacation. From all of this. Okay? I'm sorry I didn't tell you. I just..." Olivia didn't know what to say.

"You lied to me." Steve looked right at Olivia as he said those true but awful words. He let go of her hands. "Anything else you haven't told me?" Steve's eyes looked dark.

"Um." Olivia looked down and knew the double whammy of mother-lying would not go over well, but it was time to be totally honest. "There is one more thing I've been meaning to tell you."

"Seriously?" Steve hid his face in his hands.

Olivia got on her knees and pulled his hands down so he could see her. "I want to be honest with you. And it's not easy when it comes to my mom..." Olivia tried to find the right words but only the easy wrong ones would come, "because I feel like you never want me to help her."

"It's not that. It's that she takes your help and shits on it. Every time."

"I lent her money." Olivia said the words as fast as she could, hoping they might speed by Steve and all this fighting would be over.

"How much?"

"Doesn't matter. I repaid it."

"Of course it matters. And it matters that you didn't tell me."

Olivia tried to channel Patricia and say the amount as breezily as possible. "Three thousand dollars. She was behind on rent. They were going to throw her out."

"Three thousand dollars!" The amount sounded bigger when Steve screamed it.

"I was able to repay it with the money I made from Patricia. And my bonus from selling the house. And hey, now we have the tickets, so we might not even need all the money in our vacation account." Olivia saw Steve's body shake and his eyes get big. That's when she realized she said one truthful word too many.

"You gave her money from our vacation account." Steve repeated these words with disbelief. He rubbed his eyes hard, like they were no longer working.

"Yes. She was getting kicked out of her apartment. She was desperate. What was I supposed to do?"

Olivia grabbed his hands, but he pulled them away. Steve got up and walked across the room. He turned back and said, "What were you supposed to do? I don't know. Talk to your husband. Figure it out together. Not let your mother use you. Did she tell you not to tell me?" His voice wavered somewhere between angry and sad.

"No," Olivia could taste the tears falling as she talked. "I was going to tell you. There were so many times. But I knew you'd get mad. And then I started making money and I thought I could just repay it. I just knew if I told you, you'd tell me not to do it." Olivia wrung her hands. She could feel the stress of this conversation in every joint of her body.

"And why is that, Olivia?" Steve's voice was all frustration now.

"Don't you get how hard this is for me? I know my mom sucks. But how do you say no to your mother? Would you say no to your mother? Would you let her get kicked out of her apartment and live on the streets?"

"My mom isn't an alcoholic." Steve said the words nonchalantly because he could. They stung Olivia all the same.

"No, she's not. Which is why you don't get it." Olivia slumped down on the floor. Tears splashed all over her bare legs and arms. A release of a river of stress, lies, and the burden of loving a mother who couldn't love her back. She thought about grabbing pajamas to throw on, because sitting in her underwear and bra while being sad and defeated felt like the most unsexy thing ever. Right now was not a moment for black lace; right now was a moment for humongous white cotton comfort. Then again, this was her. Flesh, softness, and brokenness, trying her hardest to take her cracks and pieces and be a mosaic for her daughter and husband. Right now, she was trying to open her grip and let her mother go.

"You're right; I don't. But I do love someone who loves an addict and you don't understand that." Steve sat next to her and dried a tear on her cheek with his thumb. "Don't ever lie to me again. I'd rather know and be angry, or whatever, than not know." Although his words sounded soft, his face was still hard.

"I'm sorry." Olivia looked into his eyes. "I am really sorry. I hate that I let my mom get between us." He stared back at her, but she could see his hurt. She kissed him tentatively. "I'm sorry," she said again. "I love you," she said with her lips instead of her voice. "Does it help that I'm still wearing fancy lace underwear?"

She hoped the power of fancy underwear would be enough to mend her mistake of not telling him, but he didn't crack a smile.

"Just don't send me a dozen postcards." He kissed her back.

She kissed him more deeply. Thankful that he understood her. Thankful that he loved her—scars and all.

"Never underestimate the power of lace," Steve said and touched the rim of her lace underwear gently. "But don't ever keep anything from me again. Even if I'm being a dick about it. Okay?"

"Okay," Olivia said and kissed him sweetly.

That night they had not-vanilla sex. With sprinkles.

CHAPTER 27
DETAILS

When the sun rose the next day, it shone with the light of a new beginning. No more lies. Instead, there was the hustle and bustle of a plane ride and Sammy's early morning crankiness, which turned to excitement as the plane landed. Olivia breathed deeply, filling her lungs with the thickness of humid air. It felt good. Vacation. Olivia scanned the parking lot and waved.

"You didn't have to pick us up." She ran towards Chris.

"I wanted to. And I brought you these." Chris held up a big bag of Twizzlers.

Olivia gave him a big hug.

"Chris, this is my husband, Steve, and my wonderful daughter, Samantha."

Samantha held out her hand and said, "Friends call me Sammy."

Chris smiled as he shook Samantha's hand. "Hi, Sammy."

They passed the car ride with their chatter. Chris told them how he was going to take them canoeing. And about their beach rental. The neighbors two houses down were away for a wedding, so Patricia had snagged Olivia a good deal, of course.

When they pulled up to their beach house, Olivia felt like she had really made it. She had been through a crazy year and had accomplished new things. A journey that had started with hate and salad had brought her here to this beautiful place. Olivia looked at Chris and he looked back with clear eyes and a smile.

"Thanks, Chris. Tell your mom we'll pop over as soon as we are settled."

Chris waved to her and the three of them oohed as they walked up the path to their beach house, which was turquoise with lime green accents. It looked like one of the many postcards Patricia had sent.

"Wow, this is so cool," Sammy said, as she ran from room to room. "I want the bedroom with the pretty shells!"

"You can have whichever bedroom you like." Olivia smiled. It was nice to say yes to things. To be excited.

"Come, look at this!" They heard Sammy scream from the top floor.

Steve kissed Olivia on the forehead. The air felt like the magic of Christmas morning as they ran upstairs to see what surprise awaited them.

"Isn't it beautiful?" Sammy asked. Her voice was full of awe and wonder as she showed her parents the stunning view.

"So beautiful," Olivia agreed. The three of them stared out in silence. When the light hit the water, it sparkled like diamonds.

"Can we go play in it noooooowwww?" Sammy beamed up at them.

"Yes. Why don't you two get started and I'll go say hi to Patricia, so she knows what we are up to. I'll put my bathing suit on and then join you. Don't forget to put on lots of sunscreen," Olivia added.

Sammy opened up her suitcase and started tearing through it, throwing clothes everywhere, looking for her suit.

"It's in the side pocket." Olivia tried her best to ignore the enthusiastic mess as she handed Sammy her bathing suit with the blue stripes and cute red crab.

"Thanks." Sammy tore off her clothes.

Olivia put on her black bathing suit and threw a black cotton dress over it. She knocked on the bathroom where Steve was. "You cool if I head over? Sammy is dressed and needs lotion. It is right here on our bed. SPF50 for the face."

"Got it," Steve answered from the bathroom.

Olivia grabbed a small, wrapped gift from her suitcase. She left the house, practically skipping down the sandy beach path to Patricia's. Patricia was sitting on the porch in a straw hat and drinking lemonade. She wore a bathing suit and a colorful sarong as she read a magazine. She looked up and smiled.

"Well, hello." Olivia smiled back.

Patricia stood up and hurried to her friend, hugging her so tightly that her hat fell off. Olivia laughed.

Patricia launched into a million questions. "Is the house nice? Do you love it? Isn't this beach amazing? How was Chris? Was his driving okay? He was so excited to pick you up! I stayed here and got everything ready for you. I've got lunch prepped for when you guys are hungry, and I put groceries in your fridge. Did you see that?"

Olivia didn't know which question to answer first, so she just laughed. "Everything is great. Chris looked great."

"He does, doesn't he?" Patricia grabbed Olivia's hand. "Come on up. I made fresh lemonade with a touch of mint." Patricia gave her signature wink, and Olivia didn't even hate it.

"This is so good." Olivia tried not to drink it all in one gulp. Damn, Patricia could even make lemonade more perfect.

"So, tell me, how was your flight? How is…" she paused and asked, "everything?"

Olivia took one more sip of the heavenly blend of sweet and sour and said, "You know, everything is sort of amazing because we are here. And oh, I almost forgot. This is for you. A small thank you gift."

Patricia went to open it and Olivia suddenly felt shy that she brought Patricia a gift she had made. "Open it later. When you're by yourself. It's silly, really. Just something I made for you."

Patricia patted the present and put it on the table next to them. "I will. Thank you."

"So, I found out about my mom yesterday."

Patricia's eyes opened wide.

"She's still alive. She's in Florida."

"What's next? Are you going to see her?"

"No. The detective gave her my note, so she knows I love her and that I am here for her. But that's up to her." Olivia took a deep breath in and added, "That's all I can do. I can't be the one holding on for both of us anymore."

Patricia put her hand on Olivia's. "You are so strong."

Olivia couldn't believe the words coming out of Patricia's mouth. A woman who crushed most days with her pinky and had the balls to move to an island after her divorce. "Me? Strong? You're the strong one. I mean jeez, Patricia, look at this place. This is how you get over a divorce."

Patricia smiled, but it was tight. "I don't think I'll ever get over it," she said so faintly, the din of the ocean almost swallowed her words.

Olivia looked at her and said, "You will. One day at a time. Just like Chris."

"I wanted to talk to you again about that." Patricia sat up straighter. "Last time, right before you came, Paul called me and chewed me out. And then you arrived with Chris, and I…I'm so sorry I let my insecurity mess everything up. I should have said thank you. I should have said…" Patricia paused and stared off into the distance.

"It's what friends are for," Olivia offered.

"I've never been good at that." Patricia looked down as her hands went to play with the wedding ring that was no longer there.

"You should put it on your Me List," Olivia joked.

"I have. Every year," Patricia said in a voice that was so small. "It's actually how the Me List started. Paul made some stupid comment about how I should get more friends to improve my social life so he could spend more time golfing. I should have known then what an ass he was. But all I heard was what was wrong with me. And I thought, I'll do more than that. I'll make a whole list of things to improve upon and show him. But you know, the friend one, I never did accomplish that. Until now."

Olivia moved towards Patricia, awkwardly bent over her, and hugged her as Patricia stayed seated in the rocking chair. "The friend one is hard for me too," Olivia whispered.

Olivia rocked back and forth with the chair as if Patricia was a small child being comforted. Patricia finally let the sadness of her divorce overcome her and escape. As Olivia held Patricia, she thought of her dying mother and rocked her in her heart, holding her hand, and then letting it go.

There was nothing pretty about what the crying did to their faces, but a moment of absolute beauty hung between them in their emotional un-doneness. Two women who had grown, changed, and become friends when they'd both needed one. Two women who were opening up and letting their love and wounds show.

Patricia leaned back, then stood up and fixed her sarong. "That's enough of that. I'm going in to get lunch ready. You go find your family and enjoy the sun. Come over when you're ready to eat."

Olivia took a few steps off the porch. "Hey, Patricia." Patricia turned back and the sun streamed through the porch and around her hair, making her look like she was a person built of sunrays.

"Thank you," Olivia said, "With a capital T."

Patricia nodded and walked inside, but Olivia could tell she was smiling as she walked.

Just then, Sammy came running up the beach path and put a seashell into Olivia's hand. "Isn't this great? It's sooooo beautiful here. Come on. Let me show you."

Olivia gazed at her daughter looking so free and breathed her joy. There would come a day when Samantha's hands wouldn't shove little treasures into her hands. But for now, Olivia was going to treat each shell like the precious gift of time it was. She ran with Samantha towards the ocean and said, "Let's find some more!"

They spent the next hour taking in the sun and playing in the waves. Olivia held one of Sammy's hands while Steve grabbed the other and they jumped the waves over and over, together. Olivia wondered if she'd ever jumped waves with her own mother. She had no memories of that. They had jumped plenty of life's waves together. Divorce. Addiction. Sickness. They'd never had a chance for calm waters.

"I'm going to go dry off for a bit." Olivia let go of Sammy's hand, and Steve instinctively grabbed it. That's what a good parent should do. Always know when you need more support. She sat on her towel and took it all in. The sun, her family, the beautiful blue water, and the strange friendship that had brought her here.

Olivia watched the waves crash and then turn to white foam. She grabbed a handful of sand and let it slip through her fingers. She wondered if her mother was staring out at the ocean, too. A tear slid down her cheek. This ocean between them.

. . .

Inside, Patricia opened the gift Olivia had made for her. She unfolded the pastel wrapping paper and held the mint green board with the wooden frame in her hands. Patricia knew just where to put it—on the windowsill in her kitchen, so she could look at it every day. On the sign were the white letters Olivia had painstakingly picked out to create the right message.

It said: The Me List. 1. Be happy. 2. The rest is details.

MAKE YOUR OWN ME LIST

Think of things that excite you, scare you a little, and challenge you. Big things. Small things. Things that will make you smile. Now go ahead and make your list and make this year the best one yet.

1

2.

3.

4.

5.

6.

7.

8.

9.

10.

ACKNOWLEDGMENTS

I started writing this book after two women supported me and helped me find my voice for my debut novel, *The Things We Keep*. It takes a lot to put yourself out there as an author. And if I didn't have Jacki and Tara in my corner, I wouldn't have published my first book or taken on *The Me List*.

Thank you to Jacki for making me believe in the power of friendship. It truly can change a life. Thank you to Tara, who edited my first draft of this book and got me past the fear stage of sharing my words.

Thank you to the writing community on Twitter that supports me every week through Move Me Poetry and encourages me to keep writing. You know who you are. Your voices may be just words on Twitter, but your motivation is loud in my ears. Shout out also to the many amazing authors from the Women's Fiction Writing Association who have been invaluable in my journey.

Thanks to my sister who read a draft of this manuscript for me in a moment of panic. My husband who sits by me and proofs. My three girls who graciously play around me as I write. And to my three nephews, I know how addiction has affected your family. It's why I wanted to write about it. Thanks for letting me into your hearts—you will always be in mine.

Thanks to Kathryn and Inna, who helped me get more insight into the details of addiction and being a realtor, respectively. (Not sure how often someone writes both of those words in the same sentence!)

Thanks to the many rescue dogs and cats that I've fostered who inspired me to write a furry character. And to my favorite 100-pound rescue dog and two cats who sit next to me every day while I write.

And thanks to you, the reader. Every time I turned on my computer to write, I smiled at the file name, The Me List. It felt like I was writing it for me. But really, it was all for you.

ABOUT THE AUTHOR

Julee Balko is an author who loves writing novels with complicated women characters. Her debut novel, *The Things We Keep*, takes on grief, secrets, and family dysfunction. *The Me List* is her second novel and is full of snark and heart as it brings to life an unlikely friendship between neighbors.

You can find Julee somewhere in the woods of Washington hiking with her husband. Or at home, enjoying her three daughters, rescue hound, two cats, and axolotl.

NOTE FROM JULEE BALKO

Word-of-mouth is crucial for any author to succeed. If you enjoyed *The Me List*, please leave a review online—anywhere you are able. Even if it's just a sentence or two. It would make all the difference and would be very much appreciated.

Thanks!
Julee Balko

Printed in the USA
CPSIA information can be obtained
at www.ICGtesting.com
JSHW080353271023
50898JS00001B/59